THE POISON

THE HUNT SERIES BOOK 3

TIM HEATH

HAPPY CONTENT PUBLISHING

Created with Vellum

For Rachel—my cancer fighting ninja wife and biggest fan (cheering alongside Mia and Anya)

****

A character glossary is located at the back of the book.

1

He'd seen them driving around in blacked-out Jeeps all over the south of the city. Martin Rennold had already been in St Petersburg for two days, three nights given the time he landed. On each of those nights, he'd been walking the streets, unable to sleep in unfamiliar surroundings. Besides, he'd always been a night owl since his teenage years, which seemed too long ago to remember––but were concluded only twelve years previously. It was while taking these now ritual night-time strolls that Martin started to discover the truth of things he'd always believed about Russia––that the Mafia ruled certain districts. Martin's hotel was located near one of these neighbourhoods.

He was not a man to go looking for trouble, but trouble seemed to home in on him. It found him no matter what and this whirlwind visit to Russia was no exception.

In his left hand he still held tight––his grip as robust as it had ever been––a lottery ticket worth over £11 million. He had one day to claim it and the return flight for which he had a ticket––a ticket the airline couldn't switch––was not due out for another three days. He was broke. He couldn't afford new tickets––despite the fact he might just be a millionaire before the week was out. His credit rating––if you could call it that––was abysmal. He had no option but to approach the Mafia.

But the Mafia always found a way, his logic had slowly convinced him over hours of heavy vodka drinking. They could fence stolen goods, launder dirty money and therefore surely he'd find a compromise, a way for them to also profit from the winning ticket.

He had nothing else to try. He was out of his already very limited options. But the rush of optimism the last few hours had given him since getting his hands on the ticket was something else entirely. Energy still pumped through every vein in his body––as if the ticket itself was offering pure oxygen to his drowning body, so profoundly submerged in debt and despair. Now, though, he had hope––and a lifeline.

"Hey, are you Russian Mafia?" he said, calling across to one of two men just climbing out of a Jeep. He'd thought about what to say, how to go about it. His approach wasn't good––he realised that as the words were coming out of his mouth––but he didn't have much choice. He also rarely thought things through enough, anyway.

"Mafioso?" he repeated, a Russian accent put on this time as if that would help them understand him. He apparently wasn't posing a threat, and they were smiling, their suits crisp, clean, expensive looking. There was no sign of weapons but Martin was sure they were there somewhere, concealed under layers of Armani, or Gucci––or whatever it was the Russian Mafia was now wearing.

"Who are you? Police?" the man replied, in English.

"No, I'm a friend. I have a business proposition for you and your men. It'll be worth three million pounds to you. British sterling. But it has to be today. Can we talk?"

Both men now standing in front of Martin towered over him, he realised, despite his relatively tall five feet eleven. Neither Russian said anything to the other, though their eye contact suggested they were communicating easily enough among themselves.

"We're listening," the lead guy said, his English surprisingly good, though with a noticeable American bias.

"Can we go someplace a little more private?"

"Sure." The other Russian came over to Martin, frisking him suddenly, Martin just letting the man confirm he wasn't carrying a weapon and wasn't a threat.

"You alone? Anyone watching us now?"

"No, God no, I swear. It's just me."

"You sure?" It was already dark, though it was only three in the afternoon. That was not unusual in St Petersburg at the beginning of January.

"Absolutely!" Martin said. He was telling the truth, for his part. He had no idea a team of Trackers were watching him at that moment, had been on him for the entire day, in fact. They were always watching.

"And no one else knows you are here?"

"No, no one. I'm travelling alone." They were walking now, heading for a small alleyway that took them away from the road where Martin had first approached them. When they were standing under a little lamp which was attached at the second-floor level to the side of one of the buildings––though there were no windows down this alley––the two Russians stopped.

"So, tell me what this proposition is."

Martin took a moment but just started explaining what he'd been working on in his mind. He didn't know how much to tell them, what to keep secret, but did enough to get them interested. He knew there was a chance that once they had the ticket, he wouldn't see any of the money. He was out of options, which was why he'd approached them in the first place. He'd take his chances.

"Interesting," the lead guy interjected, as Martin came to a pause. He said something in fast, unintelligible Russian to the man standing next to him, the guy pulling out his mobile phone and making a call. They were probably trying to check whether the ticket was real or not. He'd done the same thing that morning when he'd first laid hands on it. It all still felt such a blur. The guy on the phone said something back to the lead Russian.

"Let me see the ticket," he said to Martin, the Englishman hesitant, but he handed over the ticket anyway. He had come to them for help, after all. More words were spoken in Russian, the lead guy reading off the numbers, in turn, the other Russian on the telephone then relaying them to whoever they'd called. There was a brief pause. It wouldn't take long for them to confirm what he'd found out himself that morning over breakfast––it was valid, and about to expire.

Both Russians smiled.

"Very good, it appears what you have been telling us has all been one hundred per cent accurate."

"I've nothing to hide from you; I just wanted to work with you."

"To work with us?"

"Yes."

"And no one knows you are here. You are certain?"

"Absolutely."

"How did you know to find us here?"

"I've been staying in a nearby hotel. I saw your Jeeps racing around the streets the last two nights. It doesn't take a genius to know who you are."

"A valid point."

"So are we good?"

There was a noticeable shift in both Russians at this point.

"I'll tell you what I am going to do for you. You said it was worth £3 million for us to help you, but the way I see it now is that we have a lot more than that in our hands currently from where I'm standing. Do you get my drift?"

"Hold on. I came to you!"

"And I'm very grateful that you did. Mikalai," he said, turning to his companion, the order clear. Mikalai pulled out his gun from an inside pocket, two bullets ripping through Martin's body before he could move from the spot. His body hit the frost covered ground. "Get this cleaned up," he said, moving back across to the Jeep, ticket in hand, vital funds for his organisation soon to be made available.

Inside the Games Room, the murder, enacted in front of them all on the giant screens that broadcasted to them all the activities of all three Contestants, brought little shock. The moment Twelve's man had gone to the Mafia, they knew what the outcome would be. These men wouldn't share something like this. His Hunt was over.

It'd happened once before, as well. The big question that remained now for Arseni Markovic was whether he went after those currently in possession of his ticket, or left them to it. He'd invested the £11 million six months ago in acquiring it in the first place. Losing this particular Hunt would now cost him more. Would he allow the Mafia to cash in on something that had cost him so much already? Those watching the screen were keeping one eye on their fellow T20 member.

It had been a relatively quiet day up until that point for the ten men who made up the T20. The only ticket left in play had been that of the Englishman's, which now technically still was, albeit in Mafia hands. Eighteen and Twenty had also been hosting Contestants this time around, their would-be female millionaires both captured at the airport, each within thirty minutes of the other, by different teams. These tickets were now back in possession of men working for the Russian oligarch that had purchased them––Motya's ticket worth the most at nearly €15 million, Osip's the least of the three at €11 million.

It was only Arseni, therefore, who potentially stood to lose a little from the day––he hadn't managed to stop his Contestant, and also didn't now have the ticket himself. At Twelve, however, and worth $2.2 billion, he could easily afford it.

The truth was, and Svetlana had seen it happening more and more over the last few Hunts, the Russians were all getting too good at controlling events to dictate what happened. Ever since the previous year's New Year event––a contest that left two Contestants dead, not to mention the murder of another civilian––the edge had been taken off these smaller, more traditional gatherings. A fresh start was called for.

"Gentlemen," she said, with all her Hollywood grace that she carried around with her wherever she went, "it's been another fascinating day." It hadn't been, not by a long shot. "We've not even got to four in the afternoon and all three Contestants have failed in their attempts to escape with your money." One of these very Contestants was being dumped into the back of a van at that moment, the centre screen showing this happening for anyone watching. "So we are, therefore, concluded once again. As always, it's been my pleasure to host you all here, and I will be in touch regarding our next gathering. If you'll excuse me, I have to get to another meeting. Don't feel any of you has to rush off. Plenty of champagne still needs drinking up. Enjoy!"

A chorus of *S Novom Godom* rang out--Happy New Year--as Svetlana Volkov stepped down from the small staging area and headed for the exit. The men left her to it. They knew what group of men were awaiting her next.

2

In a fourth-floor apartment across the road and not quite directly opposite the Volkov mansion, Alex, Anissa and their FSB insider Sasha continued to sit as they had done for much of the afternoon. They knew in the next door building to them––the one that did sit directly opposite the target property––was at least one team of security. Another group was at street level in a van parked just a few doors down from the front entrance, an entrance that was heavily secured.

Temple Mount––the unofficial name given to the Volkov mansion––was easily the best-protected location Sasha knew about in St Petersburg. And with men––and at least one woman––inside with a combined net worth of over $100 billion, it was easy to understand why. Wealth had a way of protecting its position.

As evening drew in, Anissa had checked off the arrival of all twenty men they now knew made up the Games, the ten wealthiest being the last group to arrive, men making up the Tio. The other group had been there for most of the day. They'd not seen anyone leave yet.

"What I'd give to have ears in that building! Are you certain there is no way to do that Sasha?"

"Absolutely not. The property is listed with my office." Sasha had been with the FSB for some years and worked from Big House, the home of the FSB in St Petersburg. He ran his own small team, which gave him an element of freedom. He'd used most of that freedom to help his two British friends over the last couple of years, having done something similar before that for another two agents. "Because it's listed, it means we can't carry out any type of invasive surveillance without it being cleared from on high––which it wouldn't be––and we would have compromised our position in the process." Both British agents knew that really meant he'd be compromised. They were not here on official MI6 business, far from it in fact. Their operation, already more than two years old, was very much under the radar. If their bosses understood what they were really up to, they would be closed down. Sasha, on the other hand, would most likely be dead. Keeping him alive was very much their top priority.

"From what we've seen so far," Anissa said, the obvious point being they'd seen very little, yet, "I don't recall all twenty men––both groups––meeting together like they are today. Could that be significant?"

There was no answer to that one. Alex said, anyway, "Anything they do en masse like this, all their gatherings, we have to assume are significant until we know otherwise. Sasha, any news on who they are using as Contestants this time?"

In the past they'd been given names––Andre Philips, as he had called himself until they realised he was Matvey Filipov's only son––had detailed certain people from various nations. These had turned out to be Contestants who suddenly turned up in Russia. This time they didn't have that kind of information. Sasha had no idea who to put a watch out for with the border guard.

"I've got a few guys watching the airport, but nothing at the moment," Sasha said, his English noticeably improving, and his accent becoming far more British, over the last two years. Anissa wondered if anyone in his office had picked up on his vast improvement, but then she figured he wouldn't have been speaking English there, anyway. "Without names, they don't have much to go on. This is one of the busiest times of the year, after all." Which was very accurate, New Year being Russia's most prominent holiday, and that in itself enough to draw tourists from around the world, but especially Europe, those brave enough to take on the cold. The real cold was still a month away.

Alex checked his watch: it was seven thirty. They'd been sitting there, just watching the building across the street, for over five hours straight. Lunch seemed like a long time ago.

"I think I'll run and get us something to eat," Alex said. Sasha had shown them a convenience store just around the corner, open twenty-four hours a day, seven days a week. Regardless of it being a national holiday, or not. Alex put on his coat and hat, something Sasha had lent him, helping him blend into the city a lot more naturally, able to disappear into the streets and go unnoticed, which was indeed needed in their current location.

Anissa looked through the pair of binoculars once more, her wedding ring catching the light a little.

"Tell me about your husband," Sasha said. "You have a family, right, though if I can say it, you hardly seem old enough for that." There was a smile on the Russian's face.

"You'd be surprised. Yes, Paul is my husband, and our two boys are called Jack and Alistair. Jack is the oldest by twelve months, though you wouldn't always know it. Jack's nine, Alistair is eight. We've been married for twelve years next month."

"Congratulations."

"What on having two boys, or still being married for so long?" she joked, Sasha not picking up on the joke.

"On the soon to be anniversary."

"I understood what you meant, sorry, English humour."

"It can't be easy balancing your two worlds?"

"My husband is super supportive. My mum lives nearby as well, so can often help with the boys. She's retired now, which makes it a lot easier during the school holidays, as well as with the school run. It's freed Paul up considerably. I'm not sure I could do what I do if they weren't both around."

"Have you always worked for the Security Service?" Somehow, being in Russia, where he knew anyone could be listening in, he still couldn't say MI6. Old habits.

"No, not as long as Alex has, anyway. I was in the army before, which in a round about way is how I met my husband."

"He's not army then, himself?"

"No, but it's a long story. I was injured and had to get out of the army altogether. Thankfully Military Intelligence came calling, and here I am."

"Alex doesn't have a wife, no?" He was quite sure it would have come up already had there been someone waiting for him back in England. Sasha had often wondered about the dynamic of the two Brits working so tightly together, if there'd ever been any tensions, any sexual chemistry between the two, but didn't feel he could ask that, yet.

"No, Alex doesn't. You'll have to ask him about that; I try not to get too involved."

"And your husband knows about your trips with Alex?"

"Yes, Sasha, and he's completely supportive," she said, a little too forcefully for what was needed, bristling a little too. "I'm sorry," she added, realising he wasn't really stepping out of line.

"Don't worry; I'm sure it's not been the first time you've been asked that."

"No, it's not."

"It's just if I was married to someone like you, I know I'd be super jealous if my beautiful wife was often travelling alone with another male colleague."

It had all got a little too heated, a little too focused on Anissa for her liking.

"And is there a lady somewhere, Sasha, someone you have hidden away from us all?" It was time to turn the spotlight onto her interrogator.

"No, there isn't. There was someone I was very fond of. She died a few years back."

"Oh, I'm sorry to hear that. Were you together?"

"No, nothing like that. I don't think she even knew how I felt, not really, anyway. It couldn't have worked. Plus, I know she was still in love with someone else."

Anissa knew about the history of Sasha and the British Security Service. She knew how he'd first helped another MI6 agent, Charlie Boon, after Anya Lobova had been killed by a bomb left in their hotel room in Zurich. She knew enough to assume this was the girl Sasha was talking about but liked him enough to keep that knowledge hidden.

"That must have been hard for you, Sasha, whoever it was. Can you see yourself one day getting married?"

"I'd like to think so. But I do think you did it the right way round, marrying first before joining our world. For men like Alex and myself, it's a lot harder to find time for romance."

"The fact you are talking about romance, and not just sex, Sasha, tells me there is much hope for you."

"Really?" but their conversation was interrupted as Alex walked back in through the door.

He emptied the bag of shopping onto the table, a loaf of bread, some cheese as well as some pies––Alex had no idea what was inside any of them––and proceeded to switch on the kettle.

"Snowing a little now," Alex said, as steam started to appear from the spout of the kettle.

"What's in the pies?" Anissa said, taking one in her hand and giving it a sniff.

"Not got the slightest idea. Just eat it, and you'll see." They all laughed.

As the kettle came to a boil, Alex poured the drinks, Sasha still over by the window, Anissa already eating, Alex then joining her, putting both their mugs onto the table, before picking up a pie and taking Sasha's green tea over to him.

"When do we expect movement again from across the road?" Alex said.

"It's hard to say. I guess there'll be some departures before nightfall––there are only so many guest rooms, even in a mansion that large. We know there are too many men inside to accommodate them all. I would expect to see a few men leave in the next hour or two."

"And then what?"

"Then, I have no idea."

They ate in silence for a little while, the three taking it in turns to watch at the window while grabbing some of the food that Alex had just bought them.

INSIDE TEMPLE MOUNT, Svetlana had left the group of men who made up the T20 within the Games and after a brief moment's pause was on her way into her other group of guests, the ten men who made up the T10. The room contained some of the most influential and powerful––not to mention wealthy––men her nation had to offer. And she was the Chair. Amongst all her starring roles in some of the biggest grossing films of the last decade, this personal role was amongst her favourites. It was her world, her rules and her style.

A noted hush came over proceedings as she entered the room. There was a large conference table for them all, and five men sat along each side––and she at the head. There were no cameras or screens needed for now. This was for the eyes and ears of only those currently present.

"Gentlemen, it is wonderful to see you all together once more," Svetlana said. It had been several months since they'd last met in her presence, and today was mainly a catch-up, hearing where each group was up to, seeing they were at least making progress. In their events, with the targets so much more significant, the time it all took so much longer, it was easy to bite off more than they could chew. This was why she kept a keen eye on proceedings.

And yet, this latest time, they were taking on targets multiple times bigger than she'd ever deemed viable before, Matvey Filipov having put forward the idea to her the last time they'd gathered. It had sounded utterly impossible at first––she'd nearly walked away from him, twice, in fact, dismissing it as such––but he had persisted.

It had been that persistence and the knowledge that he'd then suggested he go up against the largest of the unions, and his own team being the weaker of the two, that she'd suddenly taken it all more seriously. If someone would disadvantage themselves so much and yet still want to be involved in the attempt, as impossible and unlikely as it was––clearly nothing had ever been attempted like that anywhere in the business world before––then she was game for it. The more she'd looked into things, the more fascinated she had become.

"I've gathered you all here today to assess your progress in this latest, and easily the greatest, challenge I have ever laid before you. I want to ascertain that you still feel you have a chance of even getting close––remember, gentlemen, with targets this large, if you go about it the wrong way, you risk your own downfall. Bankruptcy isn't an impossibility." Dmitry Sokoloff, albeit a man only in the T20, had faced just that, most of his $2.2 billion fortune lost as a direct result of his involvement in the Games. His body was now lying six feet under, assumed to be a suicide by all, apart from the one man present who knew otherwise.

"I will meet with both groups in turn––it is only fair to do things that way, looking in detail at each team's progress without giving away anything to the other group. When I've met with you both, we will then all reconvene in an hour, and I will give my verdict on which, if any, of you I deem to be in the lead. Remember, the winner is the first team to complete the takeover. There are no prizes for second place." She stood up. "Matvey, I'll chat with your team second, so if you and your fellow team members could please step outside, I will call you in about thirty minutes when it'll be your turn." The five men stood, leaving without saying a word. The fact Svetlana had addressed Matvey, calling it *his* team, was missed by no one in the room, especially Mark Orlov, the wealthiest man present by some distance. It confirmed his suspicion that Matvey had more to do with it all than he was letting on. It was a slip by Svetlana not missed by Matvey, either, as he followed the other men out of the conference room. He hoped it wouldn't cost him dearly at some later point.

Left around the table was Lev Kaminski––the uncle of Dmitry Kaminski, who was a member of the T20, and whose Banking Union was directly being targeted by the other group. Lev was next to Roman Ivanov, the second wealthiest man in the T10, as well as Viktor Gavrilyuk beyond him. On his other side were Dima Petrov and Timur Budny, who was known as the *Iron Man* and was the least wealthiest member of the T10, despite being worth $8.9 billion.

Over the next thirty minutes, Svetlana talked in detail about their progress, Lev and to some degree Roman speaking the most, though it was Lev who undoubtedly led the team, in keeping with his image as the *Lion Man*.

"So I could expect to see some movement over the next three months? That is fast progress if you can indeed pull it off."

"We can certainly pull this off. We can see that victory against this banking empire would add great wealth and influence to our collective portfolios. So we are very much on board."

"That's an impressive position in which to be. I didn't expect either group to get anywhere close," she said, which was true. Before this latest event, the most significant business that had been put forward as a target was valued at around $500 million at the time of the attempted––and unsuccessful––takeover. That had been a single business. They were currently targeting a union of banks––there were nine in the one Lev had just updated her on, eleven in the one Matvey would soon give her details about––and the smallest of the two unions was still valued at well over $57 billion.

"And believe me, the other group haven't got a chance. They're up against an impossible target. It can't be done."

"You seem rather sure of yourself, Mr Kaminski." Svetlana knew full well that the man's nephew sat at the head of that Union of eleven banks Lev had just said couldn't be beaten. She'd also known Matvey had specifically targeted them, regardless. She was looking forward to her next meeting, intrigued at what light they might be able to shed on the possibility of taking out such a large target.

"I just know how these things work," Kaminski said. "They are too big, too protected; even against a group of men of such standing." He didn't say that he'd warned his nephew about the attempt that was soon to be heading his way, but there were no fools in that room. It was obvious Lev would let Dmitry know of the threat. It only boosted his own team's chances of victory.

"Well, I think our time is up, so I'll ask you to give me half an hour before I call you back in." The five men got up, leaving the room immediately. Moments later, from a separate door so as not to have passed the other five Russians who had just left, Matvey Filipov led in his fellow oligarchs.

In the last half an hour, while they waited for Svetlana to finish her chat with Lev and his group, they'd already started to implement their plan of action. The five men had been spending the last few months focussing their efforts on five other businesses––one man targeting one business. Like trees in a dense forest, to get to the biggest oaks in the centre, other trees had to be felled first to make space. Other trees cut down to be able to get to the prize in the middle. The eleven banks in their target Union represented those oaks in the centre––the five businesses they'd been working on these last few months were merely the trees cleared to create a clear path. And that process had just been started.

Half an hour later, all ten oligarchs were back around the conference table, fresh coffee supplied for them all, though none of the men would touch it.

It was already getting late, and Svetlana wanted to spend what remained of the day with her husband Sergej, who had been hosting family and friends at a separate function.

"I've been able to assess the progress of both teams––and I must say, I'm mightily impressed with how far you've been able to get in such a short period. Normally we take up to three years to complete a game's cycle, and yet, only months in, I see real progress already." Lev couldn't help but smile at her comments.

"Having thought hard about what I've just been told over this last hour by both groups––and gentlemen, I thank you for your frankness and openness in that regard––I have a clearer idea about which team is in pole position." Lev now glanced across to Matvey, watching for his reaction to what he thought Svetlana was about to say. "And the team in the lead is Matvey and his group." Matvey didn't move–– didn't move a muscle––and Lev couldn't help but look away. Each of the five men now sitting across from him seemed smug, arrogant even. Svetlana had said how advanced his own team had been, that she was surprised what Lev had told her, pleased that progress was so great––and yet she'd then placed the other group in the lead? A team which didn't stand a chance of going up against his nephew's Union, a Union that operated a different way to most. Did Matvey know therefore how it ran? Still, as soon as the first takeover attempt would be made, the others would close ranks. He'd warned his nephew about the imminent attempt, so he knew they would be waiting.

Yet, with all this being the case, thirty minutes in front of Svetlana Volkov, and Matvey had managed to convince her that his team, and not Lev's, were in front. How?

Svetlana stood up at that point, momentarily breaking Lev's flow of thought. "If you'll excuse me, I will leave you all now. As always, my home is open to you, but as you've all indicated that you would be making your own arrangements for accommodation tonight, these facilities have already been made available to other guests." They all knew this meant the other men of the Games. She left the room without anything further said, Lev himself standing and heading for the door, as Matvey and his team slowly started to rise.

Downstairs, the members of the T20 had long since departed the Games Room. Only the three victorious Hosts were staying the night, an ongoing tradition for the winner, or perceived victor, of any given Hunt. Lev Kaminski had gone in search of his nephew Dmitry, frustrated to find that he had already left.

Matvey came down the main stairs at that moment, passing the standing Lev as they crossed on the second floor, no words spoken between the two, though their eye contact communicated a whole batch of expletives. Matvey had made this personal, and Lev could now feel that. But a lion didn't have sharp teeth for no reason. He was up for the fight. He'd warn his nephew and do whatever it took to stop Matvey Filipov pulling off whatever it was he thought he was able to do. There was no way he was prepared to lose this particular battle––for the sake of his own nephew, and therefore hundreds of his employees who'd otherwise be out of work. He wasn't prepared to lose his honour either, something of immeasurable value, something he wouldn't allow anyone to steal from him, especially a man like Matvey Filipov, who had only joined their elite group the year before.

3

"When I was younger, I used to find the fact my birthday fell three weeks after Christmas really sad," Maggie said, a glass of wine in her hand, despite it being breakfast time. She'd slept very little the night before. "My folks were always broke after Christmas; it seemed out of all my siblings I got the least presents."

"I'm sure that wasn't true," Phelan said, himself with just a cup of coffee.

"Maybe not, but I still never liked it so close to such a big holiday. This year, however," and Maggie put the glass down on the coffee table, and sat astride Phelan as he relaxed on the sofa, "it's probably my best birthday ever!" She kissed him on the lips, which Phelan met, briefly, but she'd been drinking, not been to bed all night, and her breath was far from fresh. Just at the point his legs were starting to lose feeling, she got off him.

"Happy birthday, anyway, for what it's worth."

"Thank you," she said, this time just a kiss on the cheek, as Phelan rose to get breakfast ready.

The last couple of months had been a whirlwind for Phelan. Happier than ever with his wife and family following the news that their lives were no longer under threat, they'd been touring around Southern California and enjoying everything the Golden State had to offer them at that time of year, especially its weather. How he now missed his wife and boys.

That had all been interrupted––not permanently, he hoped, though the longer it continued, the more that fear surfaced––when Matvey had called him again, unexpectedly. The Russian, to whom he owed so much gratitude––though thinking that debt had been paid already––was demanding Phelan do one final thing. He'd been on a flight back to London before he'd really had time to process.

Here he was––wishing a happy birthday to a woman he'd once had an affair with, a genuine one that time––yet now pretending to be in love with her, sharing her bed each night, all for a man he was beginning to loathe. A man who a year and a half ago had offered the world to him, the millions in his bank account a testament to that––yet, he was no less a prisoner now in riches than he had been in the vestiges of a former life.

Maggie, for her part, was oblivious of the situation, which only made it worse. She was very much in love––contented, he could tell for sure––and probably planning to settle down with him for the rest of her life. It would make his betrayal, whenever it would inevitably come––he didn't know when Matvey would instruct him to do whatever it was he needed––all the more bitter. All the more devastating for a woman, he knew, who'd taken years to piece together her life the last time it all fell apart.

He didn't love her. Couldn't love her. And what of his wife and kids? What of their devastation if they were ever to find out what he'd been up to over the last weeks? What if his boys found out why he'd not been with them as another New Year came around? What then?

He'd been standing still in the kitchen, unaware that Maggie had been standing in the doorway just watching him, his thoughts racing away in his mind when she broke the silence.

"Phelan McDermott, you look like a man with a lot of surprises in store for me today, the way you were just standing there in silence. I can't wait!"

Phelan said nothing, giving her a half smile as his mind came back into focus, walking over to the fridge he was now too familiar with, in a home into which he wished he'd never ventured. He grabbed the bacon, four croissants in a paper bag on the side––still fresh he hoped––that he'd picked up the night before, and started to heat up a pan.

Some of her friends were coming around for a party later. He assumed it was still a surprise though he'd never been good at planning those sort of things, it was something his wife always did. And yet here he was, doing this without her––and for another woman.

"Maybe turn that bacon down a bit, handsome," Maggie said, appearing at the door again in her bathrobe, her leg sticking deliberately out through the central parting in the middle of the gown. "I don't officially turn forty until this afternoon, so if you want to enjoy me while I'm still in my thirties, why not join me in the shower," and she vanished, the shower on seconds later. Phelan's head sank, he felt sick with guilt, and as much as he tried just to enjoy it––Matvey had called it bonus sex––he couldn't. He loathed himself more with every passing day.

He reduced the heat on the hob to the lowest setting possible, the sizzle stopping almost immediately on the half cooked bacon, and left the kitchen. His t-shirt was off before he'd got up to the bathroom, an already naked Maggie with her hair under the water, opening the sliding door to the shower, as Phelan dropped his boxers onto the floor and climbed in next to her.

As January was coming to an end, the first few businesses that were being targeted by individuals within the T10––all men working with Matvey in his team, on his instructions––were starting to show signs of trouble. What had been an internal fight was now having to become a public one.

The first business declared itself bankrupt on the last Friday of the month. The fallout over the weekend news was quite extensive, a focus of the coverage being of the eight hundred employees who now didn't have a job to go back to the following week. Three of the other four firms that they'd been working on were also just days, if that, away from announcing a similar fate.

All five of this first wave of firms that Matvey Filipov had instructed his men to take down––they'd not even started focusing on the Banking Union yet––had each been vital recipients of financial aid to the tune of hundreds of millions. This funding had come from the four biggest banks in the Meridian Capital Union, the Union they were ultimately targeting, the very same one run by Dmitry Kaminski, member of the T20 and would-be President of Russia, come the March 2018 elections. He was yet to officially put himself forward––independent candidates still had until the middle of December that year to announce their nomination, with political parties given another month from that to put forward their man. By that time the following year––the end of January 2018––all names would be entered into the official race to become the next President of Russia. The elections would then be less than two months away. It was a long-held view that Putin would be re-elected for his second six-year term. Two men in the Games had other ideas about that.

In the Kaminski Union, the seven smaller banks had one vote each, but the four biggest ones had two votes each, so they effectively controlled the entire Union. These four banks had lent heavily to three or at most four, other businesses, bailout money for companies that had hit hard times during the financial crisis, money that had kept them buoyant. The four banks had been able to do this because they had themselves also taken out a huge loan. They were able to make the hefty repayments on it thanks to the interest they were charging the businesses which they had bailed out.

It was these same businesses that Matvey and his team were now taking on. The ones targeted in the first wave––there would be three more waves––were focused on the firms with the most significant repayments owing. By the time the last wave of takeovers would be completed, businesses owing as much as ninety per cent of the banks' income would have been sucked dry, bankrupted themselves and therefore the debt declared null and void. They didn't need to go after every business that owed them money––there just wasn't the time for that––but with the three or four firms per bank that they were taking out, there would be no recovery. Once they were all destroyed––the loan repayments stopped––Matvey would instruct Maggie, via Phelan, to get JP Morgan Chase to call in its mega loan that it had made to the Union, which they then wouldn't be able to repay. The four banks would have no choice but to be declared bankrupt–– paving the way for Matvey and his men to move in and take them all over––winning their contest but gaining so much more besides.

For Matvey Filipov, winning the Hunt was of secondary importance. He had Dmitry Kaminski firmly in his sights, even if the Russian in question as yet had no idea. Dmitry's uncle, Lev, who was himself heading up the other group of five oligarchs in the T10, only had his suspicions. Matvey trusted that by the time Dmitry and Lev realised what was going on, it would be too late.

"I see in the financial news that you've already succeeded in bringing down your target firm, Matvey," Valery said after the Russian had answered his mobile. Valery was the fifth member of Matvey's unlikely team, these men put together for the first time in a T10 event, and for the most part, thoroughly enjoying themselves. Success had a way of doing that to people like them.

"It's like I said. These outside firms will fall like trees in a forest, carving us a path right into the centre."

"Into the Banking Union."

"Yes, the very one."

"I'm having a little resistance with my target, Matvey. I was calling to see if you might be able to help me seeing as your firm has already declared itself bankrupt. From what I hear from the others, theirs aren't far behind yours in their announcement, either. It'll have the industry in a meltdown, fearing another crisis is imminent."

"Well, for some, it is." Matvey couldn't help smile to himself at that thought. "And yes, I will help you. This first wave has to be almost simultaneous so that we can then move onto the next. They won't know what's hit them."

"Thanks. Will they see it coming?"

"It soon won't matter if they do, the main damage has already been done. What could they do?"

"I won't try and guess that one, besides, you seem to have us well covered. I'll send over where I've got so far with my target business, and we can swap notes."

"No need, I know where you are up to," Matvey said, only now giving a hint of how deep he had men watching everything going on, reporting back to him the progress of all the men in the T10, especially his own teammates. Valery said nothing.

"Thanks for the help."

"Don't mention it." Matvey needed them for the moment as much as they needed him. Once this stage was all done, once operation Vlast was fully realised, he'd close down this whole event. Russia wasn't the place for rogue oligarchs left in secret and doing their own thing. He hoped he'd be able to offer them a new role in a rejuvenated Russia––a vital role in a nation that he believed could rise from the ashes and be great once more. And if they couldn't work with him then they would have to be removed. A time would come when they would have to decide once and for all––were they with him or were they against him? Then, there would be no middle ground.

"ANISSA, IT'S ME." It was the third call that the MI6 agent had received from Josée––a former Contestant within the Games––that month. It was the call she'd been waiting for.

"It's good to hear from you Josée. How are you doing?" Anissa had been working with a lawyer to try and build a case that would allow this Frenchwoman to bring a legal case against another former Contestant, Leona Chase.

"I'm so-so," she said, her English coming on well, her choice of phrase bringing a brief smile to Anissa's face. Josée was anything but so-so. She'd seen a man's throat slit right in front of her, while the guy was having sex with her in fact. She'd only herself escaped at the time because the attacker––Leona, who was able to claim the millions herself––had gone for the lottery ticket instead of the now traumatised French national. Josée had been having nightmares ever since. She'd not been able to work again since the incident, and she'd let herself get out of shape somewhat, which for a former fitness freak, was a huge deal.

"It's good to hear from you again. Have you made a decision?" Over the last few weeks, with the help of a French lawyer, Anissa had been able to put together a charge that she felt would stand up in court. As well as dealing with an actual crime––murder was murder after all––she hoped this was their big chance to bring the world of the Games out into the open for everyone to see what had been going on. Forced to answer questions before a judge, the defendant––and the same could be said for Josée also––would inevitably open up about those behind the event. Why she'd suddenly gone to Russia in the first place. How she'd obtained the papers to travel. When had she been approached and by whom to be deemed suitable for the event?

"I want to proceed as you have suggested, yes." Anissa let out a breath, unaware she had been holding it from the moment she saw Josée's number displayed on her screen.

"That's great news."

"I just need there to be some closure to all this. I need the nightmares to be over. I need to know why this all happened."

"I've said before, we can't promise all these things will be answered, but what I can promise is we'll do everything that is available to us to see that justice is served on all those involved. This isn't just about you or Leona––I want the men behind it all."

"I know, but this is still about what she did to that man, right? I mean, they're going to ask me about the murder? Why I was there myself, why I was having sex with him as he was murdered? They're all going to know about that, aren't they?"

"Yes, and again I'm sorry, there is no way around that."

Josée composed herself again, taking a few seconds before continuing, "I know what you said before, but I need you with me on this one. I want you there as I share this."

"I can't Josée, and we've gone over that." She'd been quite clear about that given her role within MI6. Not to mention the fact she wasn't officially in Russia at the time of the incident, shouldn't have been anywhere near the Armoury at the Peter and Paul Fortress in the centre of St Petersburg. She just couldn't be involved in her legal case.

"I just don't think I can do it on my own."

"You won't be on your own. The lawyer is a good lawyer, and she'll fight for you. She lives in Paris; I made sure it would be someone local to you so that you would be able to meet with her whenever you need to. Do you want me to put you in touch with her? I know you haven't been able to meet her yet in person, but I think you'd like her, and she is someone you can come to trust."

"I'm not sure I trust anyone anymore, Anissa." Anissa couldn't help but see how this had all nearly destroyed the young Frenchwoman's life.

"Time will heal," but as soon as she said it, she knew how empty and pointless it sounded. Josée seemed to brush it to one side, regardless.

"Will the trial be here?" Anissa had discussed this for a long time with the lawyer. Undoubtedly a trial in France, under French law, would be ideal for Josée. But the culprit––who'd yet to be charged, though now they had a witness prepared to testify, that would inevitably happen soon––was British, and the crime had been committed in Russia, the victim himself a Russian. The lawyer felt that the trial would most likely be held in Russia. Russia didn't have a good record of trying Brits on murder charges, but that was the least of her concerns. Right now it was the witness about whom she most cared. Anissa had taken her under her motherly wing, wanting to be involved as far as she could personally. Now, with yet more pleas for her to be present at the trial, Anissa did wonder if she'd been too hands-on, if she should have handed this onto someone else a lot sooner.

"I don't know," is all Anissa said after a long pause, before adding; "I'll have to consult with the lawyer about that, now that a charge can be brought against the accused."

"She's not just accused, Anissa, Leona killed him in cold blood. You were there, and you saw what she did."

"I know, Josée, it was just a figure of speech. I know she is guilty, which is why I came to you. I want you to tell your story. I want there to be justice for the man who she killed, who no doubt has relatives of his own, desperate for answers."

"Oh God, his relatives are going to be there, aren't they? I'm going to have to sit there and look them in the faces as I tell them all what I did to that man--what I let him do to me. And all for what? For a bloody lottery ticket? Am I that cheap?" She was crying again, and Anissa didn't know what to say, deciding to remain silent until the sobbing subsided enough for the conversation to continue.

"You aren't the person on trial here, she is. If it is easier for you, you'll be able to give your evidence via a video screen. They don't even need to know your identity, or see your face."

"Look, I said I'd do it, so whatever it takes, let's just get it done shall we?" She'd been living the nightmare for too long. It was time to face up to what she'd done, and then, when the dust settled, to try and somehow move on.

"Josée, we can sort out the practicalities later. You don't need to put yourself through anything too severe if you don't want to. The most important thing is that justice gets done. It's not about exposing you; it's about getting to the truth, bringing to justice a woman who has done a horrible crime, for the sake of some money."

"Millions, in fact."

"Exactly, and she's been living the good life ever since, as if nothing happened."

"And condemned me to a life of misery in the process."

"Which is why you are going to testify. It's time the world knew where the money came from."

"I still want you there with me."

"I can't; you know that."

"Please, Anissa, please." It was breaking her heart to deny this one little request, but it would expose Anissa if she were to be involved in the trial, it would open her up to a whole world of people––the Russians and their Games––who she didn't want knowing of her involvement.

"I need to go. Your lawyer will be in touch. You've made the right decision. We'll speak again soon," and she ended the call before she said anything more, anything she might later come to regret. She couldn't grant Josée her request to be involved. It was too dangerous.

Anissa speed-dialled the law firm she'd been working with that was based in Paris, and after getting put through to the lady in question confirmed that Josée was prepared to come forward.

"Very good, and thanks for letting me know," the lawyer said. Anissa agreed to send over details regarding Josée's address––she'd suggested the lawyer meet her that coming week to build a relationship with her client, someone that had been kept at arm's length from her up until then. Anissa had looked to protect Josée until it was clear what her decision was going to be.

Anissa ended the call, using the few words of French she remembered from secondary school in the process. She then went looking for Alex, wanting to fill him in on all that had just taken place over the last twenty minutes.

4

"Happy Valentine's Day, my handsome boyfriend," Maggie said, more vibrant and elated than he'd seen in a while. She landed a tray of various breakfast goodies onto his lap, jumping back onto the top of the duvet next to where he was now sitting up in bed, his face surprised. "Don't tell me you've forgotten!" He had.

"You just startled me, that's all." He thought of his wife, thousands of miles away, waking up in about eight hours, not with him on a day married folks were meant to share together. He thought of his boys–– who he'd only seen in snatched Skype calls over the last two months, made when Maggie was at work, and always from a public cafe or coffee shop. He couldn't bring himself to call from Maggie's home.

"You forgot!" she said again, teasing him now, kissing him on the lips anyway. "I've got plenty already just with you being here, so don't you go worrying about forgetting a card or not buying a nice bunch of flowers. Mind you, there's still time."

"I'll take you out for dinner, later, anyway." He'd have to find somewhere that had space. He couldn't stand the thought of an overly romantic dinner. It was all she would be expecting, however.

"That'll be lovely. Eat up; I need to get into the office early today. There's a bit of a crisis going on around Europe, London mainly. Many businesses have been suddenly going bankrupt." He'd heard a bit of the news, headlines she'd turned the TV on to watch, Phelan barely taking much notice, just noise in the background. But the headlines had been regular enough for him to pick up that something had been going on. He had no idea what it was, though.

"That's nice," he said, half heartedly, as he sipped the coffee.

"No it's not," she said, throwing a pillow at his head, which missed. "Hundreds of people are losing their jobs, tens of thousands affected by pensions and share prices. You have no clue about business, do you?"

"Not really," he lied. It had been the role he'd always had with her, the simple Irishman, a character that had sprung back on him––almost subconsciously––when he'd re-entered her life just before New Year.

It was gone seven that evening before Maggie left the office, Phelan waiting outside the main doors with a bunch of her favourite flowers, dressed up himself and a table booked at a nearby Italian. She kissed him, having run into his arms the moment she saw him there, oblivious to anyone else around her at the time. This was her man, and he'd come to meet her from work when she finished.

As always, not far away, a car with men working for Matvey sat watching, recording and tracking what was taking place. It seemed Phelan was very much in flavour with Maggie, which was an excellent thing. Because soon it would be time to move the plan forward, and Matvey knew he'd need Phelan's help to make Maggie do what he needed her to do––otherwise all he'd been working towards for months would have been for nothing. One way or the other, they'd get her to do what she had to do.

The Italian restaurant was packed mostly with couples––as you'd expect on Valentine's Day––red roses very much the order of the day, bunches standing all over the place. Phelan had opted for something different––roses were his wife's favourite.

As their tiramisu came, their second bottle of wine finished before the desserts were even ordered, both were in light spirits-- Maggie especially, who never held her drink as well as Phelan could.

"I've been thinking a lot about us, Phelan, you know; where things are going."

"Where are they going?" She smiled at him, unable to pick up on the nervousness in his voice at that moment, misreading the vacant look in his eyes, a lost soul.

"I'd like us to get married."

"What?"

"Come on, Phelan, I think it's time we took things forward. I'm not getting any younger. I turned forty last month, and one day soon I would love to start a family with you."

"Maggie, this is awfully fast. We've only just got together..."

"Rubbish. We've been together for years. There was just a long gap before we could continue where we left off the last time."

"I'm not ready."

"Not ready? What's stopping you? We already live together. Financially, I'm in a position that could support a family. I'd love to have two children, a boy and a girl would be perfect."

"Hold on right there, Maggie Thompson! We've not even talked about the future, and you already have me changing nappies. I've done all that before!"

"But I haven't! We haven't." She was speaking louder than was comfortable for Phelan now, a few heads noticeably turning, but people knew to keep their noses out of someone else's business.

"I just think it's all too soon."

"I knew you'd say that!"

"Say what?"

"I knew you'd be resistant at first, that you would act this way. It's so typical. You just need to see it happen, that's all. It's why I stopped taking the pill on my birthday. I could be pregnant already, and there would be nothing you could do."

"You stupid bitch!" Phelan screamed, standing up from his chair, pushing it back and away from him as he grabbed his coat, the restaurant in shocked silence, all faces momentarily turned their way, as the Irishman departed, Maggie just bursting into tears. She buried her head in her hands, too upset and too embarrassed to move from where she was.

In Paris, the last few weeks had seen multiple appointments between Josée and the lawyer which Anissa had put her in touch with. Josée had given her evidence, and a legal case was put forward. As February had come around, Interpol had been notified of the arrest warrant made out for Leona Chase. She was taken into custody in Spain––where she now lived––on the fifteenth of the month. The British embassy in Madrid had been notified. The case was already looking to be a complicated one.

In France's highest court, the material was put forward––including the video footage taken from outside the Armoury. While it wasn't explicitly Leona, with the other supporting evidence, including a copy of her migration card as well as the visa in her passport proving Leona was there during the reported crime, not to mention a first-hand witness, there was more than enough to detain her.

It took a week of hard talks, but in the end, it was clear the trial and case had to be taken up and made in St Petersburg, where the crime had taken place, and where the witness had herself been at the time.

An initial hearing was to be held in a month's time, where the lawyers for both women would put forward their case. Based on that, a full trial would or would not be called for, and if it were, only then would Leona and Josée be required to attend in person.

The challenge for Anissa––and she'd initially sat back and allowed developments to get as far as they had––was that Josée had not backed down from her demands. Should the trial be held in Russia, Anissa had to attend the event with her in person; otherwise, she wouldn't go through with it. Coming at a time when the lawyer was pushing for results, Anissa had agreed to that demand then, unclear as it had been if anything would get moved at all. Now she was tied to her word. If Anissa were to back out now, the whole case would collapse. Without a witness––who it could be proved was in Russia at the time of the crime, and was the one with the most to say, as she had nothing to lose by speaking up––there was no trial. It all hinged on Josée's involvement.

If there was no trial, then Anissa knew there would be no way to reveal how the Games and the oligarchs were behind the actions of both women in the first place. This had been the whole goal all along. She knew she couldn't back down now. So she'd agreed, much to Alex's dismay and repeated attempts to get her to change her decision. She said she couldn't now turn her back on Josée, not after giving Josée her word that she would be there.

Alex had relayed the situation to Sasha, who also didn't like the fact this was all taking place. Both men would appear in the video too––and while it wasn't clear who they were on camera, it would only put them more in the spotlight within their various authorities. That was a situation neither man wanted to happen––Sasha in particular. How the FSB would want to get their hands on an agent who had so blatantly broken the rules to work with MI6 as he had been doing for far longer than anyone knew. How long he could keep that all secret now, he did not know. And that thought troubled him deeply.

For now, it was just the French lawyer who would travel to St Petersburg for the middle of March pre-trial assessment which would happen before a Russian judge in St Petersburg. The lawyer for Leona Chase would also be present, but few––if any––others would be there at that point. Once the evidence had been assessed, the judge would make a call as to whether a trial would even be possible. There were now plenty of people who hoped it would never come to that.

In Madrid, the British authorities were working with their Spanish counterparts as Leona Chase sat in a police holding cell, kept away from other prisoners. Her substantial assets had been held, the court order and arrest warrants giving the authorities enough power to freeze whatever assets they could connect to Leona. If the money had not rightfully been hers, they were coming for it.

Leona had just said goodbye to her British lawyer, who'd flown down the moment the arrest was announced. She was due to fly to St Petersburg the following week to walk through every piece of evidence they had against her client. She also needed to work out who the witness was.

Leona sat in her cell, now alone, a prisoner and with a very dirty conscience. Had it all been worth it? Did what she had gained justify what she'd done to get it? How stupid she felt, now it was all catching up with her, now that her illusion of wealth––the mirage of success––had finally been shattered. They were onto her, and she knew there was no real escape. But who was it that was against her? Was it the Russians themselves? If that were the case, she'd hold nothing back. If they'd done this to her, she would give them up to lessen her guilt, lighten her sentence, if that was at all possible. She trusted her lawyer would be able to dismantle the whole ordeal before it ever came to anything. She hoped that she would soon be free and never have to set foot in Russia again.

DMITRY KAMINSKI LIVED on the road next to Buckingham Palace dubbed *Billionaires' Row* for obvious reasons. He'd been based in the UK for some time, though he was contemplating a move back to Russia in the near future––if his political aspirations led him there. The British, or at least a select few inside some of the key positions of power within the government and Security Services, certainly hoped he might win against Putin in the next year's elections.

Dmitry was leaving his residence for the day, on the way to the bank he owned and spent most of his time at, when his mobile phone rang, a number very few people knew or had access to. He looked at the caller ID, showing him that a fellow oligarch––and fellow member of the T20 in fact––was calling him. He answered the phone in the privacy of his rear seat, as his driver navigated their way through the busy roads.

"Arseni, to what do I owe the pleasure," he said, answering the call. Arseni Markovic--known as Twelve within the Games--was a man whose $2.2 billion fortune had primarily come from metals of all shapes and sizes. Unlike Dmitry, he was still based in Russia.

"I've just heard about the arrest of Leona Chase."

"Who?" Names meant little to him at the best of times, unless they were wealthy, powerful, influential or better still a combination of all three. Leona Chase sounded like none of those.

"My Contestant from last year's big event." He was talking about the New Year, which meant this Leona had been up against his Contestant that particular time, a Frenchwoman he'd thought was up to the task named Josée Allard. She'd failed, Leona pocketing the €30 million prize on offer in that particular Hunt.

"What about her?" Arseni, indeed all men of his standing--Kaminski included--didn't make calls for the sake of making calls. It apparently involved Dmitry somehow, and he was starting to feel concerned about what might be said next.

"She's been arrested in Spain, charged with murder after what happened in Peter," he said, the implications already slotting into place, before the reference to Peter--what Russians affectionately called St Petersburg--had even been said. Arseni continued; "The case hangs on the credibility of the evidence supplied by the main witness--your girl, Josée."

"How far have they got?"

"It's being heard at a pre-trial hearing in Peter before one judge next month. It could get nasty. You need to get your girl to stand down."

"She's not my girl anymore. She lost me that Hunt, remember. And I had no direct involvement with her; she doesn't have a link back to me. I'm not getting involved now." He couldn't risk the bad publicity.

"You have to!" spat Arseni, who had more at stake if people dug deep enough. "It could expose everything we are involved in––everything we've ever done."

"How? Who's going to tell them that, in some isolated murder case? I'm certainly not going to say anything. Are you?"

"Don't get smart with me, Kaminski. I know you are thinking more about your public image than you are about the welfare of those within the Games." There it was, evidence that word was getting out, and while he might not be getting Arseni's vote for President, it was clear the idea of him running was beginning to be widely accepted––anticipated even, no doubt. "That would be a mistake. You need us all just as much as we need you to help silence this situation."

It wouldn't have been the first time that such actions were taken to shut down something that might otherwise rise to bite them, to expose what was going on amongst the very wealthiest people Russia had to offer.

"Arseni, your Contestant took the law into her own hands the moment she decided to kill someone for that money. Yes, it's why we love the entertainment––the thrill and wonder at what these simple people will do when offered the chance to get rich. But she chose to kill. She slit his throat, and while that situation is ugly––certainly many would see it as wrong––we are not the ones who made that happen. We have nothing to fear." He sure hoped that was the case. "Besides, we have enough influence in all the right places to make this one go away quietly, no?"

"I'm not sure." Arseni wasn't well connected in St Petersburg, especially amongst the judicial system. And it all depended on how hard they dug. If it were just handled as a crime––if there were no deeper motive for bringing this to trial––then most likely their role behind the scenes in it all would never get a mention. But what if that was the very reason it was being brought before a judge? What then?

"Svetlana wouldn't allow anything to threaten the Games. She'll put a stop to it. Have you spoken with her?"

"Of course I haven't!"

"Well, may I suggest you do, assuming she hasn't heard already."

"You sound so pathetic, you know that Kaminski, sitting there in your lofty position, not daring to get your hands dirty in case it ruins your image. You'll need men like me on your side if you ever dream of running for Office. And believe me, if you don't do something about this situation––if you don't pull out all the stops to silence it once and for all––I'll make sure that your involvement in this whole situation comes out if it ever gets to trial. How does that work for you?"

"You're a coward, Arseni, that's all you are. Threatening me so that you don't have to do what you were too scared to do yourself. You can't threaten me. And when I'm President you'll regret you ever tried."

"Without me, you'll never be President. I can guarantee that!"

"You? You can't guarantee anything! Go to hell you…" but the line went dead before Kaminski could finish his string of expletives. He sat there fuming to himself, more riled than he had been for a while, annoyed to have been threatened personally, but the more he dwelt on it all, the more he took the threat to heart. He knew there was a lot of truth to the suggestion that he'd need men on his side if he were to run for President successfully. Though there were more influential people than Arseni, he would make a far better ally than he would an enemy. Kaminski didn't need enemies. As the car continued its slow but steady journey through the rush-hour streets, Kaminski sat there pondering what he could do to help, how he could get involved without his presence in it all ever being noticed.

Svetlana Volkov had been heading for the airport––a flight waiting to take her to America for one month of filming on her latest movie project––when Arseni called her. While the men in the two groups within the Games did have reason to connect with her––and her husband Sergej––outside of events, it was highly unusual to speak on the telephone.

Replacing the handset––thankfully her husband was meeting her at the airport, so it was only her in the car when the call was received––she sat there for the last few minutes of her journey thinking through the implications. As the car pulled in through the gates of the private terminal, she could see her husband was already waiting for her. Putting on her smile as always, she greeted him, and they both boarded the jet, which was ready to go once they were comfortable.

Husband and wife chatted freely, before Sergej reclined his chair, wanting some sleep, Svetlana pondering everything, wondering what––if anything––could be done to minimise their exposure.

5

Phelan had not gone home the night he'd stormed out of the Italian restaurant, Maggie no doubt finding it fast becoming the worst Valentine's Day ever. He'd booked himself into a hotel, and was processing a way out of the hell-hole in which he'd now found himself. Though she hadn't said anything, the fact Maggie had stopped taking the pill, the mere chance that she was pregnant--there was more than enough possibility that he had impregnated her since her birthday--brought it all crashing back to Earth for him. It had suddenly become more than he could handle.

More than just a game--more than just an errand he had to run for a man he should never have got involved with--now it was far more severe than that.

Phelan had begun to recognise the vans or vehicles Matvey's men used to keep a watch over him. He'd found out they were watching him the first day he'd re-entered Maggie's life. He'd spotted them occasionally since too and was sure they were there always, somewhere, even if he wasn't aware.

So when he left the hotel foyer that morning and saw the van just sitting there across the road, he went straight over to it, opened the passenger door and got in.

"What are you doing?" the man behind the wheel demanded.

"You shut your mouth, and you listen very carefully to everything I am about to say because I need you to repeat it word for word to your boss." There was mute agreement, so Phelan just continued after the pause. "I'm done. That's it, I'm not doing this anymore and if that costs me the money--hell, even if you dish the dirt on me with my family--I'll come clean, and I'll explain everything to them. But I'm not doing this anymore to that woman. It's gone too far. You hear me? I'm done," and he got back out of the van, shutting the door behind him before anyone could say another word. He'd made his point. Matvey would soon get the message, and that, he hoped, would be that.

The message got relayed to Matvey; his men were told to wait for his response.

That response came just after lunch, less than three hours after Phelan had climbed into the van, and before he'd done anything he might otherwise have regretted. The men found Phelan in a nearby pub--two empty pint glasses sat on his table, and they could only imagine there had been more--and they merely went up to him, dropped a brown envelope onto the table in front of him before walking away.

Phelan looked up, a little surprised, and watched the men leave--one of the two being the same man he'd spoken earlier to in the van--before picking up the envelope. It was flat, and when he slid it open, there were just three photographs inside, the first two of his sons--taken, he assumed, reasonably recently, given the look of their location and the growth of his oldest boy--as well as a similar one of his wife. Except across the face of his wife, presumably arranged under direct instruction from Matvey himself, there was a target, as if looking through the lens of a rifle. His wife, the target.

His mobile phone rang at that exact moment. It was Matvey.

"I see you have received my package."

"You bastard!"

"Language, Phelan, or maybe it's just the alcohol in your blood speaking. Listen carefully. I don't want anything to happen to your family, but believe me, if you deviate now from what I require of you, that is precisely what will happen to them. Am I clear?" He couldn't bring himself to say anything, to acknowledge anything, to give Matvey that satisfaction. His silence would have to be enough. "Good, I'll take that as an acceptance. You only need to play happy families with Miss Thompson for a couple more months, so stop having a paddy, and be the man she thinks you are."

"She wants a baby, goddam you. It isn't a game to her; this is everything."

"Grow up, Phelan, and be the man. So she wants a baby? There are things you can do to prevent that."

"She's already stopped taking the pill––stopped a month ago already so for all I know she is already pregnant. This wasn't what I agreed to at all!"

"You didn't agree to anything; this is what I ordered you to do, and until the time comes that I no longer need to involve her, that's exactly what you'll be doing, am I clear? So what if she wants a baby––start suggesting baby names for all I bloody care! But step out of line on this once more or threaten what I've worked very hard for, for many years, in any way again and it'll be your boys who'll be without parents. Understand?"

Phelan swallowed hard; "Understood. I'll do it. You leave them alone, and I'll do what you need me to do these next few months. Only, you get your men away from my family!"

"Okay, Phelan, okay. I think we have an understanding. As it happens, it should only be another two months or so before I need Maggie Thompson to play the starring role. So in the meantime, talk about kids––maybe an engagement ring wouldn't go amiss, either. Yes, that might work nicely. Offer her everything she has ever wanted over these next weeks, so much so that she'll do anything to keep it––to keep you."

"You'll rot in hell for this Filipov; you know that!"

"Less of the drama, Phelan, please, and be civil. We've both done things we'll one day regret––as you know only too well––but that day isn't now. I'm too busy living to think about whatever might or might not be awaiting me."

The call ended. Phelan ordered another beer, his mind suddenly clear. Matvey had got him focused again, and in doing so, had suggested it was just a couple more months. He could do this for eight more weeks to finally be clear. Whatever it was that Matvey needed doing, he knew he could get Maggie to deliver. She was mad about him, and maybe that made it too easy. Perhaps that was why it all felt so wrong?

He pushed those thoughts from his mind. Looking up a private clinic on his phone's internet browser, he found something suitable and made a call.

"Oh hello. I need to arrange to have a vasectomy––I'm paying cash and I'll pay over the odds for an immediate appointment. Is this something you can arrange for me?"

BY THE BEGINNING OF MARCH, the third wave of takeovers was already well underway. Matvey had spoken with each of the other four men in his team, and they'd moved their attention onto the next targets, following the successful completion of the first wave of closures. Some of the companies were being absorbed into other businesses––usually rivals, or sometimes the Russians' own empires––but most were just laid waste. It was like a child going on a rampage through a Lego city; pieces left everywhere, only destruction in their wake.

They'd slashed their way through this forest. Now the banks in the centre––those previously hemmed in, secure banks––were visible. And more than that, they were vulnerable.

The fourth wave, which would overlap the ongoing third wave and take out the final two firms that possessed the biggest danger to the Union, was undertaken a week later. In total eighteen businesses had been targeted, and once successfully destroyed––the takeover was aggressive by nature, slashing rather than pruning––only carnage remained. They weren't doing this to keep the existing businesses healthy.

With the eighteen firms out of the picture, it would represent a hugely significant hole in income for the banks--in Kaminski's case, with his flagship bank, a ninety per cent hole--and then the final stage would be straightforward.

The five men had been in regular contact--they would meet in person during the upcoming conference in Davos as they always did when the world's wealthiest people gathered annually--as well as over the telephone.

With Matvey's inside contacts--men and women he'd put in place sometimes years before to be right now where he needed them to be--the whole process over the last three months had been remarkably smooth. They had yet to hit a real glitch. Matvey had known where to hit and exactly how to do it. The businesses had fallen like dominoes.

Crucially, no one had yet to connect the collapse of these eighteen businesses with the Union, and that was because Kaminski hadn't advertised the fact they'd made these loans to bail out what had been critical national companies that the government had deemed vital at the time. Where was the government now when their help could have made a difference? A bailout was one thing--stopping an aggressive takeover was something the government rarely got involved in, however much it looked like that from the outside. It was just business. These things happen.

It was only Kaminski, in the loop via his uncle as, who knew this was not just one of those things. This was specific targeting, and of a nature to get to him personally. They'd found his weak spot, and he could do nothing to stop them coming for him next.

DMITRY KAMINSKI PULLED up outside Duke's club twenty minutes after his arranged time to see Thomas Price. The British MI6 Deputy

Director General was no doubt already there––he usually was––and no doubt expecting the Russian's tardiness.

As Dmitry walked in through the security guarded main doors–– men who knew him well enough and didn't stop him, but men more than ready to prevent others from entering if needed––the in-house host on duty confirmed that his guest had indeed already arrived–– no surprises there––and was waiting for Dmitry in their usual booth.

As always, there were very few people in the club, three other tables occupied, the rest just clear of any trappings. It was how it always was. As exclusive as you could get, there was a long waiting list for membership and the weekday allowance was even smaller. It was how they wanted it. Everyone respected the other members' privacy. It was, therefore, a place for politicians, the Security Service and wealthy businessmen to come and talk quietly, without fear of some journalist listening in from the next table. It was their domain.

Thomas stood to greet Dmitry as the Russian walked over to the booth, the Brit shaking the hand of his guest, both men's grip strong and true. Hardly old friends, though there was indeed some shared history, and politically––as well as economically––it was undoubtedly true that they viewed Kaminski as a friend to the UK. A friend who––with their backing––they hoped would become the next President of Russia.

Drinks were ordered; it was mid-morning, so these were hot and plentiful––a jug of coffee and pot of English Breakfast tea placed carefully in the middle of the table by the man working the bar that day. He left them to it after leaving some milk, and the two men poured their favourite refreshment, as Dmitry then took off a jacket.

"There's something I've not fully explained to you, that I need you to know now. And I need you to do something," Dmitry said, Thomas instantly wary of the tone, dreading he was going to thoroughly dislike whatever it was the Russian was about to tell him.

"Go on, I'm listening," is all he opted in response.

"The spate of takeovers and bankruptcies there have just been," he said. Price was well aware of the general business news, though he had not taken too keen an interest, aware enough that some scaremongers were predicting the start of a second financial crisis. "They aren't random, and these firms weren't at risk. They've been deliberately targeted, as a way of getting to me. They're coming for my Union, and I don't think I can do anything to stop them now."

"Who are? What do you mean? These firms had nothing to do with you, the ones that have recently gone bankrupt, I mean."

"There is something you don't know about them because I hadn't released it to the markets. But each of the four main banks in my Union had heavily financed the salvage packages for these eighteen companies that hit rocky ground during the recent crisis. We lent aggressively, borrowing heavily in the process. All eighteen firms were on strict payment plans––we've got billions tied up in these firms, and now they have all been either declared bankrupt or soon will be."

"You can't have only been working with these firms? You must have many other interests, too?"

"Of course, but following the crisis, we focused everything on a few firms. My bank invested heavily in the four key businesses, as we saw it, and following advice from the British government. We were trying to help. So ninety per cent of our income is now––was––dependent on these four businesses repaying the loans we made them. Now that is gone."

"Can you still make repayments yourself?"

"Probably, yes, certainly I can personally. I have my own money to use if needed, to prop up the payments, but that isn't true for the other banks. It'll swallow all our operating money, and even if I can speak with JP Morgan Chase and readjust the repayment plan a little, it'll take everything we have."

"Dmitry, how could you get so sucked into a few companies?"

"I was trying to bloody help your nation if you care to remember! Don't patronise me as if I'm new to all this. Of course, I now know it was a bloody stupid mistake––I should have let them collapse, and all those jobs just be lost. But I didn't. I was asked to help, and we stepped in––I got the whole Union involved, though it was the big four banks that carried the risk. Without having done that, there would have been no danger to any of us, and yet now, we're wide open. So I need your help. I need the British government to help us negotiate with our creditor and give both sides certain guarantees that will secure our immediate future."

"I'm not the government, Dmitry, in case you forgot."

"Screw you! You're bloody government when it suits you. You're all the same, you lot. You've been fostering a relationship with me, and for what? But what's it really worth to you all? Because I need your help now, and if I don't see what I want, it's going to have an impact on my attitude towards everyone going into the future. You got that?"

"Calm down, Dmitry. I was merely stating I'm MI6 and in that role––as it's designed to be––I am completely separate from the political sphere. But I do see where you are coming from and that, now, in your time of crisis, a solid and heartfelt response and intervention from our side would go a long way to forging a lasting relationship with you, and in time, your nation."

"You do talk a load of crap when you get going, but it's good crap." He was smiling again now. "So we have an understanding? You help me through this mess, and we'll be able to keep on meeting like this."

"Yes," Thomas said, suddenly aware he didn't necessarily have the power or role to state that categorically, but it was what his Russian guest needed to hear at that moment, so it was all he'd say. "I'll need a little time, but I'll make sure we back you in this. With all the job losses related to these other eighteen collapses, it'd be an easy sell I think to stop the rot from spreading. I know the markets are already in a little bit of a negative spin. It doesn't take much nowadays."

"Good. Please keep me informed of whatever you can accomplish. I'll do the same from my side."

"Who's behind it then? You said it was personal, that they were using it to target you?"

"That is maybe a problem for another day if I ever need your help in that regard. Chances are––especially if you do your bit––that problem will take care of itself. The priority now is that you cover my back. Let me worry about who's behind all this and deal with that myself."

"Okay, but this better not be anything that'll come back to bite us, okay?"

"You are not in a position to be able to bargain with me, Mr Price. You need me a lot more than I need you, just remember that." That didn't seem true from where he was currently sitting, quite the opposite. Thomas had not seen Dmitry so worked up in a long time. Things didn't usually seem to get under his skin––men of wealth usually always had layers of protection so that real life issues never got close enough. That was apparently not the case this time, and the Russian had been nearly pleading for help. He let it drop.

The two men finished their drinks, their meeting over, each going their separate way. Dmitry left first, followed just minutes later by Thomas, each with crucial meetings ahead of them, and now added to that, the DDG needed to find a way to speak with those at the decision-making level of one of the world's biggest firms.

6

Phelan had returned to Maggie a more controlled man, more focused--as well as an infertile man following his rushed procedure at the clinic. He wasn't going to tell her anything about that and trusted she didn't want him to jump straight into bed with her. Their last words had been harsh--he'd been harsh towards her advances--so they'd need to work through that before anything else might occur anyway.

They went for lunch during the following day, Maggie only able to give him an hour to meet her, work and the ripples coming from these apparently random bankruptcies still causing rumours and fear to spread. They met just around the corner from her city centre office, and after eating something--the food rushed down, as the ice was slowly broken--he'd been able to apologise for his outburst. It'd been a shock at the time--he didn't like change, he'd told her. She'd bought his display.

The more he immersed himself in Maggie's life, the more he felt the betrayal of his wife. The image of her with a target across her face--as if a sniper was watching her steadily, Bluetooth earpiece on their head, just waiting to pull the trigger. Phelan couldn't shift the image, nor the danger he felt his wife, and the whole family, were now unknowingly facing. And he wasn't there to protect them––in fact; he was in London living with another woman––sleeping with a woman who wasn't his wife––all for what? He wasn't sure, had never in fact been sure what it was he'd be required to do. Matvey had not yet told him, just that it was imminent; whatever that meant.

He was losing weight––not that it was evident at that moment––but he'd noticed it himself. He was drinking too much as well. Sleep had been erratic for weeks already, despite the happy front he put on when he knew Maggie was watching him. And she did like to watch him. Entirely why, he wasn't sure. Maybe it was just her contentment, her joy at seeing a man––and Phelan at that––in her life again? Perhaps it was the realisation that long-forgotten dreams of starting a family of her own were now possible? Maybe she didn't trust him, could see through his disguise, knew about his dirty little secret that he'd worked so hard at keeping from her? Maybe it was something else entirely?

He was living in limbo. It was not what he'd envisaged when Matvey proposed he get involved in the Games and when Matvey had detailed how he would guide him to a successful outcome––a very profitable one at that––which would set him and his family up for life. And they'd tasted a bit of that the last month or so before he'd left. Life had been good, great even. And then the call had come. Like a call from the hospital in the dead of night alerting those listening to some devastating news, his world had slowly imploded over the last few months. None of it was fun anymore––had he ever really enjoyed the fact he was deceiving someone so completely? What did coming through this all even look like for them? What would it do to her? How would he explain it––if indeed he said anything––to his wife and children? It'd been this lost feeling, this growing and fast expanding emptiness that had been eating away at him the longer he lived that lie in London.

With lunch finished––they'd started the conversation, but much more was needed––he and Maggie parted, Phelan agreeing to meet her when she finished work. At least they weren't arguing with one another. That was a start.

He filled his afternoon by taking a long walk around the city, hitting a few of the parks when they occurred, and just wanting space to clear his head of all the negative thoughts that were threatening to spiral out of control. To some degree, the flowers in bloom in Green Park did just that, the openness of Hyde Park and the crowds that walked the busy streets, the roads full of black cabs, all helping him lose himself in order to find a new purpose. He couldn't put Maggie's well-being before that of himself or his family. If he had to pick the lesser of two evils, it'd be Maggie Thompson to take the hit. This whole situation couldn't destroy what he'd left behind in America––what he longed with every fibre of his being to be united with once again. That wasn't going to be how his story ended.

Whatever it took, he'd play the role Matvey had demanded he play. He'd do what he needed, and as far as Phelan understood, that would be easier to do the more thoroughly he was wrapped up in Maggie's life. He should propose to her, therefore. That's what she'd suggested––marriage and a family the very thing that had caused him to blow his top with her. These things took time, and because of the vasectomy, the family bit would not be possible anyway. So he'd push that angle as much as was possible. If Matvey was true to his word––something the last month had caused Phelan to question for the first time in his relationship to the Russian––this should all be over before anything got too serious, or problematic.

He headed straight for Hatton Garden, the renowned jewellery district of London, in search of a ring. Matvey had given him ample spending money––it seemed there were few limits when it came to getting things done for the Russian––and Phelan would see how far that money would stretch now, wanting something that was eye-catching. She would be able to sell it when he was gone, recouping a significant amount of money––no doubt small compensation for a broken heart––but at least it was something. The more expensive the ring, the happier Phelan felt about doing this.

At six, he was once again waiting outside her office––in much the same way he'd done the first time he had arrived back in London, following her all the way home only to stage an accidental encounter with her as she exited a cafe. This time she spotted him right away--he'd told her he was coming anyway--and she smiled, looking happier than she'd been at the start of lunch, joy back in her soul. He handed her the massive bunch of flowers he'd been holding out front--there was no way to hide them from her--and she kissed him warmly on the lips.

If he allowed himself--and he'd nearly done that fatally once before it all came out about his marriage--he could have fallen for her. He suppressed his body's natural response to her kiss while meeting her and kissing back as best he could.

"So, where are you taking me?" He hadn't mentioned dinner, but it had been implied as they finished lunch and he'd texted her that afternoon to confirm he was coming for six and that she couldn't work late that day.

"You'll see," is all Phelan replied, Maggie just delighted to go along with her man, as in love with him as was possible for someone at that stage of a relationship, oblivious to Phelan's other life.

It was two hours later, over dessert, when Phelan produced the ring. Maggie screamed in excitement and got up from her chair and moved towards him, kissing him before saying yes multiple times. Heads had turned all around them, a few shouts of congratulations for the obviously happy couple. He placed the ring on her finger--at twenty thousand it was far from the most expensive option available, but he felt it did the job nicely. He'd also pushed Matvey's money as far as he thought was safe to go without it making waves.

"My God, baby, this must have cost you a fortune!" She didn't seem too concerned about that fact, however.

"It's nothing, my darling, all worth it if it makes you happy."

"You make me happy, silly, but I do love the ring!"

A bottle of champagne arrived--the restaurant sensing the moment, though Phelan knew it would later appear on the bill--but while Matvey was funding him during this operation, he didn't care what it cost. The higher the price, the better, not that it would ever hurt a man as financially secure as Matvey Filipov.

"I think we should get married straight away," Maggie said as they walked in through the front door of her West London home. She'd been planning a few things in her head on the way when she wasn't marvelling at the chunk of diamond now prominently displayed on her left hand. "We don't need an expensive, fancy wedding. You've spent enough on the ring."

"Nonsense. There is no need to rush the preparations. You'll need at least six months to let everyone know––much longer probably to make sure everything you want is available. That'll take us to the end of the year, which is possible if you want a winter wedding. Or maybe we should think about next spring?"

"That's a whole year away!"

"And, I was raised a good Catholic boy, remember. I don't think we should sleep together until the big day. Give us something to look forward to again later."

"You are kidding me?" She looked at him in total surprise. Yes, he was Irish, but all the months she'd known him across their two relationships, he'd been anything but a good Catholic boy.

"I'm serious." He'd been impressed with the way his plan had come together, sounding natural, sounding like something someone in his position might say. It would certainly solve the physical side of their relationship, and any talk of starting a family. While he'd had the operation, the clinic had insisted it would be six months before he'd be given the all clear, that a pregnancy could still occur before that if he wasn't wearing a condom. And since she'd mentioned about not being on the pill––and he still didn't use contraceptives, being a Catholic, albeit a lapsed one––this seemed the best solution possible.

"Then we can't possibly wait to get married until next spring. I'd be forty-one already. I think we should get married this summer. In a few months' time. We can go anywhere in the world if you want. The Caribbean maybe?"

"There's no way our folks will be able to travel at such short notice. Most have probably got their summer plans sorted already."

"Well, they can change them––or we don't need them there anyway. I want to marry you, and I don't want to wait another year before I can be with you again."

"Okay, the summer it is then," Phelan said, his face calm, a smile appearing where stress might otherwise have been attempting to creep through. Assuming Matvey knew what he was talking about—and unfortunately, he usually did—Phelan would be long gone before the summer, long gone before they applied for a marriage licence only to have it confirmed he was already married. Long gone before this all got too serious.

"Great!" She kissed him again, pressing into him, her hands running all over his back, and down onto his jeans.

"Remember, nothing until the wedding night. I mean it."

"Phelan! You're impossible," she screamed but relented. "This is going to be tough."

MATVEY WAS IN MOSCOW, which for a wealthy Russian oligarch was no unusual thing, except this particular man tried to spend as little time there as possible. For the last few years, he'd mainly based himself in Monaco, where he had a sizeable property, as well as his yacht.

He was in Moscow because that was where the men he'd come to meet were all gathering. Following the success the previous September of the Army-2016 military and technical forum, another event had been planned—this exhibition larger still—for the following spring, and everyone within the Russian military chain of command was going to be there.

Russian Defence Minister Sergei Shoigu was once again there for the opening day. Matvey had arranged lunch with the Minister before he was due to leave the event altogether—it was mainly for the publicity angle that he was there, other men did the real work. Still, Matvey wanted to curry favour with Sergei, who'd been elected to the role in the Duma one year before, meaning he still had several years in office to run—a position that would overlap whoever the next President would be. That alone made Sergei a key target for the billionaire.

Lunch had been amicable––Matvey had kept things very low key; he wasn't ready to announce too widely his intention to challenge Putin the following year––and an understanding was reached. They agreed to meet again, if needed, and to work closely together in the future, something Matvey himself had proposed, the Minister like all politicians only too happy to have another high-value benefactor on board.

Matvey's main work at the event was with the men who ran the military. These men, having worked closely with President Putin himself for many years already, were immensely loyal to the man they saw as the best fit for their country, the best man to lead their nation. History dictated in the Motherland that unless a President had the military in hand, anything could happen. A coup was hard to stop in a country so vast, an army so large. It was the men who ran these various divisions––the military, the air force, the navy as well as several specialist units––who therefore carried vast amounts of power and with that, responsibility.

As always, Matvey found that money was an excellent loyalty neutraliser. Throw enough of the stuff in a particular direction, and loyalties could change overnight.

Putin was due to attend the exhibition himself––this was on the third day of the five-day event––by which time Matvey hoped to already be on his way home, his task completed. That gave him a little over forty-eight hours to mix it up with the men, some of whom he'd never met before, others he'd bumped into irregularly down the years. What was important was that they remembered him––more than that, they respected him. He had to leave them a good impression, someone strong and leader-worthy, someone not afraid to make tough decisions, someone willing to shed blood to save their nation; a true Russian leader––a Presidential type, no less. Someone every Russian looked up to––idolised in fact––and the perfect Russian President.

The type of leader the West, in general, never understood. Matvey often marvelled how little America and its allies understood about the Russian psyche, how the people wanted their leaders to be strong and ruthless, why that desire had allowed Communism to blossom as it had before a better system was put in place. Matvey understood it, however. And he was now finally placed to become the person he hoped his country could get behind. Someone to pick up from where Putin had taken his nation, but to then take it three steps forward. To make Russia a country that the countries of the world feared once more. To become the genuinely global superpower they already should have been for the past few decades.

The nation that first sent a man into space, the country that advanced the space race so much that in turn, it spurred the Americans to make a moon landing. Russia should once more be the nation that other nations want to beat. Once again they should be significant competition. They had the resources--both natural and monetary--as well as the people; people willing to give themselves--to die even--for a cause worthy enough. Russians had never shied away from hard work anywhere near as much as those in Europe and the West had done. It was time for his nation to rise once again. Time to take their place at the head of the table. Time to no longer allow weak decisions to govern the futures of their people and their children after them.

As Matvey mixed with the military, his presence there was noted but not always warmly welcomed. As with any pack of lion cubs, whenever another dominant male entered the picture, there was always fear about what might happen. What would take place if and when the dominant man returned? Putin was due in two days--would Matvey still be strutting his stuff when the Boss arrived?

As planned, Matvey was already flying back on his jet to Monaco when the President arrived at the event. Matvey's presence there would get a mention--there were a large number of millionaires and billionaires at the event, given it was a trade fair--and Putin could only guess why that particular oligarch had made the trip to Russia in the first place.

For Matvey, he had met with each of the key commanders at least twice over the previous two days, the first encounter, especially when he hadn't ever met them before, always reasonably brief, reasonably civil. They didn't know who he was, of course, until he said goodbye and left them his card––which they would no doubt pass to someone, or check themselves, to find he was, in fact, a man worth over $11 billion. That made the second meeting all the more comfortable. When Matvey went round again, he found he got a noticeably more positive reception, especially from those who hadn't known who he was at their first encounter. He'd won their respect. He knew that was always the first stage along the road to winning their loyalty. He was sure he would arrive at that particular destination, before too long, somewhere further down the line.

Now airborne, thirty minutes into his flight back home, Matvey called Phelan once again.

"I'm going to send you some detailed information tomorrow," he said, knowing it was now time for Phelan to get Maggie to do what she needed to do. "It's important you understand everything involved. Go somewhere quiet and read it all through. Don't mention anything about it to Miss Thompson. It'll then be your job to personally convince her that this is what she has to do––this is the cost of her love for you, and all that it means for your future together. I'll include in the package information that you will then be able to give to her. It'll prove that the Union is verging on bankruptcy and that her actions are therefore justified. You can pretend this information was given to you––or you obtained it by your own means––whatever you like. I'll leave that up to you."

"And what if she doesn't do it? What if after everything I say she still doesn't do what you want? What then?"

"You'll have to make her, Phelan. But the information you hand her will do enough to convince her that it's also now in the best interest of her employer. They can't risk not acting. It'll happen, don't worry."

The call ended. Matvey didn't want to get into a conversation about the what ifs. There were, of course, no guarantees––he didn't like strong-arm tactics, but he'd get ruthless if he needed. It had all been planned too carefully, too painstakingly, for years for it to all come unstuck over a few morals. Yes, if Maggie instructed her employer to call in the loan it would be considered entirely irregular, totally unethical and a breach of trust. But it would be justified, and prove to be when the Union couldn't produce the money. Only then would her actions be seen for what they were in the bright light of day. Before that, there would be a hell of a storm, and as much as he would like to be on the inside to see what went on, he would have to be content to watch from the sidelines.

7

Breakfast was busy as usual at Anissa's house as her two boys fought over the cereal boxes and tried not to pour milk everywhere, which they semi-successfully managed. Her husband Paul was sitting in the lounge with his coffee and the paper, the television on in the background. Anissa glanced over at it when Dmitry Kaminski's face appeared, his name displayed along a moving ticker on the bottom of the BBC screen at that same moment.

"Can you turn it up please?" Anissa called, coming into the lounge, her husband glancing at the screen as the sound increased, though he soon went back to his paper.

"In an unprecedented economic move, the US giant JP Morgan Chase's London lending division last night called in the loan of $100 billion that it made less than four years ago to the Meridian Capital Union. They have stated that it had made this move based on unconfirmed reports suggesting that solvency within the Union––to which British-based Russian billionaire Dmitry Kaminski is a senior figure––was now questionable.

"Representatives from JP Morgan Chase and Meridian Capital have refused to comment, but all trading in the Banking Union's shares have been suspended immediately, the share price having dropped ten per cent at the close of business last night based on the emergence of the rumours."

The news reporter moved on to another story, Anissa standing there for a moment, the sound switched back to mute. She wouldn't have thought much about it--business never interested her all that much--except for the inclusion of Kaminski in it all, and very centrally too, from what the report suggested. She pulled out her phone and went back into the kitchen, as her boys were just finishing, each chasing the other out and upstairs, seeing who could brush their teeth the first.

"Alex, it's me. I've just seen a report on the news that was all about Kaminski's Banking Union. Something about a loan they'd been given being called in and the BBC seemed to suggest that was something the bank might not be able to do. Read up everything you can on it, and I'll see you in the office later. My gut says it's connected to the Games." Anything involving one of their target oligarchs was potentially linked to the Games, especially when it came to Kaminski, a man who they knew their own Deputy Director General was meeting with in secret, intending to support the Russian, unofficially, in his run for President.

"Okay, will do." Alex had not seen any of the reports, though a quick search on the BBC News website would get him up to speed. He spent the next forty minutes getting his head around as much as possible, before jumping in the shower and getting ready to leave for the office. He left before eight in the morning.

"You cannot just ignore this, Maggie."

He had stopped there, and his comment had hung in the air for a long and challenging couple of hours. Since then Phelan had said nothing more to Maggie regarding her role at JP Morgan Chase and what he had shown her.

It had been early that morning that Phelan had finally dared to raise the thing he'd been dreading mentioning for months. Having been sent the information promised by Matvey the day before, Phelan had digested it as best he could, thinking through exactly what he was going to do, how he could get Maggie to break faith on a billion dollar deal.

"We need to talk," he'd said, Maggie instantly on edge, the fear in her eyes assuming it was about them, not about business. When he then first mentioned the information, Maggie was initially relieved that he wasn't about to break up with her. Then the full extent of what he was asking sank in.

"Are you crazy? I can't just instruct my bosses to cancel the agreement."

Using his cover story that he was now a retired stock market trader––a lie but it explained the money and the ability to no longer work––Phelan then built on that to explain to her that a concerned friend had sent him the report about Meridian in the first place. Why he was now passing it on to Maggie.

"You have to understand, something like this has rarely been done before, Phelan. It's unethical. It would most probably bankrupt Meridian Credit for certain."

"It's going to happen anyway, Maggie, whatever you do. Better for you to get something back than nothing."

"I can't." Maggie just couldn't see herself squaring it with her boss.

Phelan then explained how billions of pounds were held in the bank, that pensioners were about to lose everything if the rumours were true. And given what information his friend had just handed him if there was any truth in the matter she needed to use her role within the firm to force the Union's hand.

"I could lose my job, Phelan. Meridian won't be happy if I do this. They'll undoubtedly file a complaint."

"And what will JP Morgan do if they find out you knew about this and did nothing?" It was a move Phelan had wanted to avoid, the threat implied but clear enough. At least he hadn't needed to threaten her about their relationship––do this, or I'm off. He knew he couldn't say that with any real conviction, though it would inevitably have produced a quicker result.

Maggie realised that Matvey would be likely to point this out to her employers after the event if she did nothing, though she wasn't going to mention any of that to Phelan.

"You cannot just ignore this, Maggie. Innocent people are going to lose everything. You have the chance to stop that happening."

It worked. Maggie was happy to destroy a multi-billion dollar Union because her fiancé had passed her some information from a friend and didn't want innocent people to be affected.

That very next day, Maggie called an emergency meeting with the London-based board––something that was rarely done. Her proposal to her bosses had initially received some stiff resistance from them all––it was not an ethical move for the firm to make––but the information she was handing them, not to mention her track record at the company, had prevailed. If they didn't get the first strike in, they would risk having to write off the entire balance of the loan. At the end of what had been a very stressful day for Maggie, the move got sanctioned. She left the office after seven that evening, exhausted but relieved.

KAMINSKI GOT the call put through to him personally at seven the previous day. He was still in his office. It had been a week since he'd met with MI6's Thomas Price, and he assumed things were working away in the background. Being told by the American office of JP Morgan Chase––though it was Maggie's decision, she wasn't going to make the call to the Union herself––that they were demanding the full and immediate repayment of their $100 billion loan, most of which was still outstanding given the sizeable nature of interest applied, was a hammer blow.

He'd screamed blue murder, demanding to speak to the chairman himself, whom he was put through to moments later, but their decision was final. If Meridian defaulted on their next repayment, they would be forced to take legal action.

Kaminski came straight off that call and immediately contacted

Price, getting his voicemail initially, before being called straight back. The share price had already plummeted ten per cent by that point, markets now closed in London, though there were still three hours to go on Wall Street.

Price worked hard to appease the man who was screaming down insult after insult, not necessarily all directed at the British MI6 employee, but sounding off in general. Price agreed to get trading stopped in shares of Meridian Capital, to limit the damage. Kaminski demanded to know why nothing had been done with JP Morgan Chase, despite having mentioned them before and asking him to intervene. The British had failed to come through for him on this one.

Kaminski knew there was no way his Union could cover the loan––they'd foolishly, as it was now clear, overstretched themselves with how they'd refinanced other businesses. Greedy for excessive interest on the repayments and now that had caught up with them. They were a sitting duck in an ocean of sharks. A slow and cumbersome tanker in a sea of submarines––easy pickings.

IT WAS EVEN QUIETER than usual at Duke's club as Price arrived, surprised for once to see Kaminski already waiting for him when he got there. It was clear that the urgent situation for the Russian caused his clock to run faster.

Neither man greeted the other, just sitting down in the same seats in the same booth they always used. They were the only ones in the club at that moment, besides the man who worked behind the bar and the two men who always stood just inside the doors to keep out those who were not on the small select list of members.

"You need to tell me what you can do. What you are going to do."

"And what is it you think I can do for you, Dmitry?"

"To at least do something, anything! Last time we met here you promised me you'd find a way of getting to them. I told you of the danger, reminded you of your commitments to me, and asked you to get involved."

"I did start to get involved."

"Well it was obviously too bloody late, wasn't it! Last night was my worst nightmare realised. Very few people––if anyone––knew that I was vulnerable in this way. This isn't chance––it's insider dealing, it's espionage."

"Look, Dmitry, you've said it yourself regarding the loan being called in, based on rumours that you aren't solvent enough to be able to pay anything back––all indeed founded on fact, not speculation. Therefore, as much as I don't like to say it, there isn't much we can do about this for you. You've brought it on yourself. You'll just have to cover the cost personally, no?" Price had no real idea what the numbers involved were but knew the man in front of him was one of the wealthiest men in the country at that moment.

"I don't have that type of money! No one does." There was worry showing on his usually calm face––Price was almost starting to pity the man.

"So what options do you have?" Price was for the first time beginning to understand the gravity of the situation.

"There aren't any. This will destroy the Banking Union––all eleven banks left vulnerable, no doubt picked off very soon by any number of groups just waiting to acquire them––and I'll be drained financially due to my own bank's role in it all. I mean, I was the bloody key signatory on the loan agreements. They could take everything from me if it came to that. I'd be ruined!"

"Isn't that being overly dramatic? I'll speak with them again, get some political power involved. There must be some way of lessening the impact on this all, slowing it down?"

"To what end? Once news gets out, I'll be finished. No one will want to support a man for the Kremlin whose face is splashed over every newspaper with the words *bankruptcy* and *fraud* bandied about as they most likely will be."

"I'll personally make sure that doesn't happen, Dmitry. You have my word on that one."

"Your word? A year ago you told me you'd do everything within your power to support my run for Presidency, and now what, where has that got me today?"

"Can your uncle step in? He must know some compelling people." Thomas was well aware of who Lev Kaminski was--he'd been thoroughly vetted in the report that was done on Dmitry, as they first looked to develop a relationship with the man they hoped would one day become President of Russia. Dmitry was distant enough from his uncle for the British not to have felt the need to get alongside Lev as well, nor would he have been an easy catch, unlike his nephew. Now that gamble looked like it was about to misfire.

"I think it's the very men that my uncle mixes with who have orchestrated this whole situation."

"Lev is involved in it himself?" The idea that the man's uncle could have been part of this whole mess was far-fetched, though anything was possible he'd come to understand when money and power were involved.

"No, not directly, he was working in opposition to those who have carried this out. But I was specifically targeted, that much is clear. It took five Russian billionaires to get together to pull this off. Here are their names for what it's still worth." Dmitry dropped a sheet of paper onto the table, Thomas glancing at the list for a moment.

"What do you want me to do with this?"

"Find out what they are up to. Find out why they've targeted me."

"Isn't that obvious? Some of them, at least one, I presume, knew your dirty little secret. Knew that there was an unsecured back door into the very heart of a Union you'd told me was impenetrable."

"It's possible, but I think it's more than that. It's been personal from the very beginning. This was about getting to me, destroying me, and goddammit, they've nearly done that. They've turned me into another Sokoloff..." and he trailed off as he said it.

"What is it, Dmitry? What have you just realised?"

"That's it; it's got to be. First Sokoloff and Krupin get dumped from the event, now me."

"Putin's two key financiers and then his main challenger? You think it's all connected?"

"I do now, yes. I was happy to see Sokoloff collapse––I mean, it was swift and catastrophic. I even smiled when he was ejected for good. It certainly levelled the playing field somewhat when it came to taking on Putin. With Sokoloff's media angle gone, there was the chance for more neutral coverage going forward. We both saw that as positive. But then it didn't stop. The attack on me––if it had only been that––might have been Putin seeing off a would-be challenger. He's certainly done that before. But what is now happening takes money––something Putin doesn't have so readily available given the fall of these two men––nor would their fall have been his doing, anyway."

"So there's another threat out there?"

"Yes," and Dmitry slammed the piece of paper on the table, the one with the five names he'd just given Price, "and I'd bet everything that it's either one of these men listed here, or someone directly connected to one of them."

Thomas picked up the sheet of paper, now reading through the names. He'd only heard of two of them before.

"We need to find a way of getting to whoever it is before they become too powerful," Dmitry added.

"Too powerful?"

"Look, at the moment these men are each individually worth a lot––it's multiple times my net worth, maybe as much as nine times my value," which was a lot coming from a man Forbes pegged as being worth $1.6 billion at the latest report. "But if they come in and pick off the members of my Banking Union and if they somehow carry on with this debt written off, their personal net worth could double, maybe even treble. Plus they would have access to substantial assets and connections for their businesses. It would make them the five wealthiest men in Russia. That makes a statement in itself."

"Who might it be, then, that's behind all this? Who do we stop?"

"My uncle told me that Matvey Filipov was leading the group––despite there being two men who had more net worth within that bunch of five. That must mean he had more than just assets to bring to the table. He had a plan. Everything that has happened over the last three months has been carefully orchestrated. It happened swiftly, and stealthily until it was upon us all and we couldn't do anything about it. I think it's him, therefore. Matvey Filipov."

Thomas had never met Matvey––his was one of the three names that meant nothing to him when he'd read through the list. Now he could only see him as a threat to everything he––and other senior figures within the British government––had been working on for the last five years, ever since Putin got re-elected on the first of what might be two six-year terms in office.

"I'll see what I can dig up on the man."

"And regarding my Union?"

"Again, whatever I can do, I will, but I think you have to prepare for the worst, Dmitry."

"Just keep it out of the goddam media, will you."

"That's easier said than done here, Dmitry, it's not Russia, after all."

"And don't you forget it!"

"Don't threaten me, Kaminski, you need all the friends you can get at the moment."

There was a frosty silence before Kaminski broke out a smile.

"Of course, you've been a good supporter through the years Price, and I hope I can count on you now."

"You can. Keep safe."

The Russian got up, taking the hand the Englishman offered, his grip as tight as ever, and left the club soon after. Price remained, looking at the names––Matvey's in particular––for five minutes, sipping a brandy he'd ordered as he pondered the possible motives of some of the planet's most asset-laden people.

8

It was an average April day in London––rain showers with the occasional sunny spell. At Vauxhall House, an MI6 briefing was taking place for all staff members, attendance at such events something Thomas Price took very seriously.

So far, little of interest had been shared. There were general updates based on intel that was being received on various international terrorist cells––it made Alex realise how long it had been since he'd personally been involved on that side of things, going on three years already since the time he first heard from Andre Filipov. What got everyone's attention, something Price happened to drop into the flow of his monotone delivery as if to watch for those who were close to dropping off to sleep, was Putin's plan to visit London in October, something announced by Moscow instead of invited from London. It would be his first visit since a brief day at the Olympic Games––when he'd also met with the then Prime Minister––at the beginning of August 2012.

Putin was planning on spending a day, at most two, in the UK capital, his complete agenda and exact travel plans as yet unclear. It was just an initial notification so that the British could start to do their part. The visit was still some months away.

Price, apparently starting to bring the meeting to a close, then landed on a more immediate situation, and focused on the JP Morgan Chase decision to call in the loan they'd given to Meridian Capital. It was hardly an issue for MI6, nor that of their cousins in MI5, but made perfect sense to Alex and Anissa, who were sitting listening as they were supposed to do. Kaminski's involvement in the bank––and Price's role within the meeting, and that of his position within MI6–– only made it obvious why the topic was even getting an airing in such a context.

What was surprising was hearing Matvey Filipov's name mentioned amongst four other Russian oligarchs––all men who the two agents knew were involved in the T10 group within the Games. Price was asking a team to look into these men. Evidently, Alex and Anissa were not being involved at this stage––despite the fact they'd been all over these men for the last two years, as their own Deputy Director General knew only too well. He clearly wanted to keep them at arm's length, once more. The meeting was dismissed.

Anissa wasted no time and went straight up to Price.

"I'd like to know why you haven't requested Alex and myself to head up the research into those five Russians you highlighted. You know we've been investigating various activities."

"I hardly have to explain myself to a medium ranking officer like yourself, now, do I?" and with that, he brushed past her, forcefully enough to push her to one side. Alex saw him leave and came over to her at that moment.

"What was that about?"

"I don't know."

Alex spotted another agent across the room, someone who'd been out in the cold for some time but had recently come back into the fold, accompanied as always by his female colleague.

"Charlie," Alex called, and the four agents stood together just to the side of the door as a few other colleagues were now filing past them to leave.

"Anissa, this is Charlie, I'm not sure if you've met before?"

"Oh, we have, Alex. I know all about the infamous Charlie Boon."

Charlie took her embrace. "It's good to see you back around here. It's sure been a little quiet without you around the place," she added.

"Infamous, you say?" Charlie smiled. "Have either of you met Zoe before?" Zoe shook their hands, the pair having not met her personally before. They knew of her and had seen her in passing occasionally but not for long enough for them to have previously spoken.

"Do you want to grab a coffee?" Alex said, the suggestion met with enthusiasm as he led the others out of the meeting room, and towards the canteen.

Now sitting down around one of the many empty tables––it was far from a break time for most staff––it was Charlie who spoke next. "You guys still sniffing around the Russian connection?" Alex had once mentioned something briefly to Charlie in passing, he recalled, though clearly it had registered and stuck with his fellow agent. An agent that had a much longer history with that particular part of the world than they did, though in fairness they were catching up fast.

"Yes, we are," Anissa said, though Charlie had addressed the question to Alex.

"Seems strange that the DDG didn't involve you with the task he just set, then."

"There's a lot you don't know about the man one office away from running the whole of MI6, Charlie." Alex launched into a rundown of the highlights, careful not to say too much in a building full of spies, but confident that no one was in earshot of anything he might mention.

"That's a lot of sensitive information you've just shared there," Zoe said, her first comments in an otherwise male-dominated conversation.

"And it goes no further than this table," Anissa said, looking her female colleague directly in the face.

"Of course."

"What's with Putin's visit to London?" Alex said, again turning to Charlie, whose history and knowledge of Russia––helped mainly by once being based there, as well as his two-year relationship with an FSB agent––was far more significant than his own.

"Putin's political party––United Russia––have their annual congress at the end of September each year. In 2011 the then sitting President Medvedev formally proposed that Putin stand for re-election at the following year's Presidential ballot. Putin accepted the invitation immediately––it was a foregone conclusion, of course, this was just the public show. My guess, therefore, is that the same will happen this year. Putin will personally announce, this time, his decision to stand for a second term, using the September congress to make that public. An October visit would, therefore, be after it became public that he was running again. It would be a timely visit to show Russia he doesn't fear anyone––especially The West."

"Will we know the other candidates by then? As we've just shared, we suspect that at least one of those five names mentioned––and specifically Matvey Filipov––intend to stand in opposition to Putin. Dmitry Kaminski also intends to challenge the President. Will this be public knowledge by then?"

"No, I doubt it. If memory serves me right, independent candidates have until December 15th to announce their intention to run in the election. The other political parties will obviously also put forward a candidate––which is normal, though usually just a formality––and this happens only in January."

"But we have to assume campaigning has already started."

"Does it ever stop? Everything these men do between now and the actual election, all either works in their favour or not. This whole situation with Kaminski's bank is a case in point. Would it even have been raised at the meeting had it not been for the connection between Price and the Russian? He's obviously come running again to our DDG, demanding something be done. He knows that if word gets out, it'll affect his public image. While the average Russian voter won't know or care what has or hasn't happened to the Banking Union in the UK, it will matter to a whole influential segment of Russians who do have a voice. If they portray Kaminski as someone washed up, someone who's failed massively, then he'd be finished."

"Thanks, Charlie, you've been really helpful."

"No worries."

"Oh, one more thing," and Anissa paused, checking around the room for a second, before leaning in closer to him, his aftershave almost overpowering her, "Sasha says hello."

"Do say hi from us both the next time you speak. And be careful. Especially for his sake."

"We will. Take care yourself. It's good to see you back. It's been too long old chap."

"Hey, less of the old now, okay?"

They shook hands and parted company, Alex and Anissa going up to their office on the third floor, Charlie and Zoe heading down one level to where their team was based. The floors had nothing to do with rank––aside from those on the top floor––where only the DDG and Director General himself had an office.

It was the day after the MI6 meeting where Price had outlined a search to be made on the five Russian oligarchs, a procedure that was to take place without Alex or Anissa's involvement, much to their own bewilderment. They were waiting in a nearby coffee shop, Vauxhall House itself clearly thought to be off limits, which only made what they were about to be told all the more intriguing.

Gordon Peacock walked in through the door as the two agents were just finishing their first coffee, having arrived themselves ten minutes earlier. Gordon was the head technician––it had been him who'd first notified them both about the Filipov transmission that never got passed on to them. A communication they should have received, which had been sat on by the DDG, who yet again keeping them out in the cold when it came to something concerning Russia. They wondered if now they had enough reason to take this directly to the Director General. You only made this move once: either you were right, and the culprit was removed from their position, or they closed ranks and claimed you were way off the mark, and the agent was out of the service instead.

As the head technician, Gordon had been called to oversee the technical side of things for the new team that had been put together, who were digging up everything they could on the five Russians Price had listed, as well as anything relating to the JP Morgan Chase situation, which was still ongoing. It was regarding the latter that Gordon had insisted he meet somewhere private with his two colleagues, people he'd come to rely on, trusting them both very much. The feeling was indeed mutual.

"Thanks for both coming," Gordon said, sheepishly taking a seat. In the scheme of things, he was just an insignificant part of a much bigger system, the agents now sitting across from him much more significant players in that process. But they always valued him and gave him equal time to voice his own opinion, something he'd always appreciated about them both, and something that he was rarely afforded by others in the same position.

"You need to see something that just came up. We were looking into that American financial services company, and the name Maggie Thompson emerged. She was the person who ran that particular account they had with Meridian Credit, the one that loaned the union the $100 billion." He placed a newspaper article on the table. "When we cross-checked her name, we found this. Two weeks ago she got engaged. Does her fiancé's name ring any bells?" They both looked down at the paper, at the section highlighted with yellow ink––the news that a Mr Phelan McDermott was engaged to a Miss Margaret Thompson. Anissa recognised the name straightaway from what they had on the record about Phelan.

"Jesus, it's him. What's he doing with this girl? Didn't he have a wife and kids and everything?" Anissa said.

"Yes, he does. That would be pretty fast going if in just a few months he's dumped them all and is already getting married again."

"I've got you an address. Maggie lives in West London," and Gordon passed Alex a sheet of paper with the details printed on it.

"I think we'll have to give the happy couple a little visit, don't you, Anissa?" He picked up the address and put it into his jacket pocket.

"There's one more thing. I got the chaps to look into the eighteen recent takeovers and bankruptcies that rocked the markets these last few months. These were what left the Union vulnerable, as we now understand. I've no doubt that they were shut down on purpose to pull off what the Russians have just gone and done through Maggie Thompson."

"Is she personally involved with the oligarchs?" Anissa said.

"Possibly, though I think Phelan's presence might better explain the connection. But that wasn't what I was going to say. We've not done an exhaustive search—I've got the team doing that today—but so far we've been able to track eight former senior personnel—people who'd been in roles of real influence within the failed businesses—all now reemployed."

"Which isn't totally surprising, is it, given the fact they'd be highly skilled people, now available to be head-hunted?"

"True, even given the fact they'd been working in a key role within a firm that had just gone bankrupt. But all eight are now in posts in companies all connected in some way to the same Russian oligarch."

"Don't tell us—it's Matvey Filipov, correct?"

"Exactly."

"I don't believe it," Alex said. All three sat there in silence, quietly pondering what they were up against.

"Did the DDG put you onto this last bit of information, ask you to dig around those eighteen failed companies?" Anissa said.

"No, I thought of it as everything came to light about Phelan's presence."

"And you've not passed this on yet?"

"No, I wanted to see what you both made of it first. You know I could lose my job for even sharing this with you."

"We know, and we know it's not the first time you've taken that risk for us. I trust you won't have to do so for much longer. Keep what you have from Price, for now, especially anything on these eighteen firms. See if you can find out any other connections, and make a list of all the names. Maybe there will be some element of criminal charge we can stick to these people at a later point if it's proved they deliberately sabotaged these firms from the inside, from a privileged position of trust and power, something they would have had to abuse to do what has happened."

"Sure, I will. Let me know how it goes with Phelan if you manage to speak to him."

"We'll do our best. You'd better get back to the office. Thanks for sharing this with us, we both really appreciate it," Alex said.

"Yes, we really do Gordon, we know it can't be easy for you," Anissa added.

They watched Gordon leave, before ordering another coffee.

"So Matvey Filipov places moles inside these companies––meaning he must have known about the risk, must have known how to really get to Kaminski and his Union."

"And that doesn't happen overnight. It takes months of planning––years maybe."

"Which is what bloody worries me, Anissa, it really does. If we think we have to tread carefully around our own DDG, then we have to be even more careful coming anywhere near a man so dedicated to what he wants to achieve, that he can place people in firms years before they are needed. All so that when the time comes, everything he wants to happen can simply happen. It makes you ask the question––who else does he have in place that we don't yet know about?"

ALEX PARKED the car a few streets down from the address Gordon had handed them.

"Nice neighbourhood," Anissa said, looking around at the mainly semi-detached presumably at least three-bedroomed properties surrounding them, each with a bit of garden out front, probably one at the back too. They were in West London, a more spacious part of the city but where your money couldn't buy you that much. It was mainly the haunt of company executives or footballers––of which that part of London had plenty.

Maggie's address was a couple of streets over––there'd been no street parking allowed on her road, so they'd had to find somewhere close by––and the two agents walked for a few minutes before arriving back to where they wanted to be. They weren't police, so couldn't sneak around to the rear of the property, neither did they have the chance, as Maggie lived in a row of terraced houses, much like most of the city––ignoring the many high rises, of course, which most people tried to.

Anissa walked up the small path, the garden a little wild, planting minimal at best. Some litter had blown into the corners of the area–– a couple of crisp packets and a supermarket shopping bag––but aside from that, there was nothing of note. She rang the doorbell, which chimed quietly away, nothing too distasteful. Seconds later, a female face peeped around the edge of the curtains, catching Anissa's eye, before disappearing quickly, presumably heading for the front door. Moments later it opened, but only on the safety chain.

"Yes?" Maggie said through the gap, her eyes red, voice patchy. This was apparently a woman who had been crying considerably in the minutes––hours for all Anissa could tell––before they had arrived.

"Maggie Thompson?" It was always good to confirm it was the occupant you were looking for, especially when arriving unannounced.

"Yes," though she still sounded just as cautious, the door edging a little closer to being shut.

"My name is Anissa, and this is my colleague Alex. We work for Scotland Yard,"––it was always better to mention the police force, their identity cards concurring with that, than to mention anything to do with the Security Service. No one knew what MI6 really did, nor were they always so well received as the police: "and we'd like to ask you a few questions about someone who you might know. Are you alone right now, or is there anyone else with you?"

For a moment Maggie didn't move––or say anything––though the door opened a fraction, so it was clear she wasn't afraid of them anymore. Alex produced his ID, which displayed on one side his name, a few details and a photo, and on the other side the badge in cast metal for New Scotland Yard, the home of the London

Metropolitan Police. Anissa did the same with her identification, Maggie taking in the details as she was releasing the safety chain on the door.

"Yes, it's only me at home again," she said, the door now opened for them both, as she ushered them inside. There was something about the way Maggie said *again* that Alex picked up on straight away, sure that Anissa would also have seen the clue. She rarely missed a trick.

They left their shoes at the door––inside, it just seemed that type of place, everything neat, the furniture sparse but well appointed––and followed her into the lounge, where a large sofa sat along one wall, two individual armchairs facing it. Maggie sat in one of the single chairs––here were magazines and an old, not quite empty, coffee mug resting on one arm––clearly, her regular spot. The two agents squeezed into the larger sofa, though there was plenty of space once they settled.

"So what's this about?" Maggie said, a tissue to her face once more, wiping away another tear.

"We'd like to ask you about your connection to a Mr Phelan Mcdermott."

Maggie put a hand instantaneously to her mouth at the mere mention of his name––a cross between heartbreak and outright rage showing in her eyes suddenly––her clenched fist willing her emotions to stay in. She lasted ten seconds before they came. Tears, a torrent of tears. She lowered her head into her hands, and wept bitterly, groans of pain coming out, her whole body shaking from the sheer rush of energy being poured into the outburst.

Alex looked at Anissa—neither knew what to do, but Alex knew that a female touch was undoubtedly going to be of more comfort for Maggie at that moment––Anissa standing up, crossing over to Maggie before sitting on the uncluttered arm of the chair she was in, one arm around her shoulders.

"It's okay, Maggie, it's okay," she said over and over again, trying her best to bring some comfort––anything would do––to a woman apparently at the point of deep soul anguish, a woman whose emotions were a whirlwind at that moment, tossed around randomly.

It was twenty minutes before they were all in conversation again. Alex had gone to boil the kettle––tea was an answer to most problems in his book––and the weeping had reduced enough for a few words to be spoken, before Alex arrived with a pot of tea, and some biscuits he found next to the bread bin.

Maggie then came out with the whole story––the last few months, Phelan turning up in December out of the blue. She alluded to the affair some years before but didn't give any more details on that. A diamond ring sat on the mantlepiece––she'd left it there the moment Phelan told her he was going, that he couldn't do this anymore, that he wanted out.

Maggie pointed to the ring as she told them this, pausing as the dam inside her once again threatened to burst forth, and said how just days before––a week or so maybe––she'd felt as happy as she'd ever been in her entire life. Everything had come together, she was in a relationship––getting married in fact––and the future looked good.

Then he'd mentioned something about her work––up to that point he'd never really taken any interest in what she did during the day. She put it down to the fact he'd retired––that was the story he'd told her, anyway––so maybe wanted to disconnect from the world of office life, so he just never asked her about it. Then he had all this information––pages of it––and she explained how Phelan had asked her for a favour. She was so in love with him––so overawed by the beautiful ring that hung heavy on her finger––that she wasn't really thinking straight.

The information was damning, for sure. It was clear the Banking Union didn't have the funds secured to pay her employer back–– didn't even have the money to guarantee all that the investment capital firms and individuals had deposited with them. That was a severe breach of FSA rules. It was all there in the information she'd been given––all of which she'd given to her bosses so didn't have a copy of any more, when Alex asked about it––and she'd been convinced it was the right thing to do.

Then yesterday, she explained through sporadic tears and deep breaths, Phelan just upped and left.

"And he gave no hint, no sign, that this was what he was going to do?" Alex said, Anissa glaring at him as he said it, but it was too late to stop him.

"No, nothing," Maggie said, relatively calmly.

"Do you have any idea where he went?"

"No, I don't."

"Can I ask you a few questions about your role at JP Morgan Chase?" Anissa said, wanting to move the conversation away from Phelan for a moment, onto something she hoped would be less emotive, where they were less likely to ask her a question that would be like walking into a minefield.

"Go ahead."

"You ran the Meridian Capital account?"

"Yes, I did. Worked on that account for the last eight years already, the last five as key account handler."

"So nothing got done with that particular account without your say-so?"

"Not with Meridian, no. It was my account."

"And presumably you were in the team that brokered the $100 billion loan? That must have been quite something?"

"It was my first role as the account handler, yes, and it was quite something at the time. With a firm like mine, these kinds of deals--much larger ones too--aren't rare, though this was the biggest done in London that year."

"Had you ever met Dmitry Kaminski during those negotiations?"

"Of course--he chaired the Union. I dealt directly with him, though mainly through his team. We met personally at least half a dozen times."

"And he approached your firm for the loan?"

"I think so--I don't know. They were already a client before I started working there. I came into the team that handled the Union eight years ago, before then running that account myself."

"Have you ever heard of the name Matvey Filipov?" Alex said, sudden and swift. Maggie's eyes darted to his––she'd been mainly answering Anissa's questions, her focus therefore on her––before looking at the carpet, then up again at Anissa.

"Who?"

"He's Russian," Anissa said, herself picking up the cue that Maggie just gave them.

"No," she said, far from convincing.

"How did you get the job at JP Morgan Chase in the first place, Maggie?"

She paused––another quick glance to the floor, her eyes fixed on nothing in particular; this girl was not a good liar––before she said: "I applied for a position, of course, like everyone else."

"They didn't headhunt you then?"

"No," she said, looking them in the eyes. That at least was the truth.

"So Matvey Filipov didn't have anything to do with you getting the position in the first place?" Alex said.

"No," the word coming out far more forcefully than she needed it to, "no, like I said, I don't know who that is."

"Thank you," Anissa said, standing up now, Alex following. "You've been most helpful." They walked towards the door, both putting their shoes back on. Maggie opened the front door for them, Anissa handing her a business card.

"Here, in case anything further comes to mind. Sometimes people remember something they want to then let us know."

Maggie took the card. "Thanks, but I think I've said everything I know."

"No worries." Both agents moved out through the door, before Anissa turned, and as if just wanting to add an explanation to their questioning. She very matter-of-factly said; "Oh, we were just asking about Matvey Filipov because we believe he employed Phelan McDermott to come back into your life, and do all this to you," and she turned back, both agents leaving at that moment. The grenade had been tossed.

Maggie had still not moved from the doorstep––the door wide

open behind her––as the two agents rounded a corner and went out of sight. She'd been thumped with the realisation that Matvey––a man who had done so much for her––could have been working behind her back the whole time.

He'd asked her to call in the loan months back––she recalled refusing point blank to do that. How had he then known about Phelan? Had Phelan been working for Matvey all along, even those years long before when they'd had their first affair? Was any of it real? Or had Matvey found out about that––her one weakness, her one big regret––and worked it all for his own good? Maggie knew that Anissa and Alex could tell she was lying about not knowing the Russian. It was apparently why Anissa had made that final reference as they'd been leaving, to see if it would prompt her to say something more.

Why wasn't she? Why didn't she just go with her urge to call out to them, to bring them back, and to tell them everything? To say to them the whole truth. Why had she hesitated? Why was she still believing that Matvey was good for her, was kind to her? His actions––which she'd outworked on the prompting of Phelan––had put thousands of people out of work, many of whom would struggle to get a job again. He'd also caused her own heart to break into more pieces than she ever thought possible to recover from.

If she could turn her pain into anger––an anger directed at someone who'd portrayed themselves as a friend––maybe she'd heal. If not heal, perhaps she'd be able to move on, to focus on revenge or some form of punishment she could dish out. Maybe then she'd feel again––if not love, then hate would have to do. Anything was a start.

She played with the card Anissa had left her, moving it in and out of her fingers, pondering, before she went back inside, closing the door finally behind her.

9

Phelan was mid-air crossing the Atlantic, heading towards America. He had completed his mission for Matvey, served his purpose. Now it was time to leave that all behind him—once and for all. No longer would he allow Matvey to have any more of a hold over him, though the more he dwelt on it all, the more Phelan thought that now more than ever he would be forever in Matvey's grip. The Russian was now able—willing, certainly—to dangle before his eyes the threat of exposure, the risk that he could reveal all to his wife if he so pleased. The danger would never go away, therefore, not properly. Men like that never let these things drop.

Phelan had fled Maggie's two days ago, saluting the two men in the black van that had been parked outside her home as he'd made his exit, one final act of defiance before he'd run the other way. There was no going back now.

Neither could he immediately go to his family, much as he longed for them, much as he missed them and just wanted to be united with them once more. He had to get everything together, he had to work out what to say. He'd been away for the best part of five months—

having given little information at the time he'd left, nor anything during the intervening period.

He was sure he reeked of betrayal--his wife would smell it on him, see it in his eyes. There would be no way of hiding the fact, no way of brushing it all under the carpet. Surely she would find out, if not immediately when the euphoria of his arrival would be met with hugs and kisses, but later. In the quiet of the evening, when it was just the two of them. When they'd got through the physical stuff--the greetings and warm embraces--and when the heart connections needed to be restored, where intimacy happened. Intimacy--there was an awkward word. Could he ever be really intimate again, did he know what that was anymore? He'd played that card a lot those last few months, being intimate with a woman who wasn't his wife. Had he ruined it therefore for the one woman he wanted intimacy most with? Was that his problem, would that be where he was found out?

He'd thought about going on to mainland Europe, but that took him a little further from his family--insignificant as it was, it still mattered--and nearer to Matvey, with all the Russian's connections and middlemen. He, therefore, booked into the same hotel he'd stayed in on the night he first collected the money. It was funny how things came around again. Then, his thoughts were only euphoric. He'd pulled off a fantastic victory, an extraordinary coup, and got to pocket the millions himself. Then, that money was already racing around the planet, various holding banks used to safely and swiftly get it to where the Russians--and Sokoloff in particular--couldn't see it. He felt free.

Now, this money sat in his bank with millions of pounds in easy reach--and yet he felt more trapped than ever before, weighed down by the guilt and shame of all he'd had to do to Maggie, someone who deserved better. Things his own wife could never know.

If the hotel had known who he was, they didn't let on. He booked into a similar suite to the one he'd used before--the exact one had been already taken--and quickly emptied the mini bar. If the distance from Maggie wasn't able to settle his feeling of guilt, maybe the alcohol would?

He woke at half six the following morning, head banging but otherwise happy for the hours of sleep he'd managed, still fully dressed, having dropped off on the sofa, the bed untouched. He didn't have any tablets for his head, and the breakfast area wasn't open until seven, he was told. The girl behind the reception desk did have a packet of paracetamol in her bag and offered him a couple of tablets, which he gratefully received.

Showered and dressed by nine––this after a hearty breakfast––he'd got his head together enough to begin to think about his route home. The flights were one minor element to that––his story was the primary concern––but he figured he could perfect the latter over the many hours it would take to finally reach his loved ones.

He was on the morning flight out, and following one change in Chicago, would reach LAX sometime late that night, probably needing to stay in Los Angeles itself before seeing his family again the following morning. He thought he would make his return a surprise, which might go a long way to lessen the cross-examination that would inevitably come. He just hoped he was ready for that.

THE CANNES FILM FESTIVAL, now celebrating its seventieth year, ran for twelve days in the second half of May. Svetlana Volkov, two of her films being featured at the festival, was one of the big draws, especially for such an important anniversary event.

As always, the gathering saw many of the world's social elite–– and the wealthy––congregate for what was a crucial fixture on the social calendar. Svetlana had invited all the members of the Games to join her at that year's event, most being regular attendees themselves for decades. It gave Svetlana the chance to touch base with the men, as she did at similar events throughout the regular business calendar, and set forward the details about what was coming up. The summer event for the T20 was top of her agenda for that particular group. The results in the T10, if not yet quite final, were undoubtedly nearly ready to be called. That in itself was extraordinary, something if she'd been told just over six months before she wouldn't have believed to have been possible.

By the second day of the festival, all the men had arrived, the Russians mainly disappearing into the crowd, where the world's press had come to catch a glimpse of some of the biggest names in the film industry, both on screen and behind the camera.

During the afternoon of that day, Svetlana gathered the ten men in the T20 at a small private venue a little outside of Cannes itself––this was a meeting she didn't want to be photographed at.

"Gentlemen, it's good to see you all in this context once again," she said, the room silent before her, her statement white fur coat hanging as it always did so well on her. A low cut black dress was elegantly visible underneath, despite the warm temperature, too warm undoubtedly for the need of such a coat, though it was one of her most iconic statements. She was the Russian bombshell in the white fur.

"As you all know, next month we gather in St Petersburg for our annual mid-summer event. And having been assessing the last few events, and the fact you are all getting too good at defending your tickets," a little murmur of amusement went around the room at that, before quieting as their Chair continued, "I thought we'd go a little old school with this summer's Hunt." That phrase brought some trepidation for those men who'd been involved since the beginning, blank looks from those who had only known it in its current format. What they'd all done at the ten-year celebration a year and a half ago, had been an entirely new thing––a one-off they believed, and hoped.

"As some of you who've been around long enough will remember, before the time of the many lotteries we now have, and before the days of selecting your own Contestants even, we used to pick random people––usually Russians in fact––and offer them a blank cheque. The challenge was always could they get it cashed in time." That was in an era, even though it wasn't that many years ago when the average Russian didn't have their own bank account. Many still didn't. Russia very much remained a cash culture. "When banking went online, more people had the option of an account, and cheques started to go out of fashion. Now, no banks in Russia will accept them. So we switched to lottery tickets and changed the focus to foreigners. The modern era of the Games was born," and she spoke like a mother would about one of her babies.

"I thought it would be fun for us"––fun was always a very subjective word when it came to this group of people. Fun was also always at someone else's expense––"if while still supplying a lottery ticket, the Contestants for this summer's Hunt would be randomly selected from general tourists who are in the city at the time. People travelling in groups, and especially families, would offer the most captivating Contestant. Would they leave and abandon their kids and spouse to pocket some millions? I think you can see the interest." She didn't need to state the obvious, the idea was cruel yet intriguing, and where that occurred, the rest always followed. "Under no circumstances are you allowed to pre-screen or pre-select anybody who is going to be in St Petersburg during these dates. Each Contestant––and I want you all involved again this time, so you'll each need to provide a ticket––has to be a genuine tourist, and your first challenge will be to lure them into the trap, get them interested enough to make a run for it. I know that is not as easy as when it's a pre-selected Contestant, but I'm certain it'll make for a more extraordinary event. I think it's about time we injected a little of the unknown back into our events, don't you?"

There was a general agreement, though no one voice could be heard above the others, it was as if they were each content for once to just be one of the crowd, to not raise their own head above the parapet. But there was a consensus.

"Very well, we'll go ahead with that in mind. I think it promises to be a truly fantastic time, one that is likely to bring much laughter, and I hope not too much heartache, as you each once again bet against your fellow Hosts, hoping to be the one to come out on top. May the best of you do just that."

She moved away from the front of the room––it was clear what she had to say was over––and headed towards the door. A few of the men thought about saying something, but it was always best to keep a little distance in the room, an invisible barrier between them and her.

Foma Polzin, Eleven within that context, eyed the room like any dominant male lion would. He caught sight of Dmitry Kaminski, who stood quietly––it was far from public knowledge regarding his own personal financial peril––though Foma wondered if most men in that room, if not all, would already have some sense of what awaited their fellow oligarch. Would Kaminski even have anything to bet come the June event?––would he be there at all? Picking off these men had become as much an event for Foma as it was to be involved in the Games as a whole. He was enjoying both immensely, taking genuine delight in the downfalls achieved so far, even if he wasn't able to share that publicly with anyone else in the room, besides Andre Filipov––who was, like him, a co-conspirator.

It was half-past four in the morning, Anissa fumbling for her still ringing mobile, as she tapped her alarm clock to both confirm the time and give her a little light to see into her bag. Thankfully the sound had been muffled somewhat by the contents of her handbag––why she'd placed it next to her bed last night she was still at a loss to remember––so it did not wake her husband, who was sleeping soundly next to her. He'd sleep through a hurricane and not stir. She was the opposite, something that went with the territory of being a mother––though her job had also trained her to sleep lightly.

"Hello?" Anissa said once answering the unrecognised number displayed on the handset. It was a UK number, anyway, a London one, too.

"Anissa, it's Maggie. Maggie Thompson." She repeated her name with her surname as if the first name alone was not enough, but Anissa understood the moment she heard the name, despite it being some time––a few weeks in fact already––since they'd paid her a visit. "I've been thinking about everything you said to me when you stopped by. Everything you asked me, especially what you said as you were leaving. It's been with me ever since." That had been the intention, though truth be told Anissa had assumed as the days pressed, Maggie wasn't taking the bait. Yet here she now was--Anissa standing in their en-suite bathroom so as not to make too much noise--speaking with her again.

"I was a total mess when you visited--still am, actually. I've not been back to work since. Couldn't face it all. The doctor says its a combination of stress and depression. The meds didn't help me to focus, but I've taken myself off them now--can't sleep--and need to talk to you finally. Need to tell you the truth."

She paused. Anissa, tired but alert to this conversation, still didn't want to waste time. "Go on," she said.

"I had heard of Matvey Filipov--it was him who got me to the front of the line in the interviews and then basically made sure they spoke to no one else about the job." She knew it. Alex had looked into the recruitment process with Maggie's firm, but records were not precise. It detailed the interviews, her results for each one, everything from the company side, but there was nothing--on paper, anyway--that suggested Matvey had delivered her to them. That conversation would have taken place behind closed doors somewhere, one man possibly doing a favour for another or some other deal.

"Why you? What was your connection to him before the appointment?" They'd looked for any cross reference but hadn't found anything.

"I worked with his group here in the UK. We'd never met personally, but then the whole thing with Phelan happened. I don't think he knew at first, but when it all exploded--when the affair became public knowledge, and his wife found out--I had to move on. I changed my surname," which explained why they hadn't come up with anything, "and Matvey allowed me to reenter life in another of his firms, before opening the opportunity at JP Morgan Chase."

"Did he suggest back then anything about getting involved with Meridian Capital?"

"No, but it was what I already did, within his firm I mean, on a much smaller scale. The new job was for that role. I just landed the client through a promotion, signed off on the $100 billion loan, and kept moving forward from then on."

"Has Matvey Filipov been in touch with you in the last six months?" There was a noticeable pause at that second as if Maggie was taking one final moment to decide how much she was going to say.

"Yes, at the end of last year--I'm not sure exactly when--but he called me, and said he'd soon need me to call in the loan."

"What did you say?"

"I told him that was absolutely out of the question." Interesting, seeing as six months later she seemed to do exactly that after a few words from Phelan.

"How did Matvey react to that?"

"He was angry. Threatened me, but then seemed to go away. I didn't, I haven't heard from him again. It was only during your visit, since what you said, that I recalled it was Matvey who first suggested the idea to me. Once you said Phelan was working for Matvey, it all made sense. He'd sent Phelan to do what I'd refused to do before. My entire world was a sham."

Anissa let the emotions clearly flooding Maggie at that moment subside for a bit.

"You had no way of knowing this was being done to you, Maggie."

"I should have seen it coming. Phelan never talked about what had happened. I just ignorantly wanted to believe she'd kicked him out, that he was a free man, and that what we had--what I thought we had--was real. But none of it was, was it?"

"I can't imagine how that feels, Maggie, I really can't."

"I know you're not Scotland Yard, by the way."

"Sorry?"

"I planned to make this conversation in person and went to Scotland Yard myself yesterday. The front desk said you didn't work there. They didn't know your name but said you were a government official--whatever that means--and then I remembered you gave me a business card. At least the number is real. So who are you?"

"I'm a friend, who can help you, Maggie. That's all I can say."

"I think that says enough, then." Anissa could hear a long intake of breath from the other end of the line, as if she was trying to control her breathing, trying to calm herself. "Will you promise me one thing, Anissa?"

"Sure, what is it?"

"Find a way of getting back at Matvey, will you? Bring him down."

"I'm not sure what you expect me to do or who you think I am."

"I suspect enough to know that you have probably been on his trail for some time. Phelan, I might be able to forgive--but Matvey, he's betrayed every trust I ever placed in him. He can't be allowed to get away with this. You have to hurt him." There was urgency in her voice, hatred too. This was very personal for Maggie, that much was already apparent.

"I'll do everything in my power to do just that," Anissa said, deciding there was no point in trying to answer too vaguely. This was a woman who needed to know there would be a day of reckoning--even if Anissa had no idea if that were ever really possible.

"Good. Then our conversation is over," and with that, the phone went dead, Anissa not able to add anything to what had been said, no words of encouragement. She was now too awakened by it all to attempt to get back into bed--she would have to get up in just under an hour's time, anyway. She slipped back out and across the bedroom, therefore, her husband still sound asleep, though he had turned over since she'd left, and she went downstairs.

As the kettle boiled, she dropped Alex an email updating him on what she'd just heard from Maggie. It was yet more connections for her growing wall of evidence. Still, she didn't have enough to truly nail Matvey. A man that powerful would take much more to bring down than what they had so far--would they ever get that shot?

10

As the seventieth Cannes Film Festival came to an end, Foma Polzin, who had stayed for the whole event, was concerned. He'd remained because Kaminski had stayed––a man potentially running away from his own nightmare headlines in England, yet increasingly confident as the event went on.

"He's got a backer," Foma said, speaking to Matvey on his mobile, as the celebrities and billionaires alike were making their final departure. Foma had expressed his concern a few days ago––in person––with Matvey before he'd left with his son for Monaco, suggesting Foma stay around and see what he could dig up.

"Who?" The fact Dmitry Kaminski wasn't already dead and buried––figuratively speaking, though that literal eventuality wasn't off the table, either––suggested someone else was in play.

The last two weeks, and especially the time during the actual festival, had seen the full collapse of the Meridian Capital Union, with legal suits pending. That should have been enough to sink Kaminski. JP Morgan Chase's claim alone for whatever assets they could seize should have been enough to wipe the smile from his face. Yet, two weeks on, he was still standing.

Foma had followed Kaminski around closely. Though not

apparent to anyone else––it took an oligarch to know the secret dealings of a fellow oligarch––it was clear that Aleksey Kuznetsov, Twelve within the Games, a position he had taken over from Sokoloff, was the man in question. Kuznetsov had been the big winner––fortuitously as it had happened––when Phelan had come out victorious in a Hunt Sokoloff assumed he had already won. That had been his first mistake. He'd never really recovered.

"It's Kuznetsov."

"The sewage guy?" There was disdain in Matvey's voice. He didn't like being held up by a man who dealt in piss.

"What are we looking at?" For these men, it was always about the numbers. How much wealthier––by that they implied more powerful––was one person over another?

"Two point two." The combined wealth of the two men talking was over $20 billion, with plenty of change. He was small fry, in other words.

"Then he becomes another target we'll just have to remove." There were a lot of men who were just being shoved to one side, and for the first time, Foma felt that edge of caution rise in him, voicing it before he'd thought anything of it.

"Do we just keep crushing everyone that stands in your way?"

"Yes we do, Foma," Matvey said, no trace of hesitation, no flinching in the face of conflict, "unless you've lost your nerve and in which case you'd cease to be of any use to me. Have you lost your nerve?"

"Of course I haven't," he said, angry that he'd opened himself up for that––angry that he was being talked down to.

"You have my son at hand within the T20 to work with at the next event." Andre was only there because Foma had loaned him a significant amount, on Matvey's instruction, though it was true he'd already seen nearly forty per cent repaid. The boy knew what he was doing. "Make sure you take out Kuznetsov, and Kaminski won't have a leg to stand on."

"We'll do what we're best at, don't you worry."

"Oh, I don't worry, Foma. I never worry."

The call ended. Foma stood there in silence, his view of the sea before him tranquil––completely the opposite to how his stomach was now churning, yet another Russian oligarch in Matvey's sight, yet another man to be destroyed. Without great sacrifice, came no victory.

AFTER THE NEW YEAR HUNT––IT was the most significant holiday in Russia, as well as the most prominent event within the Games––the mid-summer Hunt was the next highlight. For the last few years, they'd reduced mainly to just those two events, though in the past had had up to six such gatherings a year.

It was looking like a hot summer. That was good for St Petersburg's prospects, with tourists making trips to the cooler north, getting away from the close heat of cities like Moscow, and southern Europe too.

Air conditioning was not yet commonplace in St Petersburg, or in Russia as a whole, though for the wealthy it was old news, and the Volkov mansion was a refreshing retreat as the various guests arrived at the front entrance, leaving the hot granite pavements behind.

As always, they were gathering on the eve of the shortest night, with the actual event starting the following day. For the first time in many years, none of the Hosts knew who their Contestants were going to be––nor did these Contestants yet realise they were going to be involved, either––as all would unfold in real time the following morning.

There was an air of expectancy, of interest, floating around the Games Room as the various technical staff made the final adjustments––it was quite an endeavour to assemble everything and then break it all down for each event. The room got returned to what it usually was, a large conference facility that neither Svetlana nor husband Sergej, otherwise used.

As always drinks flowed freely, made available before any of the Hosts arrived, in a building where secrecy and anonymity ruled. The men talked amongst each other, the atmosphere surprisingly carefree and buoyant. It was the calm before the storm. Tomorrow they would be competing against one another again.

The Odds Maker sat in his usual position, the men giving him some idea as to the size of ticket they had on offer. The higher the ticket value––and thus the higher reward available––the better the odds, not that losing even an enormous sum for a lottery ticket payment was anything for men so wealthy. But there was a noted pride in being able to put forward a ticket worth thirty, forty or even upwards of fifty million. It all mattered.

Foma circled around in the background, not entering into any particular conversation, eyeing up the men like a champion fighter does when facing a worthy opponent. Kaminski and Kuznetsov were deep in their own conversation. Andre entered the room at that moment, presumably back from the bathroom, and came straight over to Foma.

"So, do you feel confident, young man?"

"I feel ready, anyway. Confidence comes with progress."

"That it does." Foma knew Andre was a bright lad. As sole heir of the Filipov estate, he would one day have more than Foma had now, if he didn't reach that point within his father's lifetime––the rate he was going. In some way, he was entirely unlike his father––in appearance, his approach with people––but Foma had been around both men long enough to see that same streak that existed in father had indeed been passed on to his son.

At that moment, Kuznetsov came over towards the two men–– they were standing next to where the drinks were anyway, so that helped––and Foma grabbed the shoulder of Twelve before he could get to the table.

"You seem to be dragging an element of dead wood along with you lately. You know that'll only slow you down." Foma had nodded with his head towards Kaminski as he'd spoken, though it was clear enough what he was implying.

"And what is that to you, Comrade?" The use of the old Soviet-Russian phrase having more impact on Foma than he'd care to admit.

"It's just that when his losses become your losses, it'll swallow you whole."

"His losses are his losses. I'm just here to secure his next twelve months." That would be enough time to get Kaminski through the election, and if successful, to become President. Then the losses wouldn't matter. There were a million ways a new President could recoup anything he owed. It was clear that had been the deal Kuznetsov––or Kaminski––must have struck with JP Morgan Chase. A couple of billion as collateral held in good faith for something much more significant to come.

"Just make sure he doesn't drag you down with him now, Comrade," and Foma tightened his grip momentarily on Kuznetsov's shoulder, before releasing the man, and letting him go on his way. The exchange had taken barely twenty seconds, though Kaminski had watched it all from his position across the floor. Foma looked across at him at that point, patting the returning Kuznetsov on the back as he passed him again, Twelve shoving off the gesture as best he could, though he had two champagne flutes in his hand at the time.

"What was that about?" Kaminski asked, taking the drink which was offered to him, Kuznetsov downing his in one go.

"He was warning me about you."

"It doesn't surprise me."

"Are you worried?" Foma was by far the biggest fish in the T20 pond. Combined with Andre––their wealth totalling $9.6 billion at the last update––they were easily four times the net worth of any other player, making any Hunt where it was one oligarch against another an unfair battle. They knew they couldn't really take on directly a man as powerful as Foma without a lot of help––and help in those circles was hard to come by. Though direct confrontation was not allowed, the Games Room had always been that type of arena. A conflict was inevitable and given a chance––despite what Svetlana Volkov might say––it was a dog eat dog world, especially amongst the super-rich.

"What worries me most is that boy's father," Kaminski said, his eyes glancing briefly to Andre. "I think we know those two men standing over there are just puppets for Matvey."

"Can we do anything about them?"

"Not much, especially now. Get me to the Kremlin, and I promise you then I'll be able to really strike them. You're my wingman, I told you. You look out for me over these next nine months, and I'll make sure your place at the very top table is a great one."

They toasted to that, Kuznetsov having grabbed another drink as it was offered to him by Nineteen.

"See, they aren't all out to get us," Kuznetsov said, once Pavlov had moved on.

NEITHER ALEX nor Anissa were in St Petersburg for the summer event. In the past their information had always come from Andre Philips--Andre Filipov as he'd turned out to be, a man now part of the event himself--so without that steady, sometimes infrequent, source of information, they were a little out in the cold as to what was happening when.

That still bothered them both, Anissa more so than Alex. To have built such a picture, to have learnt so much and yet always mostly be on the outside was frustrating. It was like being two-hundred pieces into a thousand piece puzzle, but to have only covered the edge. There was no centre, nothing to really link these men--and woman in Svetlana Volkov's case, at least--to anything criminal. Anything that would hold up before an uncorrupted judge, an untainted jury--assuming they even got that far.

It often felt like there was just too much against them to make it worth pursuing, that however far they got, whatever charges they thought they could make, when it came down to it--especially as they were dealing with Russia--it would all fall flat, for one reason or the other.

Someone would get paid off--or knocked off--and the case would collapse.

That felt wrong to Anissa––it was wrong––even as part of her knew it was probably all inevitable. And that really bothered her. She'd never felt like she knew so much about an organisation––they weren't exactly that, but it's what both agents had long been calling the Games, despite nothing official ever existing about them––and yet was so powerless all at the same time.

Their one other source, one other contact man, was Sasha, their FSB insider, a man who had got them in and out of Russia several times over the last few years, involving himself more in their investigation without really seeing it all coming. He was now as equally invested in it all as they were––more so if you considered what he had to lose should his assistance ever come to light with his employers or his government.

Anissa had had to warn Sasha a few times to back down from something, to hold off a little, fearing that her Russian friend was racing into situations that would put him at risk. He'd apparently made someone's radar, being spoken to by Foma Polzin––warned off at that.

Yet it was Anissa who now risked exposure. She'd agreed to go with Josée to Russia for the trial that had finally been called together, holding the hand of the witness but most likely invited to take the stand herself. It would alert the authorities––who were sure to be watching, or at least taking notice at some point after the trial––that a British MI6 agent was operating without their knowledge, or authorisation, in St Petersburg. By bringing to light the murder of the janitor––something that Josée was an eyewitness to––it would also expose her presence. She was sure both the FSB and even MI6 would start asking questions. The latter might also conclude Alex would have to have been involved, something she hoped wouldn't get him into trouble.

She was a week away from travelling––this time with authorised papers, through the usual channels––for the trial to commence the first week of July. Anissa had primarily been spending the last couple of days focusing on the criminal case––not really her speciality––but she understood more than ever, if she could get this one crime brought to justice, if she could get these two women on the stand, then from there she could start to expose what was really going on. She was sure that parts of Russia––important parts that still mattered, like the FSB, police and government––didn't know what their oligarchs were up to. Of course, some would, but if she could raise the issue enough, expose what facts she knew, she was confident the Russians would then take the reins.

Alex calling on her mobile at that moment broke her train of thought.

"Anissa, you need to come. They've found Maggie's body at her home."

Nothing more was said.

Anissa jumped up from her desk, hurriedly collecting some of her personal things––this was the last thing she needed before her trip to Russia––but something in which she had to be involved. She'd been the one Maggie had called, she'd sounded broken, clearly––that much was obvious––when they'd last spoken a month before, but Anissa had been watching from the sidelines. Maggie had gone back to work the previous week. That was deemed a good thing.

Less than an hour after the call from Alex, she joined him at the address, where police had taped off the gate to the small front garden, with crime scene tape also on the front door in the shape of an X.

Neither said anything to the other, the two agents showing their details to the officer standing on duty, and they were allowed through. Opening the front door, they were met by another female police officer.

"She's out the back," she said and led them both through.

Maggie's legs were visible as they entered the kitchen, still dangling where she'd been found. Maggie had hanged herself from the upstairs window, her body slumped against the outside of the kitchen wall, her legs level with the window. There were two muddy heel prints on the glass where her boots must have connected with the window as she jumped out from the upstairs bathroom.

"There's a suicide note upstairs too. No sign of a struggle, no signs of an intruder. Forensics is doing a thorough sweep now, and once the photos are taken, the body will be examined by the pathologist," the officer said. She left them to walk out of the back door, which they did, a crime scene photographer just finishing up, a three-person team standing behind him with a black body bag ready, waiting to cut Maggie down.

"You think it was a suicide?" Anissa said to Alex, looking away now from the body, having seen enough. Anissa was still in shock.

"Let's not make that call until we have all the results in."

"It can't have been a suicide, Alex, come on. It's them."

"Who? They can't be responsible for everything. Why kill Maggie now?"

"I don't know." She was angry, and couldn't be there when they started to remove the body, which was obviously about to happen, so she went back inside. "One way or the other, Alex, they did this to her. They made her life a misery even if this does turn out to be an unassisted suicide. It's ultimately his fault."

"Whose? Phelan's? Matvey Filipov's?"

"The Russian, yes. The last thing Maggie urged me to do was to get Matvey. She knew more than she told me, I was sure. Maybe that's what killed her."

"We don't know this was a murder, Anissa, let's not jump the gun."

"How can you be so bloody calm? So protective? After all we've been through, after all we've learnt? How can you stand there––another body being zipped into a bag––and think anyone else is responsible rather than these...these...these barbarians?" She pulled away from Alex before he could offer an answer, before he could say anything. Alex let her go. He knew she wasn't angry at him, it wasn't about what he thought. She was upset, deeply troubled by everything they'd been going through. Maybe it was getting too much? Perhaps they should have seen this coming, got in extra help, counselling maybe months ago when it might have been of better use.

Alex climbed the stairs, joining the forensic guys who were focussing on both the bathroom and her bedroom, two people visible carefully taking samples from the bed. In the bathroom, the rope had been tied around the handle on the side of the bath, which sat along the wall under the large window. Alex peered out the window, the rope still hanging there though thankfully her body had been taken away already.

Nothing seemed out of place in the bathroom. There were no signs of a struggle, nothing broken, no blood anywhere. The items--two jars of soaps, bottles of shampoo and conditioner, and a lady's razor--which he assumed would have usually been on the window sill, had been moved instead to the top of the closed toilet seat. She'd carefully moved them in the moments before committing suicide, so that she could climb out of the window a little easier. That seemed bizarre, that someone at the end of things--so desperate that they took the only escape they could find--yet still were rational enough to remove the clutter from the window.

Alex went into the bedroom, where the forensic team were still working on the bed. The note was on the dressing table, pen neatly lying next to the A5 scented notelet. Alex read the note, which was written in precise, crisp cursive:

> *I'm sorry you had to find me like this, I'm sorry if it comes as a shock. My life had become not worth living anymore, my work a place of ghosts—my home no longer a sanctuary. I tried to keep going, I decided to start again, but I couldn't. My heart was tired of living, and so was I. I'm sorry. MT.*

She couldn't even bring herself to write Maggie. Alex left the note there, wanting to go and find Anissa. She didn't need to see the upstairs--she could process all that, cover everything at some later point from the reports that would be made--right now she needed time to talk. That couldn't be done there, not in Maggie's home.

Anissa was outside on the street, standing next to the officer but neither was obviously saying anything. She looked up as Alex came out through the door, a smile on her face her way of saying sorry for the outburst. Alex smiled back; don't mention it, you were in shock.

"Let's go," he said, walking past her, Anissa following. She didn't want to be there anymore.

"Want to catch a coffee and talk about it?" Alex said.

"Not now, Alex. Some time, but not now. I have to get ready for Russia, I have to help Josée come through this. I have to be there for her, to make her see there is light at the end of the tunnel, there is hope where now she feels only brokenness."

Alex didn't say anything. He knew what she was saying--she wanted to make sure Josée didn't become another Maggie.

11

It was Game day in St Petersburg, and more so than usual, there was an air of expectancy––of the unknown––floating throughout the room where ten men waited. Svetlana was yet to join them.

For only the second time, there would be ten Contestants, each oligarch present therefore a Host. This time, no one knew who would be their Contestant. These were currently unsuspecting people in the general public––which was normal––though that morning they were unsuspecting tourists, couples and families just enjoying the White Night's season in beautiful St Petersburg, oblivious to anything that might be about to happen to them. For some lucky souls––it was the Hosts who would use that term, though being lucky by being included was anything but certain––they could get their hands on some serious money, millions in fact, if they could only escape with the ticket from Russia. Would they deem it necessary––vital even––to just abandon whoever it was they'd travelled with, and flee? Going to wherever it was that the ticket had to be claimed.

It was the same fundamental principle the Games had always been based on. There was entertainment to be had––and money to be won or lost when you pitted billionaire against billionaire––by merely putting the prospect of unimaginable cash before otherwise ordinary people, people who weren't wealthy, people sometimes struggling to make ends meet. The more significant that struggle was, the more the oligarchs enjoyed watching what they saw as a performance, a good show.

Indulgence of the most severe nature. Just a bit of fun for them. The fact people got hurt occasionally––whilst there had been deaths, it was still quite rare, if not a more frequent occurrence––it was a minor concern. These weren't people the oligarchs knew or cared about. They were just playing pieces, like any number of their employees were. Dispensable.

On the dot of ten that morning, Svetlana glided in through the main doors, her entrance as dramatic as always. She had to be the centre of attention, this was her show, her home, her audience. Their involvement in her world had built its own level of loyalty towards her, which was a rare position for a woman to hold in modern day Russia. She felt invincible around such men. It was empowering. Of course, her husband's presence in the background––she always turned to him when a financial hit was required––went a long way to gaining their loyalty initially.

"Good morning, gentlemen," she said, taking the stage straight away, addressing the group as a whole. She rarely did small talk, rarely spoke one-on-one, especially in that context. A little distance was always good, a little unfamiliarity kept people in line. "I think the next two days are going to be a wonderful time together once more. Let's raise a toast to our Summer Solstice, and to an exciting Hunt!" The men raised their glasses and made the toast, repeating her phrase, before emptying the contents of their glass in one gulp.

"I can see from our Odds Maker that there is a good range of tickets out there today. May I congratulate you all once more, gentlemen, on your ability to source such rewarding prizes for our would-be victors," though none of the men standing there wanted to contemplate losing. Someone usually did, however, especially when it was ten Hosts involved at the same time.

The tickets ranged in value considerably––the lowest at €11

million, the most at £22 million. Five of the tickets were from the UK, and therefore in pound sterling. The other five were all Euro Loto tickets––two claimable in France, the others in Spain, Portugal and Ireland. All but one of the tickets were claimable up until the following day, so that gave thirty-six hours from that moment. It was one of the two French tickets that had an 8pm deadline that same day, which was the best the Russian could come up with. It was worth €16 million should someone manage it.

"I think we had better get things underway," she said. "As always, we have a large number of teams on the ground to keep a live feed on anything and everything that happens," and the screens jumped to life at that moment, three different camera feeds coming through.

The images displayed changed every five seconds, as it worked through the ten teams broadcasting at that moment. Of course, until there was a Contestant, the images showed very little, just the busy streets of the city as people went about their day. A city of granite that once again would unsuspectingly play host to the Games. Such extravagance and waste when you considered the fact that the cumulative total of the ten as yet unclaimed tickets was more than £167 million. If successful––and no Russian there would want to be a loser––these tickets would remain unclaimed, the money untouched. It was what made them feel so strong. To be so reckless.

As well as the teams of Trackers that Svetlana provided––people who were neutral, just there to report the action like a sports crew would––each Host had teams of their own people working for them. Their first job was to find a suitable Contestant, limited this time to the pool of people who were already in the city. That made their job much harder. If they chose someone who had no chance of getting away––nationality didn't matter––there would be no contest. If there was no Hunt there was no risk and therefore no reward. None of the other oligarchs would bet against them. Thus there would be nothing to win, nothing to play for. If, on the other hand, the Contestant was too prepared––maybe they were travelling alone, from the country where the ticket was from, and flying back that day anyway, it would be too easy, too risky for the Host. In that case, all the other Hosts would bet against them, and if the Contestant was able to claim the prize, the losses could be substantial. Not to mention the kick to their pride and honour––which would hurt more than money ever could.

Creating a dilemma was undoubtedly the way to go––finding someone who had the means to travel, in that they had a valid passport or visa to go elsewhere in Europe––but also had dependents, people they were visiting the city with. That made for an exciting prospect. Would they leave those they'd travelled with stranded and go for the money? Would they try and flee with them? Would they try and get help? These would be the best bets, the kind of Contestants who could divide the room. If a Host found someone along those lines––if there were a whole room of men with such Contestants––it would make for one fantastic contest and an exciting Hunt.

Following Svetlana's confirmation to get things up and running, each of the ten Hosts was busy speaking on their mobile phones to their various teams––some men preferring to use multiple teams, others with a trusted few.

The Games Room fell into a hum of hushed conversations, men busy on phones like you would see on a stock market trading floor, but the noise was noticeably less. These were conversations they didn't want the others to hear.

It was Aleksey Kuznetsov––Fifteen at this event––who found the first Contestant, definite bragging rights going his way, though catching the first nibble on the end of a line was far different from actually reeling it in. Just ask any fisherman.

Wilma Baines was originally from the UK but lived in Poland. Fifteen's team had spotted her in a cafe. She was eating with a friend, both staying in the same hotel. Her Facebook profile had her down as single. However, once the men had made a check at the hotel––something all teams would be doing, no doubt, for all potential Contestants––they found she was not only staying in the same room as her friend but had explicitly got them to change the room from a twin to double. Clearly, this girl didn't want certain people to know her actual status.

With live Contestants like this––as opposed to the pre-screened ones, where information was usually passed under their hotel room doors on the morning of the event alerting them to the location of the ticket––the Hosts had to be far more blatant. These people, unlike the usual Contestants who had been flown to the city especially, weren't expecting anything unusual to happen. The Russians had to make it clear that what was being offered was possible––was real, and not a fake. Either the Contestant bought into the idea immediately, or the team moved on and found someone else.

That was the pattern they had settled into in the early days––when Contestants were found similarly––blank cheques on offer in those Hunts, just begging to be signed and cashed into an account before the six months were up. The cheques were always dated so that the day of the Hunt was the final day. That phase had grown stale, and they'd moved onto lottery tickets instead, which promised so much more opportunity and fun. And so it had proved. Like any drug addict would say, however, each high was never as good as the last one. They needed more.

The New Year warehouse event had been that for them––nothing since had proved anywhere near as appealing. They knew it, and Svetlana knew it, which was why she'd proposed this latest change. They were getting bored. She hoped, for her sake as much as her Hosts, this time around there would be that hit they were all longing for again.

Confronting Wilma as she left the cafe––her partner, girlfriend, lover, whatever she called her still at the table––the team working for Fifteen made their move. The Trackers homed in on the unfolding situation, keen to record what might be about to happen.

"Wilma Baines, this is a take it or leave it moment," the dark-haired Russian female had said, standing across her path, blocking Wilma's progress should she have wanted to keep walking and ignore the interruption. Instead, she eyed the Russian up and down carefully. She'd been warned about homophobic elements in Russia, though had assumed St Petersburg was a little more Europeanised.

"What?" she finally said, the standoff longer than she was happy with. She wasn't a fighter, but by the look of the girl in front of her, neither was she.

"This lottery ticket is worth £12 million. It expires tomorrow. If you want to claim it, it's yours––on two conditions. One, you don't ask any questions, and two, you leave right away, immediately, as you have to find a way of getting to London before tomorrow evening. On these conditions and as I stand before you, are you in or out?"

Those watching in the Games Room were now silent, the audio ringing through clearly, each man––and that especially true for Fifteen––craning forward just a little closer to the screens.

On the street, Wilma remained silent for a moment, checking around her, before looking squarely into the face of the Russian in front of her.

"Find a way of getting back to London," the English woman echoed, the Russian raising an eyebrow, before Wilma said, "That wasn't a question, I just find it funny you suggest it's hard for me to get to London. I'm in." She took the ticket when it was handed to her, almost expecting it not to have been. This had to be some kind of joke––a prank somehow—though the Russian had known her name. That meant this wasn't a freak coincidence.

"Make your lover proud," the Russian said with a wink. The realisation they knew about her love life, her reason for being in St Petersburg, hit hard. She felt exposed. Before she could say anything––she stopped a question forming on her lips at that moment as she remembered the first condition––the female was gone, turning and disappearing into the crowd almost as quickly as she'd appeared. After a few seconds, Wilma could no longer see her.

"Stand by," came the voice from the Trackers, the sight of a Contestant with ticket in hand, not an uncommon one. They knew what would happen next if they were genuinely hooked––it was always the same.

Wilma grabbed her phone. She looked back towards the cafe which she'd just come out from, as if thinking about going back, maybe to tell her partner. Instead, Wilma turned back to her phone, using the internet to search the National Lottery website, finding the history of previous draws. She got to the date listed on the ticket, and it confirmed it for her––£12 million still unclaimed, the option to cash in the prize expiring tomorrow evening, at six. Wilma swore, then swore again, this time louder, a smile on her face.

"Game on!" came the response from the Trackers, and inside the Games Room, Fifteen stood there proudly. He had a Contestant in play. Her details were now being updated on another screen, the first odds appearing within two minutes. How long would she last, how far would she get? Might she even cross the border? Could she possibly claim the prize? As the first Contestant in the Hunt, she had an advantage of time over all the others––especially over whoever got Eighteen's ticket, which had to be claimed that day.

Wilma's initiation into the Games prompted a flurry of others to follow shortly after. Within half an hour––by half past ten that morning––all ten Contestants were now in play, the tactics employed in each of those encounters similar to what had been proposed with Wilma: take the ticket and run now, without asking questions, or walk away and carry on as if nothing had happened.

All ten took the ticket.

No one turned down the potential of millions for the chance that what they were being told was actually true, as improbable as it always sounded initially. As unlikely as it was that a stranger would hand you a lottery ticket worth millions and just let you walk away with it, then disappear, no suggestion that they wanted anything in return.

What no one asked themselves––if they had, they would probably have walked away immediately––was why someone would do this? What was in it for them?

Twelve––Arseni Markovic––had managed to get a British woman and the only single person in the ten, but she had travelled to St Petersburg by car after touring around Finland. She'd never flown anywhere before, an apparent fear of flying picked up in her background check. That made claiming her possible €16 million prize in Paris somewhat of a challenge. It made her an interesting prospect for all the men in the Games Room.

Thirteen––Rurick Sewick and the only non-Russian in the two groups, being Ukrainian—got the next Contestant, a Swede. His men handed her a UK ticket for £15 million. She was the first family person involved––she was on holiday with her husband and three kids––which made her involvement in the Hunt equally fascinating.

The run of females being selected continued with a Scot, for whom men working for Sixteen––Akim Kozlov––handed her the prospect and a ticket for €12 million, claimable in Spain. She lived in Edinburgh with her Scottish husband, and they were in Russia with their one-year-old for a long weekend.

At the same time that she was taking the ticket, the first male Contestant was also declared to be officially in the Hunt. A German man from Munich was handed Nineteen's ticket––chemist Pavlov—worth £13 million, one of the five UK tickets in that day's Hunt. The German man was visiting a lady he'd met online––a Russian girl, beautiful and desperate to start a family––and it was once again fascinating as they watched the man just take the ticket. He showed no apparent regard for who he was leaving behind, maybe blindly assuming he would get to explain it all later. Not everyone got that chance, as history had shown.

The last five Contestants to enter the Hunt were all found within a few minutes of each other, as the screens went epic, mirrored with the activity now happening in the Games Room, as the Russians who already had a Contestant in the Hunt were working out their plan of attack.

A Dutchman and father of two got Eleven––Foma Polzin's––day going. The Irish ticket was worth €17 million. Then it was an English wife with four kids––she having the largest family of those competing in the event––taking Seventeen's ticket––Dmitry Kaminski having shelled out £22 million for the day's highest value prize. Nothing like trying to impress his fellow Hosts.

That was immediately followed by the lowest value ticket of the day--€11 million claimable in Portugal, which Twenty--Osip Yakolev--had put forward. An Irish woman--the couple didn't have children with them in Russia--was his Contestant.

The final two Contestants were basically announced at the same time; a Frenchman who had travelled to St Petersburg with his wife and two daughters at the start of a week's holiday--or so he thought--taking the £19 million UK ticket when offered and apparently prepared to not look back. That brought Fourteen--Andre Filipov--into the Hunt, pipped to the post for the last position, by Eighteen--Motya Utkin's Contestant, an Englishman from London who was travelling with his partner and their one child. He had the most laborious task, having just that same day to get his €16 million ticket back to France before the opportunity to claim was over.

BY ELEVEN, the atmosphere in the Games Room resembled that of a trading floor--which to some degree, it was. Certainly down the years there had been times when in frantic minutes of action in that room inside the Volkov mansion, more money had been put on the table than might have been spent in a week of trading on the London LIFFE floor. In examples like Sokoloff--a man who wasn't missed around their closely guarded circles--whole empires had been destroyed. Billions lost.

Svetlana loved events like those currently happening before her eyes more than anything. She loved to stand back--from her elevated and sideline position--and just watch the men. Watch them in their silence as well as their action. Catch the glances they always gave towards other Hosts, which only hinted at what they were thinking, who they were watching, where they were hoping to make their next killing--or maybe, and this she loved to observe most, where they saw the most significant threat coming from. Who these men feared.

Fear was such a rare thing for men in such circles as theirs that she found it fascinating to dance around the edges of it all. It was what thrilled her most about it. The danger, the power, the risk.

It was almost sexual, this drive inside, the energy it created, the thrill it gave her.

To watch men she knew to be strong and fearless, protected by their billions, for the first time maybe face the fact they might lose. It was drama she couldn't have acted out herself. It was priceless.

And there was a noticeable charge in the atmosphere that morning. Svetlana had sensed it the moment she walked into their presence. There was more on the line than just finance––there always was––but now, if anything, it seemed even more than that. She watched the room's wealthiest Host––Foma, who was unchallenged at Eleven––walk around, dropping in and out of conversations, continuously in connection with his team via his headset. He looked towards her occasionally––more so than most of the others––and he looked involved, as involved in it all as she'd ever seen anyone. She knew it wasn't just about winning his own particular Hunt, she could see by the actions of the man––he was after blood.

She watched Andre––riding high at Fourteen now––the newest member of the group. He was young––the youngest by far––but it seemed as if that fact made him work twice as hard. He was driven, focused, characteristics he shared with his father, though to look at them, the way they carried themselves, the way they dressed, they couldn't have been more different. She found that fascinating.

Andre had conducted himself well so far––he'd won the only Hunt he'd been put forward for. Today might challenge that perfect record.

She looked over to her Odds Maker. The role had been held by a few different people down the years, though the current man had held it for the previous five. He was well adjusted to the demands of this particular arena. She could see bets were being made––they were piling up in fact––each bet confirmation listed on its own dedicated screen, as if the men in that room needed reminding precisely what they'd laid on the line. Maybe they did? Billions were already invested so far that day. It was not always in cash––rarely did that come into play––but business agreements, regions, rights. Anything that could be quantified was included, and the monetary value estimated by the Odds Maker. What he said went, and no one now bothered to ever question his judgement.

She looked back at the screens, which displayed a rolling feed of the ten on-going Hunts, all of which were in their very early stages, the exciting part where it still wasn't clear which way each would go, the nets of their Hosts still far enough away for escape to seem possible.

It was usually the actions of the Contestant that closed the net around themselves.

Where they chose to try and leave the country from, often played into the hands of the Host. If it was the airport and that particular oligarch had strong connections that way––be it the border guard, the airport security or maybe he even owned the airline the Contestant was trying to use––they would instruct that particular contact to shut the Hunt down. Therefore all the fellow Hosts always kept an eye out for what the other Contestants were doing––because it worked both ways. If another Contestant happened to come into an area they were strong in, the bets could be placed, and that competing oligarch would then use his own connections to help that Contestant on. Winning came in many forms.

Hosts therefore not only had to lay their own traps––something that their fellow Hosts couldn't see coming, and so would keep betting against them right up until the point it was too late––but also had to stop their Contestants getting into any of the hundreds of areas where another Host might be stronger than they were. It was a multi-layered multi-faceted puzzle––something that kept them all coming back year after year, and something Svetlana loved to watch happening right under her own roof.

On the floor, the men could feel the highly charged atmosphere. Foma's presence––he'd only been allowed in the previous year––had shifted things. He was too strong, too big for them. They all saw he had Andre Filipov on side, as well.

Dmitry Kaminski, who was only too aware of their threat, had his own mini alliance going on, something which gave him at least a fighting chance in the room. He was sure that others could well have thought the same as he did--where those alliances might be, he couldn't tell, besides Andre and Foma. They were seen talking closely with one another often. They never looked over to Dmitry once, but he was sure they were discussing him.

It was Kuznetsov, however, who formed the content of most of their dialogue, as Andre once again stood alongside Foma, both of their Contestants in a state of waiting. They too were waiting to see where each escape would be attempted from. They had one eye always on Wilma Baines--the first Contestant into the Hunt--and the one representing Kuznetsov. They were both working on the double mission of winning their own Hunt, while setting up such a giant ambush--with equally large betting--against Wilma, that it would threaten to destabilise her Host. They hadn't yet found the right opportunity, nor was he seemingly prepared to go head-to-head against them. He'd matched a few bets so far--something in the region of eighty million on the table--but nothing substantial; he'd placed the lowest value in stakes so far of them all.

He'd also not met any of the bets Foma or Andre had proposed. They apparently had to entice him with something he couldn't resist--the poisoned chalice--something all Hosts dreamed of making.

It was precisely what Kuznetsov had unknowingly walked into with Sokoloff when Phelan McDermott had been in play. Both men had known sure victory--Kuznetsov actually acting recklessly at the time--a trait they hoped to exploit in him once more today.

Kuznetsov should have pulled out of that encounter when he had the chance. That's why Sokoloff had tasted blood and had moved in for the kill. Kuznetsov had been weak, he'd taken it personally and gone in way over his head. It was only because of the outside actions of Matvey--who controlled Phelan in that Hunt--that Kuznetsov had then come out on top, and massively so. That apparently left him thinking more of himself than was merited. If they could catch him in a similar mood again, they would have him for real this time.

So far, he was cautious.

Maybe it had been an error for Foma to threaten him before the event. Perhaps he was wary of being their target now? Only the next two days would ultimately tell. As it stood, little damage would be done to either man––Kuznetsov or Kaminski––which wouldn't please Matvey at all.

For the other Hosts, Foma was a fascinating target. You put someone into the mix worth nearly four times anyone else's worth, and of course, they all wanted a piece of the action. If three or four of them could take a billion or two from him, it would cut him down to size, and they would all be able to leapfrog him as a result.

His mere presence brought that focus––of course, it also offered great danger too. You didn't get as wealthy as Foma without having connections all over the place. The fact he'd dropped down from the T10 to join their group as the new Eleven only added to the risk. In the T10 were much wealthier men who might have an alliance with Foma who he could pull in favours with.

12

That same morning, at Vauxhall House, an MI6 briefing was starting, the meeting focused on the official visit of President Putin which was due to happen in the autumn. Alex and Anissa had been called in to be a part of this team––asked to oversee it, in fact, something of a complete shift by their DDG when it came to them and all things Russia. Maybe the fact it was a visit to London––and therefore kept them firmly rooted on British soil––was the primary incentive for their involvement?

Anissa was due in Russia the following week as it was––signed off on by her employers, the DDG not happy about it at all but agreeing to it anyway––and neither was in jovial spirits as the meeting got underway. Anissa was particularly downcast following the discovery of Maggie's body the day before.

"Alex, I want to hand the floor over to you now, so that you can take things on from here regarding what needs to be in place," the DDG said, stepping to one side as Alex came forward. He didn't actually then stay around himself but just walked straight out the door and left them all to it.

"A few of you were involved the last time Putin was in town, back in 2012. You'll know he has his own team, and we won't be told his itinerary until the morning of his flight." It was the same with the Americans––maybe even worse in their case––as with similar high profile figures. "Gordon, as always, I'd like you to put aside a few technicians to watch for any cyber chatter based on his visit over these next months," he said, which was now standard practice. Much intelligence information had been gathered that way, saving vast amounts of time later on, when threats might otherwise arise. Most online comments never led to anything. But they would be watching.

"Anissa, I want you to head up a group of people who'll work out his most likely points of contact. The Russian Embassy, the Prime Minister and such. Build a likely list of who Putin will see, and the related security implications these visits would involve. I'll work with the guys who'll actually man the ground during his day in the city. We'll liaise with his own security people when the time comes, working with them as best we can. But you know how it is." They all did. It was often challenging to work alongside such teams, who had their own way of doing things, their own people they trusted––which usually was only the members of their own group anyway.

Alex dismissed the meeting, Anissa coming over to him. He put a hand on her shoulder.

"I know you don't really want any added responsibility at the moment, but I felt it was important you were seen to be heading up a section. You can delegate everything to the team. I just want you leading them."

"Thanks," she said. With everything on her mind for the upcoming trip to St Petersburg––never mind what had happened with Maggie, which she couldn't forget, and not having slept a wink the night before––she didn't really want anything else landing on her plate. After Russia, she wasn't sure how secure her role would be within the Service. She could see Alex was only trying to include her, and she was, in fact, the best-qualified person to be doing that, anyway. It was kind of him.

"You okay?" he said.

"Just tired."

"Didn't sleep either?"

"No."

"Want to talk about it?"

"Not really," she said, with a smile. "Not right now, anyway."

"Fair enough. I'm here whenever you need to."

"I know. Thanks."

As the afternoon pressed on, Foma had been able to set what he thought was the perfect trap, calling Matvey who waited on the outside to help implement things. If Svetlana found out, or if any Host reported what he was now doing, he would be out. They didn't care about that, however, nor would she be allowed to find out.

Wilma Baines had not been making much of a move––and this had given them their chance. Her girlfriend had been left in the cafe and despite going back to the hotel, had been unable to find her lover. Matvey had managed to set it up that at two in the afternoon, someone approached her, saying she'd seen Wilma being grabbed––kidnapped––from outside the hotel.

She called the police immediately. The hotel helped her make the required report. Matvey then simultaneously reported in the details to the FSB––a report of a kidnap coming in from the police, following the girl friend's call, as well as from him, would get the required attention Matvey needed on the situation. Matvey sent the FSB video footage Foma had had his team snatch from the Games Room broadcast of Kuznetsov's men watching their Contestant. Watching, but not kidnapping anyone, not that the FSB needed to know that. Matvey reported it as an ongoing kidnap situation of a foreign national. A team was dispatched. Once done, Matvey confirmed it to Foma, who made his move.

Kuznetsov had been playing long enough, and it was time to call it a day. There was no way he was letting Wilma escape with his ticket––with his team watching her closely, she was about to fall into his hands. Kuznetsov stated to the Games Room there was no contest, the Hunt was over––he was boastful and all assuming. Foma made a bet––which Kuznetsov couldn't meet as things stood, his team about to grab the English woman––that Wilma would be caught before four. Foma stated it was obviously a foregone conclusion; *Well done Kuznetsov, but I bet she couldn't make it any longer.* Seeing a chance for money, Kuznetsov would have to keep things running a little longer. All he needed to do was to call off his men, for the time being, giving Wilma the time to make it past four, now with his team's protection. He would make sure Wilma was safe, at least until the time was up. Kuznetsov jumped at the chance to get one over on Foma. He matched Foma's bet. Andre also wanted in on some of the action. It wasn't much by either man, but it was a start.

Matvey gave the instruction to the FSB to hold back the unit that was, unknown to Kuznetsov's team, watching the oligarch's team as they tracked Wilma, the FSB waiting, poised to intervene. This was when Sasha, his own team on standby should the kidnapping escalate, became suspicious. He knew straight away this was Games related and went out in search of the unit that was sitting in an unmarked van, but apparently doing nothing. The fact Matvey had such influence with fellow agents was surprising––and highly alarming.

Four o'clock was allowed to come, and pass. Kuznetsov had won that bet––Wilma was still walking free. Foma and Andre looked suitably riled––Svetlana could recognise good acting when she saw it and found the spectacle highly amusing––and Foma came back with another stab at things. He doubled what he'd just lost and stated categorically that Fifteen's worthless excuse of a Contestant didn't have a chance of making it past five. Kuznetsov checked with his own men. They reported there was no one watching them, no one even close––they had her just where they needed her. Kuznetsov once again matched their bet.

Five o'clock came and went. This was becoming somewhat profitable for Kuznetsov. He loved the look on Foma's face after taking one hundred and fifty million from him.

"You son-of-a-bitch," Foma said, though he was calm. "You've got men protecting her, haven't you? She didn't have a chance."

"Better check your sources, Eleven, and don't believe everything your own guys tell you. I've got this one––she's mine. You think you can outmanoeuvre me on this? Name your price, asshole."

Foma had him. He had him exactly where he wanted him.

"European operations." Kuznetsov was the water treatment man, and while he ran businesses across the world, Europe was his hotbed, his most asset-rich area.

"And what could you possibly have to match that?"

"North America. Telecoms." Both men looked to the Odds Maker. Foma's North American operation was easily worth over $2 billion, significantly more than Kuznetsov's European business network.

"I'd say the deal is clearly in your favour, Fifteen, if Eleven's happy to offer that." He clearly was. It was a basic rule that you couldn't go back on a verbal offering. Once spoken, the bet was as good as made, unless the weaker party refused. Kuznetsov could double his value with this one trade. Win it, and he'd significantly expand his influence.

"What's the bet?" They'd apparently agreed on the terms, now they needed to settle on the outcome.

"Your girl claims the ticket."

"You're switching, now? An hour ago you said she wouldn't last until evening, now you think she'll get out? Don't you know that I control everything about her?" Again, being the stronger party, as soon as Foma had spoken the offer it was Kuznetsov's privilege now to either accept or decline. There was nothing further Foma could do about it.

"Do we have a deal or not?"

"I just have to close down this Hunt immediately, and you hand me North America? It would be my pleasure!"

Deal done. Foma had just lured him into instant defeat. Nothing more was said, both men turning to attempt whatever trick they thought they had up their sleeve, Kuznetsov speaking to his men about stepping in and stopping Wilma, Foma confirming with Matvey that the trap could now be sprung.

It was less than a minute later––the call put through to the FSB unit waiting in the unmarked van––that the screens displayed the agents surrounding those working for Kuznetsov. Weapons were raised, orders barked out that each of the five men place their hands behind their heads and lie face down on the pavement. Wilma could be seen fleeing the area.

"Damn you, Eleven!" Kuznetsov shouted, but he was not going to give up that easily, he had too much on the line. He was frantically getting another team in place––teams in fact––as it didn't matter what they did to her now, she was a stop on sight target. With $2 billion riding on the outcome of this Hunt––money Kuznetsov couldn't afford to lose––a bullet through her skull wouldn't be so far off the mark. She would do well to claim the money then.

He wasn't allowed to leave the Games Room while any Hunt was still underway, that was another rule. While the Games were unfolding, they all had to control everything from within those four walls, in front of their fellow Hosts. Otherwise, he would have personally driven and shot her through the temple. He didn't care what happened to her now––he wasn't losing that money, he wasn't going to lose to Foma.

Within the room, the other Hosts picked up on the life and death struggle in play between two of their fellow oligarchs, focus soon narrowed to that particular Hunt, some men altogether ignoring what their own Contestants might or might not be doing. They would get notifications from their teams if things became critical.

For now, it was irresistible to watch the personal duel that was unfolding within their midst.

They could see the growing desperation on Kuznetsov's face. He wore the same expression that Sokoloff had worn when he first realised his time was up. Yet it was about to happen again––and it was fascinating.

Like watching a lion devour its prey––this time another lion.

Part of you didn't want to watch, as it was too horrible to look at, but for the most part, you couldn't help but stare, transfixed by the last moments of a considerable force, a notable presence.

Foma couldn't be seen directly interacting with another Host's

Contestant––so to just have the FSB pick her up and take her to the airport was not an option. It would forfeit his bet and allow Kuznetsov to get off the hook. So they had to be a lot smarter than that. They had to know when and where Kuznetsov and his men would attempt to stop her. A sniper taking her out wasn't beyond the realms of possibility, either. They'd have to be on their A-Game.

Like an invisible force working out of sight, the FSB unit continued to take out the men Kuznetsov and his heavies had been sending to apprehend Wilma. This was helped by Matvey having invested heavily in the past to map out Kuznetsov's entire empire––and more importantly, the men he turned to in such a situation. That meant now, he had them all tracked. He knew who the men were that would be spoken to, long before Kuznetsov had even made the call.

It was through this knowledge that Matvey guided Wilma towards the train––Kuznetsov's influence reduced dramatically, but he had guys working within the airport, as well as a team at Heathrow. If she could cross the border into Estonia or Finland––it didn't really matter which one she chose––she could fly out from those airports and hit any number of other destinations.

Of course, that might still have alerted Kuznetsov's men in the UK had the Trackers still been on her tail. They too had been grabbed by the FSB team investigating the attempted kidnapping. The fact that the Trackers had been watching Wilma with cameras, only added to their guilt in the eyes of the FSB. With the live video feed brought to an end, no one in the Games Room had any idea where she was. Only Matvey did, and therefore Foma. She was well on her way.

Sasha, however, was still on her trail. He'd been there when the arrests were made––first when they arrested the men working for Kuznetsov as they closed in on Wilma and then when they had captured the team of Trackers, their camera equipment visible. Sasha's own unit, in his absence, had been called in to track Wilma, and Sasha was yet to rejoin them. Sasha knew this was a live, real-time Contestant, and he saw firsthand what was going on.

He called Alex––getting only his voicemail, where he left a short message anyway––and continued his pursuit.

AS EVENING FELL, confirmation came through that Wilma was on her way to the UK by plane. It didn't say where she was heading. Kuznetsov's men watching St Petersburg international airport, Pulkovo Two, had not reported her leaving from there, suggesting she wouldn't be landing at Heathrow where he had another team stationed.

Kuznetsov knew his game was up, knew he'd been set up, his own stupid temperament causing him to walk into something he apparently didn't know anything about. He'd trapped himself by his own rash presumption. It would cost him dearly.

He knew Foma had done this on purpose. It was personal, and according to the so-called sacred ethics of the Games, these things should not have happened. They were not meant to be tearing one another apart, yet over the last two years, that was what had started to happen. Sokoloff was destroyed, Krupin dumped from the event himself, and all to allow Foma, and then his side-kick Andre, into their group. Kaminski had been run dry––he didn't know how that situation would work itself out now after the day he'd had––and they'd now come for him as well, too. It'd been all too personal.

Foma had to go. If he were out of the way, the bet would not have to be honoured. Kuznetsov made a call to one final man––the only one of his contacts not caught up in the now flawed pursuit––and had him take up residence in the building across the street from the Volkov mansion. It was actually the same apartment that MI6 and Sasha had used to spy on the Russians earlier that year. Now, the instructions were to take out Foma Polzin as he left the mansion that evening. A bullet through his skull would go a long way to removing what might otherwise be an impossible debt he owed to the fellow Host.

He deserved it; Foma had struck out at him, but he would be the one to strike back with the genuinely fatal blow.

As the evening came to an end––three of the Contestants were still on the run, including Wilma who was flying to Gatwick airport, south of London––the men were heading out for the evening. It remained to be seen whether they would, in fact, come back the following day.

The imprisonment of one team of Trackers––something Svetlana was trying to get others to sort out––had been a sour note. The unfolding events between Eleven and Fifteen were something else entirely. When that result was called––the Contestant was yet to claim, but it was clear she would be doing just that––the event was effectively over. How could anything else compete with that? It was drama of the highest order, albeit not for the losing party––Aleksey Kuznetsov.

As the oligarchs gathered their things together, finally leaving the Games Room after an exciting day, their own security personnel now joined them, and they descended the stairs. Kuznetsov was in the rear, mobile phone to his ear, keeping his distance.

"He's coming out of the building any second now, in the third group. Get ready," he said, his security men around him unaware of what was about to happen.

After Osip and Motya had left the building, their teams of men with them, it was Foma who then stepped out through the doors. He'd taken three steps when shots were heard––the sound of three, four high calibre bullets filling the night––Foma going down, his men instinctively on him, before they dragged him to the waiting car.

Inside the mansion, the men stood frozen, the shots coming before any of the others had stepped out, their own security now kicking into gear, guns drawn, as were those of the men already on the street.

"What in heaven's name is going on?" Svetlana said, hearing the shots and coming down the stairs at that moment.

"It's Foma," Andre said, still in shock. "Someone has just taken a pop at him as he left the building," and he was looking up at Kuznetsov, but then rested his eyes on Svetlana, who stood there with a hand to her mouth. If someone was watching her home, then others knew about the events going on in there, unless it was someone connected to the men she'd just been amongst. The fact the target was apparently Foma, made Kuznetsov the most obvious culprit.

"If I find out that this has anything to do with you in any way at all, Fifteen, I'll personally make sure you hang for this, do you understand?"

"Svetlana, how could you suggest I had anything to do with this?"

She left it at that. Her head of security came up to her at that point.

"Aren't you supposed to be watching us?" she said.

"We have been. They accessed a property across the road from a rear entrance. We have men onto it at the moment."

"Any news on the target?" She wasn't assuming anything at this point.

"Foma and his entourage seem to have been the intended target. His men were surrounding him and got him into the vehicle before we could see what might have happened. We'll have to await word from them before we confirm anything."

"And the shooter?"

"We have men moving in now. The Russian Guards have been informed. They had two teams on their way. We've secured the exit from the building we know they've used."

"Good, keep me posted."

"Can we get out of here from another entrance, maybe?" Kaminski called up to Svetlana, not keen to be seen leaving through the front entrance now, even if the threat had gone. Foma and his men had been the third group out––he'd seen that first hand––so if they'd all been targets, then it would have been Osip who would have been fired upon first. He was confident the shooter was long gone, if indeed he had managed to escape. But police would be showing up shortly. A crowd, too, no doubt gathering on the pavements nearby. This wasn't a situation into which a future President––President-elect, anyway––could be seen emerging.

"Yes, of course," she said, leading the remaining men to a rear door, one they'd never used before. It led to an underground parking area, big enough for three cars, of which one space was taken. A ramp led up to street level via a side courtyard––a shared entrance at that––so that it wasn't obvious which building the driver had been coming out from. "You can get your drivers to pick you up from here. I'll make sure the shutter is opened," and she left them at that moment, the first car two minutes away, each one allowing enough time to load the car and depart before the next would pull into the courtyard and navigate its way into the basement parking area. Soon all the men were leaving, Kuznetsov himself the last to go. He'd not heard anything back from his man by that point––maybe he was already dead. Presuming he had in fact done his job––and killed Foma––the shooter was now nothing more than a loose end, anyway. If he had been taken out by the Russian Guards as he made his escape, or if that was about to happen, it would only tidy things up nicely for Kuznetsov.

Foma had known nothing about what was about to happen to him. Matvey had seen the sniper being called to action. He had not been able to directly monitor Kuznetsov's call, but the result of the call was only too evident. Matvey's men saw the sniper heading towards the centre––to the mansion––confirming what he'd been ordered to do. Having tracked the man to the building opposite the Volkov mansion, Matvey's men had reported in, their boss then confirming they storm the building and take out the shooter. He was killed therefore twenty minutes before Foma even stepped out onto the street.

A photo lying on the floor beneath the high calibre weapon––Kuznetsov's sniper was a pro––confirmed Foma was the target. Matvey's men deposited shell casing from the same gun on the floor, four empty cartridges, before removing the bullets from the weapon and replacing them with four blanks. The attack still needed to take place, but Matvey would ultimately just manipulate the outcome.

The mobile on the floor had rung––it was Kuznetsov confirming Foma was about to step out of the building––and the team counted the first two groups out, their cars pulling up as the oligarchs got to the edge of the pavement, speeding off into the dark night soon after. Then Foma stepped out.

One, two, three then a fourth bullet fired. When the shots rang out, and Foma had instinctively hit the ground, the impact of his team of four men on him––forceful arms and hands that might as well have been bullets––made it impossible for him to tell if he'd been hit or not. They bundled him into the Land Rover and sped away. If the bullets had not been blanks, Foma would have been a dead man. Certainly, Matvey would let it look that way, for the moment.

He called Foma, who was shocked by what had just taken place, and told him what had happened. Lie low, for the time being, play dead.

Matvey's men quickly exited the room––going instead up to the top floor. They would hide out there until the police had discovered the sniper, and only then would they make their escape.

Everything was then reported to Matvey, the operation had gone smoothly. He said he would make sure the police were out of the building as quickly as possible. He would later send one of his own cars to pick them all up, promising it wouldn't be too late. They sat down, a bottle of vodka already open, a deck of cards being shuffled, and waited for everything to run its course.

With Foma apparently murdered––at the hands of a fellow Host, all the evidence would suggest––the Games would have to be postponed, maybe even shut down altogether. That was Matvey's ultimate plan. When he was in power, he didn't want groups of influential people meeting together as they currently did. He wanted them out in the open, either for him or otherwise detained. He wouldn't have allowed what was happening now to be taking place if he'd been President. And he soon would be, he knew it. No matter what Kaminski thought––a would-be pretender to the throne––or Putin himself, a man who'd got so secure in his role, it was as if he didn't expect anyone to challenge him.

But a challenge was coming and from multiple angles. At the moment, Matvey had the element of surprise. While the challenge was unknown, it held greater fear for the current President. As soon as the names were announced, it would be a level playing field. Then it would be the last man standing who would come through. Lion on Lion.

That moment was still a few months away. He would remain in the long grass to one side for the time being, which suited him well, picking off those that needed picking off, until the end was in sight.

When that time came, all runners in the race would do everything in their power to win—there would be no rules then, no codes of conduct. It would be the survival of the fittest.

13

"Sasha speaking," the Russian said, the number not displayed on his handset.

"It's me," Alex said, confirmation that he'd got the voicemail Sasha had left him a couple of hours before. "Where are you?"

"Still following the crew. They escorted a female--British I think--to the Baltic Railway station where she boarded a train to Tallinn." They'd watched someone on that route before, it offered a direct flight to Gatwick, once they reached the Estonian capital. "I returned to the city behind the FSB unit--my own unit in fact. I'll reconnect with them soon, stating that I'd been looking for them and will find out where the orders came from. If I can trace it back to whichever Russian it was, we might have a bit more to go on."

"That's great work, my friend." They were keeping names as much as possible out of the call--barring his opening greeting, neither man referred to the other by name, as they didn't know who might be listening.

"One more thing. I was there when they first made the arrests, getting a good look at the teams following the Contestant. I have a better understanding now how it all works. When I get back into the office I'll run my own checks, work out who the first team are associated with. I suspect with some digging it'll give me the name of the man at the top of that particular tree," he said, Alex understanding he meant the man within the Games. "There was a second group, too, which was interesting. They had broadcast quality cameras, directional sounds, the lot. Really well kitted out."

"Something to do with it all as well?"

"I assume so, but probably connected to the event itself, as opposed to any one man. I'll run their details too, see where it leads."

"That's great. We're still running things at this end. Pineapple is coming out next week," which was their code name, slightly humorously suggested by Sasha for Anissa, because of the similarity of her name with that particular fruit in his own language. It worked well in this context, "and I don't need to ask you to look out for...it," Alex realising he didn't want to give her a gender, which might otherwise connect Anissa to their investigation of the Games. True, she was in St Petersburg for the trial, and that implicated her enough. But anything to keep others guessing.

"You have my word." Alex would communicate later via their draft email process, something they'd continued to use well, ever since it had been suggested. He would share there about his involvement with the Putin security for his trip later in the year. Alex really wanted to know if Sasha might be involved in it from the Russian side, though he doubted that would happen. Putin probably had his own dedicated team, and even if he did use the FSB as well, it would be men who were based in Moscow. Why would they consider Sasha, based in St Petersburg with no apparent connection to the UK, to be a suitable candidate? The more Alex pondered, the more he hoped his friend would have nothing to do with it.

They finished the call, nothing more said, therefore nothing more given away. Alex then called Anissa and filled her in on everything. She was a few days away from her trip but intrigued to hear the development.

"Do let me know when he's got back to you regarding the associates."

"Of course. He'll keep an eye out for you."

"You shouldn't have mentioned that. He doesn't need to be involved, it only implies Sasha knows more than he's said if they see him taking an interest."

"Nonsense, it's a trial in his city with a known British MI6 agent in attendance. I'd say that gives him more than enough reason already to be showing his face. The Motherland keeping their eye on a foreign spy."

"Less of that, will you. I'm trying to play down my visit, not turn it into some big political situation."

"Sorry. Do you feel prepared? Have you been in touch with the witness lately?"

"I spoke with Josée yesterday. I'll meet her in Paris, and we'll fly out together with her lawyer."

"And Leona, where is she?" Alex had primarily left that whole situation––something that didn't come within his working remit, anyway––to Anissa, only occasionally showing interest, like he was now, his concern solely for his colleague.

"She flew out yesterday. They'll hold her in custody until the trial, but under house arrest effectively. She'll be allowed limited freedom, at least until the verdict."

"Any idea how long you'll be away for?" He'd tried to get this info out of her for some time, though the answer was always the same.

"Still don't know for sure. Could be a day, or a week. I really don't know. As long as it takes, Alex, as always. It's important we push every angle on this one. It's the first time anyone has got anywhere near a courthouse."

"Just be careful."

"You worry too much, Alex, especially about me."

"Well stop giving me reasons to worry, then, will you," but he was laughing. A text message came through at that moment from Gordon Peacock, head of MI6 technical surveillance. "Hold on there Anissa," Alex said, having scanned the message as the notification came through. "Gordon says there is news on the web about a shooting outside the Volkov mansion, unconfirmed reports linking it to a wealthy Russian being assassinated, though he's said the mainstream media are silent on the story."

"Get in touch with Sasha, see if he can find out who is involved and if the story is genuine. The fact there is a media blackout would suggest there is something they don't want us to know. Given the security in place at that address, it could well just have been someone trying to access somewhere they shouldn't."

"But that would suggest others knew what was going on. Besides, he mentioned it was a wealthy Russian. That's news speak for an oligarch. Someone has taken out a fellow member, is my suspicion."

"Let's see what our friend finds out before we jump to conclusions. Keep me informed," though it was true she was heading to St Petersburg herself in three days. If there were something still going on, she would most likely be close enough to find out what that was. During the day she would be involved in the trial, but outside of that––and assuming she had the energy––she could have a look around, see what more she might be able to find out. It was going to be strange being in St Petersburg without Alex this time. They'd made all their trips together––always under the radar thanks to Sasha––but this time she was flying solo, and very much exposed.

Sasha was back inside his office at Big House. He'd just had a full debrief with his unit. They had received their instructions directly from Moscow, and in his absence, they had been authorised to go back to their regular duties when the situation had been resolved. Sasha left them to their other responsibilities, shutting his own office door so that he wouldn't be disturbed, and accessed his system to find out where that particular command had come from.

It wouldn't tell him––which meant it was senior, only a few people at the very top of the FSB had that level of clearance that their intervention would not be displayed. It told him all he needed to know. He'd seen Matvey do something similar in the past. Someone had apparently made a call again, to someone in the senior ranks, and that person had then put the two teams into action. It had probably been the same person who had sent a team the previous year to intercept an Irishman named Shane––two agents had been killed in that exchange with the Russian Guards––though it had been a grenade from the escaping Irishman, and not Russian fire, that had killed the FSB agents.

Still, that call had come from someone senior. They had only been there because of the instruction of someone not even in the FSB. Money always had a way of gaining influence over people who could make a difference.

Sasha then picked up the latest message from Alex, the news about a shooting in his city something he'd not been told about. If there had been a shooting––and if the target was one of the oligarchs, men who always had their own security around them––Sasha knew how to find out. Most of the guys that were employed to babysit his country's wealthy were most often former FSB or police personnel––some doing both, in fact, working as bodyguards when they were not on duty. The pay was especially good to make the added workload, for those still juggling the two jobs, worthwhile. And because that was the case, he knew at least a few contacts in every team where he could start getting some answers.

The confirmation came during his fourth batch of calls. No one was answering. He'd been calling the men responsible for the safety and protection of Foma Polzin. Sasha then cross-referenced Foma's name with a highly sophisticated piece of technology which he ran through Yandex, the Russian version of Google. In a few seconds it threw out the handful of reports there were––none of them still live stories anymore––which suggested Foma had been shot, one actually naming him, another calling it an assassination.

None of the main news channels were covering the story. That either suggested it was true and they were limiting the damage it would do to his empire, making sure everything was sufficiently secure before the news was released, or that it was fake, or that there was some truth in it all and it was being kept quiet for another reason. His own knowledge of the Games suggested the third option had weight, and while it was possible it had all been a fake, there were enough reports and comments to suggest otherwise. Besides, it was highly unlikely that all of Foma's security personnel would be uncontactable at that precise moment if everything were in order. Clearly, something had happened.

Sasha wanted to get to the scene of the alleged crime––all reports confirmed it happened in the same street where he knew the Volkov mansion was located. One reference had mentioned an upstairs window on a building facing the Volkov home. He'd been there. Svetlana's own security occupied the building directly opposite––was it possible that this had been an inside job, someone who'd stepped out of line and needed silencing? But Foma? A man worth over $7 billion. Or maybe the shot had come from the next door building––a building he'd used himself when Alex and Anissa were over, and they were able to watch the New Year event unfolding, to some degree.

Pulling up outside the basement restaurant that was a few doors down from the mansion––a place where a van was always parked whenever anyone was at home, telling him the mansion was therefore currently empty—Sasha got out of his car. High above on the building opposite, without looking directly at them, Sasha could tell the men were still in place, a twitch of the curtains enough to give away their presence. They would most probably know who he was, too, at least guess he wasn't just a tourist anyway. His car gave him away to those in the know, not that the team of security in an upstairs apartment was a concern to him at that moment. He wasn't there to attempt an entry into the mansion.

Most noticeable of all was the smashed glass on the ground––yellow police tape still visibly marking off that section of pavement––the window in the same room they'd been watching from at the beginning of the year now noticeably boarded up. So the shooter had been in that next door building. It wasn't an inside job. That made it particularly intriguing.

He wouldn't risk going up there to have a closer look. The apartment might well be guarded anyway, and while his role within the FSB would warrant his presence there, it wasn't his case. Some agents within the service didn't like other agents stepping in on their toes. He left that thought there, turning from the building––the glass and the tape––and faced the Volkov mansion once more. Little evidence remained to suggest anything at all had taken place. That was the first thing that stuck out. If, as indicated in at least two of the reports he'd seen, there were multiple shots––at least three were heard, one report said it was four––then the police would have combed the area for the impact craters. Sure, a direct hit from a less powerful weapon might have meant the bullet never passed through, but he suspected it was, in fact, a sniper's weapon and four shots, and a falling body would have left some trace. There would be signs of the bullets hitting concrete, tarmac, brickwork––anything. There would also have been blood residue left from the victim. He'd been around corpses enough to know how the blood got everywhere. Even after sawdust was applied––and there was no sign any had been––it took heavy rain or a thorough clean of an area before it was gone entirely. That gave strength to the feeling that it might have been a fake story.

Why had there been multiple reports, however? Granted, they had all been taken down already, but that could have been done by anyone. It didn't mean the stories were wrong. And what about the broken glass, the police tape? Clearly, something had happened here. Someone apparently knew a little more than was being said.

He needed more. He knew he needed to gain access to the property the shooter––assuming there was one––had been watching from. There was no other way of being more certain. Sasha carried on down the street, turning the corner where the open all hours convenience store was located. Taking that turn, he looped back around and in through a courtyard, which led to a rear entrance to the block of housing that made up the opposite side of the street to the Volkov mansion. The door had been left open.

Sasha climbed the few flights of stairs that were needed to get up to the third floor, taking a corridor that led him deeper into the building, passing other apartments on the way. There was nothing evident on the door to the apartment in question. He remembered it had been empty when they used it––run down and unused, which is why he'd been able to source it for the stakeout––and assuming someone had just used it for the same purpose, he presumed it was still empty. He forced the door, which gave way without much of an effort.

Everything was as he'd remembered it, if not a little more dusty, a little more run down. Clearly, it was still empty. He felt the breeze coming through before he got into the main room, the window boarded up, though a slight gap appeared down the left side which allowed a little light, as well as air, into the dank room. A small patch of sawdust lay on the floor underneath the window.

Sasha went over and moved it around with his boot––blood was immediately evident. As was the smell of gunpowder. Shots had been fired from this location––and evidently, a body then found as well. Was it possible that this, in fact, had been the murder, these were the shots that had been heard? A stray bullet or two smashing the glass on their way through the victim? That thought had some merit, but there was no crime scene tape, no report about such an incident taking place. Something had apparently happened, but as far as he could see, there were no police reports on record.

The fact it was this apartment––the very same empty apartment they'd used months before––all but ruled out it being a murder. No one lived there. Why else would something like that happen in an empty home? It was also a perfect vantage point for the Volkov mansion. When you put men together who had so much wealth, there would be a long list of names who might want to take revenge.

Given the amount of blood, there must be a corpse, or at least a severely wounded individual, who wouldn't just disappear, but the story was being brushed under the carpet.

Someone, somewhere, knew something. It was his job to find out.

If he could get access to the body, he might be able to work out who had sent him. If he could figure that out, it might lead on to other things.

He left the apartment with the thought that Foma might well have been the target––not clear if the attempt had been successful or not, and the blood suggested not––though what had really happened, and why it was all still so silent, he was yet to work out.

14

Trial day had arrived in St Petersburg, a day Anissa thought would never come, though as she woke in her hotel room that morning, she wondered if she was even ready for it now. It had taken an enormous effort to get things that far. There had not been a trial in Russia of a British suspect charged with murder since the William Hackett scandal, the repercussions of which were still being worked through some time on.

Anissa's aim all along––as well as achieving some level of justice for Josée, and to some degree, the family of the victim––had been to expose before the Russian judicial system the very existence of the Games. There was nothing like being forced to reveal their dirty laundry in public to make them give some answers.

Nothing had come up in the news about the case––which was a little disappointing, though the less profile Anissa received during the ordeal, the better. It had been kept quiet because of an agreement by all three countries––the French for the protection of their national, and key witness in the trial, the British for the protection of a Security Service member who was deemed vital for the witness to give her evidence, and the Russians––which was the biggest surprise of all––unless you understood that those with so much to hide had apparently made this one proceed in the shadows.

Walking into the courtroom, Josée just ahead of Anissa, it wasn't anything like Anissa expected. The space was light and modern. There was also apparently no space for a jury. Anissa had been looking forward to watching the faces––and in particular, the reactions––of the jury members as everything got disclosed.

When the judge arrived––his English clear and understandable––he quickly set the tone as they all took their seats. Leona sat to one side. It was the first time since the incident that the two Contestants had been in the same room at the same time. Neither looked at the other.

The trial was to be conducted in English, and the reason immediately became apparent.

"Seeing as today's hearing will be solely before me––there will not be a jury," the Judge stated. Anissa immediately wanted to interject, to demand why on a murder trial such a move––though not without precedent––had been made, but she stopped herself. Of course, she should have expected this. They would have made sure no ordinary Russian was there to hear what was said. It meant the Judge must already be in the know. Her trip and potential exposure were most probably already pointless. She'd certainly put herself on the FSB's radar, without being able to open up before an impartial jury the goings-on by one particular group of Russian men. "I will speak in English, the native language of the woman who stands accused of the crime I will be assessing the evidence for. As I understand it, all persons present have a good level of English, so a translator is not required." He looked at Josée––the intended person of that last comment––and moved proceedings on.

Over the course of the next few hours, both lawyers made their initial opening arguments. Crucially, Leona was not denying being in Russia at the time of the incident. They would get to question her more directly about why she was there later, they hoped. But her defence team obviously realised trying to argue that element was not in her best interest. If she denied being there only to be confronted by video and documentary evidence, it would blow a massive hole in her credibility.

Where they would argue the case, however, was who––if even either of them––had killed the janitor. Leona's lawyer finished up her opening address with the stark statement that her client was adamant the janitor was alive and well when she left the lovers to it––that she had nothing to do with whatever may have unfolded, she had just been there looking for the ticket.

So the ticket had come up. The Judge asked for no clarification––there was no confusion on his face as if to wonder what she meant by a ticket––it was clear he already knew all about it and wasn't going to press that angle. Josée's lawyer also knew about the ticket, so couldn't really ask those questions––much to Anissa's frustration––instead she just focused on doing her job, which was to get justice for her client.

As the afternoon progressed, Leona was called to the stand. This was when at least the prosecution could get the chance to lay into the defendant. By instructing her lawyer to say the janitor had been alive when she left––instead of outright denying being there, which is what Josée's lawyer had imagined would have been the case––it suddenly brought her own client a little nearer to the crime, in theory. Potentially in the eyes of the Judge, Josée suddenly became a possible perpetrator––maybe not the innocent witness after all––maybe a cold-hearted killer instead? She should have seen that coming. Perhaps she'd been foolish to bring this to trial at all?

Anissa––who was there as a support for Josée as well as a witness not to the actual crime but of Leona being there––now had less of an upfront role to play. The defence lawyer had just admitted her client was in the room where the crime had taken place. The British agent was growing increasingly frustrated. All the things she wanted to expose, all the progress she wanted to make in the case against the Games, seemed likely to fall on deaf ears. She couldn't even guarantee the safety of Josée, someone she'd personally harassed to bring this all to trial.

As the defence lawyer summed up at the end of the first day, she'd gone to town at painting a potentially very different picture. That her client, Leona, a successful and now wealthy woman who'd won her competition––she'd repeatedly referred to the Games, and the ticket in particular, as just that––was having her good name and reputation dragged through the mud by an out of work, depressed and suicidal woman, who was looking for someone to blame for her defeat and subsequent downfall. That despite having sex with the man––Josée had not been put on the stand yet but already her life was being exposed––she hadn't won the money, something her own client had rightfully claimed. She then finished with the sting in the tail––that after seeing her client with a lifestyle of wealth and apparent happiness, Josée envied her. That it was her own jealousy and self-loathing that had brought them all to trial in St Petersburg that day, that maybe in fact the blood was on her own hands. Perhaps in her anger at losing sight of the ticket––having promised the man sex in exchange for entry into the Armoury––she'd lashed out at the one person she could. That in fact, she was responsible for the murder, that it should be Josée on trial, and not her own upstanding and valued member of society––who had done nothing but good to others both before, and especially after, her good fortune.

Josée was in tears, breaking down at the closing statement, dramatically presented by the defence lawyer before the Judge. The day was officially ended, the Judge then immediately leaving the room, as both lawyers returned to their clients.

"It's all complete lies, she's even trying to implicate me now, Anissa. You never said that would be the case."

"She's just trying to cast doubt."

"What if they don't believe me? What then?"

"We haven't shared our side of things yet. You'll see, it'll be a better day tomorrow." She didn't believe it. Josée and her lawyer then spoke in French with each other––the words fast––tears flowing before long. Anissa couldn't imagine what she must now be going through. It'd been a rough first day, and the defence seemed to be throwing everything at them to place doubt in the mind of the Judge. By implicating Josée in the actual crime, it questioned her entire character as a witness––if she had committed the crime, of course she would try to blame someone else for it. Anissa hoped the Judge would be able to see through it all. Nothing about the first day had gone to plan, however.

They left the courthouse together at five. Leona had already gone––she was still under house arrest, though after a day like that, there was no knowing how long that would even last. Josée was staying with the lawyer––they had booked their hotels separately, so Josée was in a different one from Anissa––which suited the British agent. She needed nothing but a little space and time to think. She would most likely face some questions herself tomorrow, as well, and needed to be ready. The defence lawyer was after blood. If she could find a way of implicating MI6 in the murder––what were trained killers doing in Russia in the first place?––Anissa was sure that bitch would. For the first time since agreeing to go with Josée, Anissa wondered if she'd made one colossal mistake. How the Russians would love a British spy in prison for the murder of one of their own.

After a shower and some food, she called Sasha. As a British MI6 agent, she'd had a tail since landing in St Petersburg. However, it had been Sasha and his team who were assigned the task. He had men outside the courthouse during the day––standard stuff, just Russia keeping watch on a foreign spy. Sasha would take all the evening shifts, allowing him to meet with Anissa without anyone else knowing. He joined her in the hotel's bar at nine.

"Rough day?" he said, Anissa having filled him in a little over the phone, the two empty glasses that sat in front of her telling him the rest. They chatted for half an hour about the day's events in the courthouse, then Sasha brought her up to speed somewhat on what he'd found out.

As the first day of the trial had been taking place in St Petersburg––Sasha had made brief contact with Anissa, though they both knew they would have to connect properly later––the Russian agent was himself still continuing to run his own investigation into what exactly happened––and to whom––outside the Volkov mansion.

He'd managed to track down the body, using his own connections in the police force as well as FSB seed money, to buy himself that information. He'd also paid to then have his own pathologist take a look at the body.

Sasha received those results during his lunch break that afternoon. The report detailed the man's DNA and fingerprints––something he would later run through the FSB database to see if he could identify this as yet unnamed dead sniper. The report, on Sasha's express request, also detailed the startling fact that there was no gunpowder residue found on the body. If he'd fired multiple shots––three or four shots from what those early reports suggested, though he'd been unable to clarify how many exactly––there would have been something showing on the shooter, particularly on his hands or arms. Somewhere, and something. But there was nothing. Aside from the kill shot to the back of his head, the sniper's body was clean. The fact the sniper had been shot in that empty apartment they found him in––where the rumoured shots at the Volkov mansion would have had to come from––and yet for there to be nothing on the body, suggested that the sniper was already dead. He hadn't fired his weapon.

To have killed the original man then still to have made the hit was an interesting thought. Had the target therefore changed? Had Foma ordered the initial hit, his man now lying in the morgue, only to become the target himself once his plan had been discovered? And Sasha still needed to track down Foma, to find out for sure if he really was the target.

As Sasha sat in his office that afternoon––one eye constantly on the clock with an internet feed that slowly updated the events taking place in the trial––he ran the prints and DNA for the body he'd had tested. He found a match.

The shooter was a former soldier––a sniper at that––and Sasha printed out the details of the dead man. Frustratingly, however, he was not able to make a connection to anyone else.

The sniper apparently worked freelance. If he could trace the man's address and bank account--assuming he even had one--maybe that might highlight a connection to someone else further down the line. Right now, he would settle for a name and had the beginnings of a theory as to what might have been going on.

Clearly, there had been a shooter. Given the reports and the physical evidence, Sasha had to believe that there had indeed been multiple shots fired; that the stories which had long been removed were in fact based on reality. That much made sense. However, until a connection could be made between the dead sniper and whoever it was who had initially employed him, there was nothing more concrete Sasha could piece together. Sasha realised he needed to find this missing information, and seeing that the police were not pursuing the matter--he'd checked, the investigation had been closed off from on-high already--he would have to do it himself.

Working alone, he hoped he would slip under the radar somewhat of anyone watching out for him. His role within the FSB gave him an element of anonymity, though as always he would have to be careful. The dangers in life were never the threats you could see--someone, as trained as he was, could always take down a physical attacker coming at him--but those you couldn't, like a predator waiting in the grass. That was what he most feared and what his nightmares consisted off.

15

It was sunny and scorching in Monaco––as you would expect it to be at the beginning of July. Matvey stood looking out to sea; the local harbour––his yacht included––lay down there, out of eyeshot from where he currently was. The sea looked calm, inviting. He held a warm drink in his hand as he slowly stirred the sugar into it with a spoon, tapping the spoon three times on the edge of the cup before he laid it on the saucer. An old habit, one of many his son Andre had also picked up without realising it. Foma sat down on a sofa to one side. It'd been a challenging few days for him.

He'd been angry because Matvey hadn't warned him about the shooting. When he'd heard the shots fired––men in his position, with security always around them, still feared that sound––he thought his number was up. Knowing that it could only have been a fellow oligarch who'd commissioned the kill, such men paid for only the best––these snipers didn't miss. Yet, as his men bundled on top of him, and dragged him into the waiting vehicle, something he'd thought about since, impressed by their reaction––his own money well spent, it seemed––he knew he hadn't been hit.

His body hurt, that was for sure. That came because a man of his age wasn't used to being thrown to the ground, with eighteen stone men manhandling him forcefully.

But there was no blood––he was still alive––so whatever had just happened, it hadn't been a kill shot.

His first thought had been that maybe one of his men had been hit––though as they raced away across the city, that was soon clarified, everyone in his party accounted for. He was delivered thirty minutes later to the private terminal at the airport, where Matvey's own jet awaited him. Then it all started to become clear.

As he boarded and the flight took off, he was on the phone to his fellow Russian, who then shared what he'd done. Their conversation had been heated––Foma wasn't the type of man who liked to be kept in the dark about anything, especially his own attempted assassination. However, Matvey had assured Foma he'd personally been in control the whole time, that there had never been any real danger to him, and that Foma should let him finish explaining, which he did. Matvey then went on to say how it was all a great opportunity. If Foma was presumed dead––and that was why he was leaving on Matvey's jet, and not his own, to lie low for the time being––once it was proved that Kuznetsov had something to do with it, Matvey would then use that information to blow the Games apart.

Despite the fact he was now a part of the T10 and his son, alongside Foma, was a part of the T20, Matvey was only there to destroy the world of the Games. Any context that put such men together––maybe giving them a common cause––was dangerous. Like a pack of lions, you couldn't ever overpower them as a group, no matter how strong any one individual lion was.

But on their own, they could be tamed––and if not tamed, destroyed.

That's why Matvey had laid careful plans that had begun many years before. He was a diligent strategist. He knew that victory couldn't be won overnight, that any short-term successes would never stand in a nation with so much going for it, so many people with their own agendas. The fact Svetlana Volkov––the people's darling––could have been conducting her own private group for over a decade, was a testament to that point. How many other secret allegiances there were, he didn't know. Svetlana's one--because of the men it involved--was undoubtedly one of the most influential, and therefore the most dangerous.

He'd worked hard to get the right type of people--he always prided himself on being able to employ a workforce with particular skills, and a very dedicated outlook--in place at the right type of firms. They'd been his deep sleepers, getting on with their jobs, becoming fully integrated into the companies they'd been placed in while receiving substantial payments from Matvey for doing so. It had been that group whom he'd used to beat the Banking Union--his target being Dmitry Kaminski all along--and he'd since found suitable positions for all his key people who would otherwise have lost their jobs.

Staying on the outside as Matvey had been up to that point, it had been easier than he had expected to gatecrash the T20 event two years before, getting his own man--Phelan McDermott--chosen as a Contestant, something he had started working on months previously. He'd carefully set the trap. It was important that Sokoloff's men thought they were the ones discovering the Irishman. Like an expert fisherman setting out to land a mega catch, Matvey had set the bait just right. The rest had taken care of itself, and once Sokoloff had gone in person to watch his man--something Sokoloff always prided himself on doing--Matvey knew it was a done deal.

Matvey had provided Phelan with help and protection and enabled him to get away and claim the lottery win. That single event had destroyed Sokoloff. He'd never really had the chance to recover, nor had Matvey allowed it. With both of Putin's money men out of the Games--Sokoloff dead in fact within months of that Hunt--his attention turned to the group as a whole, as well as to Kaminski, who had his own political ambitions.

Matvey had already laid that trap, with his people in place awaiting further instructions from the man who'd made this his single obsession. Once the Hunt had been set, it'd been executed flawlessly.

"This trial," Foma said, turning around from the window. He didn't like last minute rushed jobs. He planned well, and he planned long. "It does give us an opportunity." They'd only heard about it relatively late. No one had ever brought a case against the Games––directly or indirectly––before.

Matvey had immediately managed to get to the defence lawyer, a considerable retainer paid and much more promised. He now had an inside track on the trial. It was after speaking with his own legal team––men and women who'd been finding loopholes for decades and knew how to argue their way out of an awkward position––that he suggested to Leona's lawyer that she shouldn't deny her client had been there. Admit to it in fact. Matvey pointed out––after the lawyer's initial protest––that the prosecution would undoubtedly be able to prove Leona had been in Russia.

Matvey had also managed to swing another thing in their favour, getting just one judge to hear the case. While he wanted the Games destroyed, he didn't want it done publicly. He was also now currently involved himself in the group, so would get his own name and reputation muddied along with the rest of them. Keeping the trial low-key, therefore, would limit exposure. The press was shut out.

The fact Josée was a witness––with an MI6 shadow around her, too––made it all the more interesting. Josée had been representing Kaminski at that Hunt. Matvey saw another golden opportunity, though he hated having to rush anything. Despite his reticence, it was an advantage too good to miss out on. His team had once again gone to work.

The second day of the trial, happening thousands of miles away from the mansion he was standing in on the coast there in Monaco, would force Anissa onto the stand.

The defence lawyer would call her up first, in a surprise move, where the involvement of MI6 in Russia would get brought out for all to see, even if just before one judge. News would spread.

Then they would go for Josée.

They would dig hard into her, reveal the whole picture. If they could get the name of Kaminski connected to her--the man who had only recently seen his Banking Union collapse, leaving hundreds of thousands of people in an uncertain financial situation--it would be another bright stain on Kaminski's character.

16

Anissa had slept soundly but woke early. As she opened her sleepy eyes, the room not instantly making sense to her until she remembered where she was, she became fully awake.

It was day two of the trial, and she would most certainly that morning watch Josée take the stand. The lawyer said Anissa might also be called personally to give evidence, but it wasn't certain. If she could keep Anissa off the stand, she had insisted she would.

Anissa showered and went down for breakfast, which had not long opened up for guests when she entered the restaurant. She was the only one in the dining area. Anissa ate very little, her appetite vanishing after just a little bread and a glass of orange juice. She left everything else on her table and returned to her room.

At nine, the lawyer and Josée swung by in the hire car, Josée quiet and reflective in the back seat, the lawyer behind the wheel. Anissa got into the rear seats. She felt for the woman next to her, knew today wasn't going to be easy for any of them, especially for Josée who'd been right there at the time. Today she would have to relive that nightmare--retell the things that had kept her awake for many nights at the beginning--and had woken her during many dreams since.

Yet, still, on the previous day the defence had started to suggest there could be doubt over who actually made the kill––thereby implicating Josée directly––which was the most significant shock of all.

They pulled up outside the courthouse just before nine forty-five. There were fifteen minutes before the trial was to resume, and they wanted to be in and preparing their opening questions well before then.

Inside, Leona was already there. She wore a dark pinstripe suit––very expensive looking, very respectable. Very much the wealthy woman so manifestly unfairly targeted for her money in this whole beastly affair.

Anissa had been there that day––she'd chased Leona on foot––and there was nothing expensive or classy about her back then. She was just a thief––a murdering one at that––who'd got lucky.

The picture she was now portraying of herself––clearly something orchestrated by her expensive lawyer––couldn't pull the wool over Anissa's eyes, even if it might temporarily do so for the Judge.

When proceedings started––at quarter past the hour, the day already running a little late––Anissa was shocked to be called immediately to the stand. She had a few words with the French lawyer––she was just there as a material witness, she was assured, so just go up there and tell the truth.

The truth, that was an interesting phrase. She was an MI6 agent who'd been covertly––against Russia's knowledge as well as that of her own Security Service––operating in St Petersburg. The truth might not be so easy to share.

"Anissa, if you would explain me this," the lawyer said, her English well rehearsed, a smile always kept on her well-presented face, her tone steady, voice calm, "because I've not been able to get the confirmation from your employer. If you were in fact in St Petersburg––and I'll be clear, when speaking with MI6 they were not able to say that you had been in fact operating within their remit in Russia––what were you actually doing here?" And there it was. Before she could answer, as if wanting to strengthen her own position as the person asking the questions––as if to ascertain certain facts before everyone listening––she added; "You do work for Military Intelligence Six, do you not?"

Anissa glanced across at her lawyer. It was open knowledge to those present that she did, so there was no danger in confirming that point.

"Yes, I do."

"And you are still employed by the British Security Service?" She had a way of drawing out the full name of her employer as if to press home to the Russian Judge that this woman standing before him was a spy––a foreign one at that.

"Yes."

"I just wanted to check, in case they'd fired you already." A cheap jab. Anissa didn't flinch, though inside she was already beginning to hate this lawyer. "So to come back to my opening question: an active service British MI6 agent is in St Petersburg without either the Russian FSB being informed nor with the permission or knowledge of your employer––tell me, why were you even here, therefore?" Going on something she'd been given, the lawyer had made the jump. She hadn't spoken with MI6, nor would anyone have confirmed or denied anything to such a lawyer had she done so, but Anissa wasn't to know that, and at that moment, the bluff had worked.

"I was conducting an undercover, ongoing and therefore covert operation that involved British nationals. I just happened to be at the Peter and Paul Fortress outside the Armoury when the crime occurred."

"Whoa, whoa, whoa there, Anissa," she said all too slowly, all too deliberately. It was becoming agonising trying to stay calm in front of her.

"So you were doing spy stuff? Here in Russia?"

Anissa looked over to her lawyer, who stood up at that moment. "Objection!"

"Okay, let me reword that," the lawyer said, not waiting for the Judge to no doubt confirm the objection. "You stated," and she looked down at her notes at that point as if she needed to confirm word for word what she'd just said about a minute before, "that you just happened to be outside the Armoury at the time of the alleged crime." She paused for effect. "There was nothing, however, random in your being there though, was there? You were specifically waiting there, watching, weren't you?"

She thought about what to say, how much to let on about her original aim in getting the Games the public exposure she wanted. Clearly, that wasn't going to happen now before a jury or the press––they were conspicuous by their absence––but there were still other officials around, people who weren't otherwise tainted by that particular group of oligarchs.

"That is correct. It's my personal belief that some high profile Russians gather to conduct events that innocent members of the general public are caught up in. That is why I was at the Armoury on that day. I'd found out that one of the lottery tickets that was used as a big cash prize had been securely located there. I was waiting for whoever had found themselves caught up in this criminal business to show up." There, she'd said it––aloud, too. The lawyer didn't appear too disconcerted, which should have been a warning.

"All this talk of entrapped people and lottery tickets...my oh my..." and she paused, taking a sip of water from the bottle that rested on her table. "How did you find out that there was a ticket apparently inside the Armoury? Who gave you that information?"

"My witness does not have to provide that information," Josée's lawyer stood up and confirmed.

"But you must have been working with someone else in St Petersburg?"

"I was by myself," is all she replied. She'd been clear with Alex that she wasn't going to implicate him or Sasha in any way.

"So," and the lawyer picked up a piece of paper as if she needed to recall to memory something from her notes that would otherwise just have slipped from her mind. "Alex Tolbert, also of MI6 and most often your partner in crime over in England; he has nothing to do with any of this?"

Anissa flinched instinctively but barely noticeably at the mention of his name. With her eyes fixed on the defence lawyer, her voice as calm as she could manage at that moment, getting as much confidence into her words as she could muster, she said; "No, he had nothing to do with this."

"Okay," the lawyer said, though it was obvious she didn't believe the lie. "How did you gain access into Russia?"

"Objection," the other lawyer interjected, "my witness is not on trial here. That is an irrelevant question, as is anything to do with her employment, as she well knows!"

"I'm merely trying to work out if, in fact, your witness was even at the Fortress. You see," and she held up some papers for good measure, "I have the migration information for every visitor into Russia during the days around the alleged crime. There were tens of thousands of arrivals. My client is listed amongst these names, as is that of Ms Josée Allard, who sits before you. But your name," and she turned back to Anissa at this point, "does not appear anywhere on this information. Can you explain that?" She could, but she wouldn't.

"I'm not at liberty to disclose that information."

"Oh, so you do have some inside help here in Russia, is that it? Someone within the FSB perhaps?"

"Objection!" the shout went up from her lawyer, not for the first time.

"Yes, please stick to the case in hand, will you. Where are you going with this line of questioning?" the Judge said, the first time he'd spoken in a while, though he was apparently taking copious notes throughout.

"Your Honour," though it wasn't a phrase that often got used in Russian courtrooms, "I'm merely trying to ascertain, if––in fact––this alleged witness was even in St Petersburg. If she isn't able to explain how she managed to be somewhere she says she was––and the Russian authorities clearly have no record of her entry or exit––I would then say that would be grounds enough to remove this so-called witness from the stand. Unless, of course, she can concretely confirm how she was there." She returned to her seat, the Judge turning to Anissa and looking her in the face for the first time.

"Are you able to confirm your presence in this context?" he said.

"No, I am not," Anissa relented. She wasn't going to give up Sasha.

"Then I'd like to ask you to leave the stand. Your evidence will not be considered in my verdict," he said, Anissa stepping down from where she'd been, catching Josée's glance, the Frenchwoman looking distraught.

"I'd like to call Ms Josée Allard to the stand," the defence lawyer instantly said.

THE AFTERNOON SESSION was no less brutal. Leona's lawyer barraged Josée with question after question, accusing her outright of killing the janitor, something she denied through many tears. Her own lawyer was then allowed to the floor, the pressure changing in the room, as she carefully walked Josée via some clever questioning through the whole ordeal as she'd seen it.

The defence lawyer went at her answers a little after that, though held back from a full-on assault. By four, much to her own personal relief, Josée was asked to step down from the stand.

"I'd like to now call in the police forensic expert who was the one to closely examine the crime scene, as well as the pathologist who inspected the body." The Judge looked at his wristwatch––despite there being a large clock that showed the same time on the wall of the courtroom––before nodding to his men at the back of the room. Two men in suits walked in through the open doors, one carrying a black briefcase by his side. They stopped at the defence lawyer's table, the man with the briefcase taking out a few sheets of paper, before walking directly to the stand. He confirmed his name and occupation––pathologist––to the Judge before answering his first question.

"Tell me," the defence lawyer said, loving being the one to be in control, to dictate the way this trial was going, "after a full and thorough examination of the corpse, were you able to find any physical evidence or DNA that would prove helpful for this courtroom?"

"Yes, I did," he said, his English broken, his voice not sounding confident using that foreign tongue.

"Could you please inform the Judge what you found out?" As part of the pre-trial, when it was determined Leona and Josée would have to fly to St Petersburg to stand before a Russian judge, DNA samples were taken from both women as part of that process.

"I found clear samples of DNA on the victim's genitals."

"Were you able to get a match for that DNA?"

"Yes," and he glanced at his notes, "they matched the sample obtained from Ms Allard." Nothing new there then, she'd stood that afternoon on the very same stand and shared how they'd had sex together.

"Did you find any other physical DNA evidence, that didn't match either the victim or Ms Allard?"

"No, I didn't."

Josée's lawyer then asked a few simple questions, but there was little more she felt he could tell the court, and he was allowed to leave. Then it was the turn of the forensics expert, who confirmed skin tissue samples had been found in the vault and by the narrow exit she'd obviously later squeezed through, which had matched Ms Allard's sample, but that nothing else was found in the Armoury.

"Nothing?" demanded the prosecution. "You mean, despite there no doubt being hundreds of visitors into a place that is a tourist magnet in St Petersburg, there wasn't a trace of anyone else?"

"No, there wasn't. As far as I'm aware this room is off limits to the public," which was true, and Josée had said that herself earlier, which is why she'd first approached the janitor to gain access. "Also, the Fortress confirmed that the whole room had recently been cleaned just days before the crime."

"That's not true!" Josée said, standing and shouting out her annoyance for the first time. "That room was filthy dirty, and you know it!" Her lawyer motioned her to sit back down. Outbursts in any courtroom never helped anyone.

"Ms Allard, I'll warn you that any behaviour like that again will mean you are expelled from my courthouse," the Judge barked. "Am I understood?" Her lawyer answered for her.

"It will not happen again, Your Honour." She turned and put her arm on Josée's shoulder, Anissa also now comforting her.

The defence lawyer then moved to the centre of the room--speaking aloud but with her focus solely directed in front of her, to the Judge, the man in power. "Your Honour, I propose you be allowed time to consider your decision. We've just had it confirmed from two renowned and respected Russian experts, that my client's DNA was not found anywhere near the victim nor was it evident anywhere in the room Ms Allard claims my client was in. That's because she'd already obtained the ticket; not from the Armoury--where Ms Allard claims it was--not even from the Fortress, but in a small boat that runs along the canal next to the Fortress. My client has freely admitted to being in St Petersburg at this time, but no evidence connects her to this horrific murder.

"Aside from Ms Allard's own testimony--remember, this is someone who has freely admitted to consenting to sexual intercourse with a complete stranger just to get into a room she believed she needed access to--there is only the apparent word of Mrs Edison. An MI6 agent who can't explain how she even got into Russia, despite the fact that your own country's border guard--an agency that prides itself in keeping your borders safe--have no record of her ever doing so. I propose that her involvement has been fabricated. She doesn't even have the backing of her own employer!

"We've seen nothing to suggest that my client, Ms Leona Chase, has done anything deserving of the treatment--the suspicion--that she is currently under. In fact, I go on record to state that it was only after losing the ticket, seeing the happiness of my client and the life that she is now living, that Ms Allard conjured up this whole episode. It's an attempt to get my client's money, while trying to atone for her own heinous moral failings and crimes, including that of first-degree murder. That once she realised she'd given herself sexually for nothing--the ticket wasn't where she thought it would be--she then killed that man in her rage."

"Objection!" Josée's lawyer screamed, angry now how the trial had suddenly turned into something far more significant than she'd bought into. Her own victim--her own client in this--now having the spotlight turned towards her, now being made the perpetrator of this horrible murder.

"If I may speak," the Judge said, "I think I will call proceedings to a close for the day--and the trial in general--pending my full exploration of the facts and then my verdict. Both women," and he motioned to Leona and Josée with each hand, "are to be held in the custody of the court overnight, before my answer to the original charge is brought first thing tomorrow. I will speak with both lawyers immediately in my chambers, but for everyone else, the court is dismissed," and he stood and left, the two lawyers gathering their things together.

"What does that mean?" Josée said, a police officer already coming to stand next to her.

"I'll do everything I can to get you released tonight," her lawyer said, "but I need to see him now. Anissa will stay with you," and she started walking, though Anissa held her by the arm.

"Take this," and Anissa handed the lawyer her own mobile phone, the video displayed on screen being the footage taken from outside the Armoury at the time of the crime. "It shows Leona entering the Armoury at the time of the incident." It also showed the legs of Alex and Sasha too, and their shadows as they were fired upon, though not enough of them to give away their identities. The lawyer took the phone, glancing briefly at the screen, before walking off towards the Judge's chambers.

Inside, the Judge already sat down behind his desk, two chairs facing him--one already occupied by the defence lawyer--she took a seat. She handed the Judge the phone.

"What's this?" he said, holding the device before him.

"It's the video feed from outside the Armoury at the time of the crime," she said.

"Your Honour," the defence lawyer interjected immediately, "if they have a piece of evidence to present, it needs to be done in the right way. As it is, we spoke with the security guys at the Fortress to ask them about possible CCTV footage from the day of the crime––you know, anything that could prove my client's innocence––and they confirmed there wasn't any. The cameras were having their annual maintenance during the week that the crime occurred."

The prosecution lawyer had no way of knowing who to believe. She'd never been shown a video––the first she knew about Anissa having anything was the phone she'd just been handed. She had no way of knowing what was right. The Judge played the video anyway, which showed some movements, some people outside the doors before one figure entered, another appearing some seconds later. Nothing was obvious. It was not possible to make out who any of the people were.

"I'll check myself with the Fortress to see if they can confirm this footage," the Judge said, "but need I remind you––and I'm sure the law is the same in France as it is here––such evidence needs to be presented before trial, so that its authenticity is able to be confirmed."

"It only just came to my attention."

"From the agent, you mean?" the other lawyer said. "The one who can't prove she was even in Russia," and she threw her arms into the air as if it had finally got too bizarre for her, as if it was amusing to the point of hysteria.

"Tomorrow morning, ten o'clock. We'll reconvene, and I will share with you my verdict," the Judge concluded.

17

Sasha had spent the second day of the trial tracking down where the dead sniper had lived. As much as he wanted to be around Anissa––especially after what she'd said last night, knowing she was most likely taking the stand that day, and therefore was most vulnerable––he knew he couldn't be seen anywhere near the courthouse. That would risk giving him up to anyone who was watching––and from what he'd heard from Anissa the night before, they were undoubtedly watching. The trial, or whatever it really was, seemed to have the oligarch's influence all over it. But from whom that control was coming––who was really behind it all––was frustratingly hard to find any real evidence for. He hoped at least he would be able to come up with something himself.

He drove to the edge of the city––where the blue metro line stopped at its most southern end. It was the same metro station one Contestant had previously escaped from after pushing another to his death. The buildings were taller in that part of the city, many storeys above the five they were limited to in the centre, where foundations of buildings built a few hundred years ago on the marsh, really didn't allow any greater height.

The building he was looking for––the address coming up on the dead sniper after searching through the FSB database of previous Russian army employees—was the third row back. He waited outside the closed metal door until someone left—a building that size, there would always be someone coming or going before too long—and he climbed the stairs until he got to the fourth floor. Apartment three-zero-three was the fifth one along the corridor.

Sasha knocked hard. There was no answer, and after a second knock, this time a little quieter—as well as a look around to make sure no one was about—he took out a device that he then used on the lock, and was into the apartment thirty seconds later.

"Allo?" he called out, his gun ready, as he quickly scanned the compact two-roomed home. There was no one there. What there was on display was neat and ordered. Army discipline still seemed to prevail, and the one photo on the wall was the sniper in his uniform, presumably—given the age of the picture and how young the man looked in it—from when he'd first joined. Military service started as young as seventeen.

He checked the fridge. It was well stocked, the milk already souring. This wasn't the home of someone expecting to be dead anytime soon. This was a home waiting for the return of its owner.

The bedroom had very little in it, besides a cupboard and double bed, though there was only a pillow on one side at the head. The small bathroom held even less. One bottle of shampoo on the floor of the walk-in shower, and one toothbrush in a small glass on the edge of the sink.

The kitchen, which formed part of the central living area, was kept tidy. In the centre of the room was a sofa, which faced a television and some shelving. There was very little paperwork, no documentation of any kind that Sasha could make out. Clearly, this was where the guy lived, but he apparently didn't do much work from there. There were no weapons or other equipment anywhere—and he'd checked as he went around the small flat—which meant the man kept all that, and presumably the links to who employed him, somewhere else.

The one thing he did find—a key with a BMW emblem—was

hanging on a hook on the kitchen wall. Sasha put it in his pocket, the hope being that these were a spare set of keys, assuming the sniper hadn't indeed taken the train to the city centre when he'd left for his last job. He undoubtedly would have had too much equipment to bring with him for that to have been a possibility. If he had in fact driven, the car might well be still parked up somewhere near the Volkov mansion.

Seeing as there was nothing else in the apartment of note, he closed the door behind him, again checking no one was in the corridor outside and left. Finding the car was his next challenge.

It took him an hour to drive into the city. A journey that would probably have only been marginally quicker on the metro, given the fact a change of lines would have been required in the centre, further confirming his suspicion that no highly paid, highly trained sniper would have used that form of public transport. He would have had to drive in.

Parked cars were not in short supply in the city––charges for street parking never having been implemented in Russia––but with the key in hand, and the knowledge he was looking for a BMW, Sasha started to comb the area. The sniper would not have wanted to lug the bag or case containing his weapon too far on his own, the weight alone would have made it a hard job. At only the third BMW Sasha got to, the lights flashed, and the locks opened as he once again pressed the button. He got straight in.

It was a new model, the car kept as clean and ordered as the apartment Sasha had been in earlier. Putting the keys into the ignition, he turned them enough to get the electrics working without engaging the engine. The car's inbuilt satellite navigation system flashed up. Sasha scrolled through the menu options, finding what he wanted, which was the car's inbuilt history of its last ten trips. The most recent had been to where he was now sitting, of course. The one before that was somewhere in the south of the city––he noted down the coordinates––and the one before that was where he'd just been that morning, the sniper's home. He assumed the sniper would have left home, gone to whatever lock-up he used to pick up his weapon before he had then headed to the Volkov mansion and positioned himself for the kill.

Sasha switched on the ignition. He had his own car nearby, but there might be other things hidden inside the BMW that would tell him more after a thorough search was done, and he couldn't do that from where the car was currently. He tapped the navigation--pressing the location that was second to last on the history--and headed south.

Fifty minutes later, he pulled off the main road as directed into an area of metal garages, standard right across the city, storage space for those who could afford them. He was now only about fifteen kilometres away from the apartment he'd been at that morning, thus making perfect sense for a convenient location for the dead man's lock-up. The challenge was, there were hundreds of garages.

Weaving his way through a few of the turns--the navigation directed him a little closer--it only got him to the furthermost row, when the car's inbuilt system confirmed he'd reached his destination. At least there were just about twenty garages along that part of the site, a few he could see were also apparently no longer used, rubbish mainly occupying the space where the garage must once have stood.

He searched the car--in the boot was a box of ammunition for a high powered weapon. There was nothing else there that was obvious. The back seats were clean also. In the front passenger seat footwell compartment, there was a key for a padlock. Sasha grabbed it and walked down in front of the garages. Only three of the doors were secured in place by a padlock, and thankfully the key had opened the first one he tried, not that there was anyone else around the area at that moment. Still, no owner would like the sight of someone attempting to gain entry to their lock-up.

Inside the garage, it was a sniper's dream. Three different weapons sat on special wall mountings along the left-hand side. At the back was shelving, containing everything from boxes of ammunition to scopes and silencers. A small array of handguns was on the right-hand wall, as well as a desk, a filing cabinet and a safe. In the middle of the garage was a table, with specialist equipment on it that Sasha knew to be for checking and cleaning a weapon.

The safe was locked--he was sure that was where he would have kept his cash--though the filing cabinet, which contained three drawers, opened with a little effort. Each drawer was full of information--it was a career's worth of material.

The paperwork housed in the cabinet was remarkably organised, though that fitted with what he'd seen about the man so far. Sasha pulled out his phone, opening up the email draft that he had going with Alex. He scrolled down the message until he found the list Anissa had added of all the known Russian names within the Games. He started looking through the files, which were ordered alphabetically, one name at a time, sometimes having to open different drawers, until he found one that matched--Foma Polzin.

He pulled out the information, which wasn't all that much, but it was recent. At the very end of an encrypted email that had been printed off and placed into the folder, was the name he was after--Aleksey Kuznetsov. So it had been Kuznetsov who had ordered the killing, Foma clearly being the target.

Sasha locked everything back up. He would maybe come back and try to work the lock on the safe another time--the garage was a gold mine of equipment, too--but for now it was better to keep it all hidden. He placed the folder with all the information there had been on Foma onto the front passenger's seat and drove the car back to the city. It was possible that the police would eventually find a car key on the body--though that enquiry had already seemingly gone cold--and then come looking for the car themselves. He wasn't going to take the chance that they wouldn't be able to find it.

Pulling up at almost the same spot where he had found the car earlier, Sasha spent ten minutes wiping everything down. He wasn't going to leave any trace that he'd been in the car. Sasha then switched on the navigation, deleting his recent trip, as well as the garage location from the entire history and after giving everything one final wipe down, Sasha got out of the car, folder in hand. He locked it up again and went to find his own vehicle. It was nearly five, and the second day of the trial would be drawing to a close by then.

Now heading back to the office in his own car, he called Anissa.

"Sasha, it's good to hear from you. Today was a complete disaster," she said, not really the words he wanted to hear, as she went on to relay some of what had happened. They agreed to meet at nine that evening, Sasha needing to show his face a little in the office, tying off a few loose ends in the process, and she needed to shower and sleep. He would then meet her outside the hotel later.

It was five past nine when he pulled over, Anissa out in the sunshine, oblivious now to the fact it was even getting late. She got in, and they sped away. She'd declined the offer to go out to his dacha––his other property that he owned some way out of the city––as it was already too late in the day to make it there and back before midnight. Instead, they opted for a bar on the other side of town. Both had already eaten, they just needed to chat and probably down a few too many stiff drinks. It'd been that type of day.

"Sasha, I'm worried about what the Judge will say tomorrow. The whole thing's been mishandled. I'm not sure how qualified our lawyer even was. It's all now been turned firmly against Josée. I'm distraught for her."

"It can't have been easy for you, standing there and having your own life––your own motives––questioned?"

"That's just the thing. She said she went to MI6. She didn't, I just checked that with Alex. There was no official record of her ever speaking with them before the trial. She made all that up."

"And yet she still knew about it."

"Exactly, and she knew Alex's name, asking me outright if he had come with me."

"Jesus," Sasha said, taking a deep breath, "someone has given her everything on you."

"She was pushing for who my FSB connection was. That's when I backed away. I was asked to stand down, didn't even get to share what I'd seen. The Judge then closed the trial down––he's making his decision, but ordered both women to be kept in custody overnight."

"She'll be okay, you don't need to worry."

"It's not that. I made Josée come here and do all this. I needed her to do it so that I could prise open the whole secretive world of the Games. It seems that all I have managed to achieve, however, is to put Josée directly in the firing line. I mean, you should have heard them, Sasha; all the physical evidence now places only Josée in that room at the time of the crime."

"Then whoever is working behind the scenes is using this to get to someone."

"Get to who?"

"Whoever put Josée forward in the first place. Has she ever said anything about that?"

"No, she doesn't know. I've asked her."

"Then I think we need to try and find that out. Might Andre know something?"

"Possibly––but given who we now know he is, does that make anything he might tell us valid?"

"True. We could always try and see, take whatever he says with a pinch of salt until we can be certain of it, or otherwise."

"I'll speak to Alex, see what he can do."

"Good. Want another?" She'd worked through vodka shots––two so far that night––and accepted a third. Sasha, after doing the first one with her, was himself having a coffee, which he also re-ordered. He was driving later, anyway.

It was eleven––the sun only now starting to show signs it was on the way down for the night––as they walked towards his car. Sasha said he'd drop her back at the hotel, Anissa a little too far gone with shots to otherwise be left to find her own way. She didn't know the city well enough to even be able to do that had she still been sober.

Ten minutes later, the streets much quieter at that time of night, they were outside her hotel.

"Come in for a nightcap if you want," she said from the passenger seat, Sasha with the engine still running, needing to get some sleep himself by that point.

"I think you've had enough for one night," he said, reaching over to open her door, Anissa kissing him hard on the lips as he reached in front of her.

"I'm so sorry," she said, both of them sitting upright again in their seats, "I don't know what came over me," and she got out of the car, walking immediately towards the hotel, not once turning around to glance back at him. He waited until she was out of sight, laughed to himself and pulled away.

18

Anissa woke at eight, her head pounding. It took her some time to work out why her head hurt so much. Then she recalled the drinks, the ride home—the kiss. She caught sight of her face in the mirror at that moment but looked away immediately. She had no idea now—in the harsh reality of morning—what had come over her. She'd been drunk, that much was obvious. It was what drunk people tended to do—stupid, unthinkably silly things.

She called her husband and left a video message for him and the boys. Hanging up, she felt a little guilty. A shower should help with that.

Twenty minutes later she was down for breakfast, ravenous that morning, and took a good half hour to savour most of the offerings, particularly liking the meats available.

At nine, she was once again waiting outside the hotel—dressed smartly and presentable, the respectable MI6 agent—as Josée's lawyer pulled up a few moments later, the car noticeably empty of her client. She opted for the front seat that morning.

"Sleep well?" she asked the lawyer, the response being what she had imagined.

"Hardly a wink. God, I don't know what to expect at all today, but in the pit of my stomach, I feel sick."

"Yes, I know the feeling." For Anissa, the alcohol from the night before probably added to that sensation a little.

They were at the courthouse just after half past nine, the earliest they'd managed that week. Josée was already waiting for them, looking scared and upset. She apparently hadn't slept much either.

"How are you holding up?" Anissa said.

"Probably had my worst night since this whole thing started." That bad. She felt for her.

At ten, the Judge came into the room, and once he was seated, everyone took their places. He had some notes in front of him, some obviously handwritten, some probably typed, though they couldn't tell from where they were sitting.

"As you all know," he started, his tone fatherly, authoritarian too, "we've taken the last two days to hear the trial of Ms Leona Chase, accused of being in St Petersburg on January 2nd last year and committing the murder of Mikael Davydov. We have one witness, who doesn't deny being at the scene of the crime when the incident happened, who has stated that she believes Ms Chase committed the said crime. I've heard from experts who have failed to prove there was any trace of DNA left by anyone else at the scene of the crime—besides Ms Allard and Mr Davydov.

"Indeed, the prosecution's only other witness appears to be someone who wasn't even in the country on the day in question. I was then presented with a video last night after I left this courtroom, which was given to me by Ms Allard's lawyer, claiming to be footage from outside of the entrance to the Armoury at the time of the crime but the figures are too indistinct for it to be used as evidence."

Leona glanced up at her lawyer at that point, having not been told anything about the video. The lawyer subtly put her hand flat, leaving it there and saying nothing else. The Judge continued; "I have since contacted the security team in operation at the Fortress, and though the footage they store does not go back that far, they did confirm as suggested by Ms Chase's lawyer, there had been planned maintenance during that week. None of the cameras would, in fact, have been operating on the day in question." His voice rose noticeably at the end of that last sentence.

"I can find no just reason for continuing, therefore, along this current course we are travelling. I, therefore, drop all charges raised against Ms Chase with immediate effect. You are free to go," he said to her, the relief and delight instantly visible on the British woman's face. He turned to the other table, his face still deadly serious.

"As for you, I have filed my own complaint. Ms Allard, there is enough evidence to suggest you had more involvement in the murder than you have otherwise stated. You will now face trial yourself on these same charges.

"And you, Mrs Edison," he said, turning to Anissa as Josée was breaking down in tears beside her. "I find it puzzling as to why a member of the British Security Service would find it necessary to fabricate such involvement--which you've been given substantial opportunity to explain--in a crime which had nothing to do with you. I'd like to find you in contempt of court for having had the brazen disregard to even walk into my courtroom, but all I can now do is to deport you--effective immediately--from this nation, with a five-year ban coming into effect forbidding you from setting foot in Russia."

Anissa looked up at the Judge, disbelief written all over her face. "Take her out of my courtroom," he added, not even looking up from the papers that he was collecting together. Two police officers came alongside Anissa--another two already securing handcuffs into place on Josée's wrists--and the British agent was hurried out of the building.

"Can I make a call?" she said as she was marched to a waiting car.

"Only when you land. Our priority is to get you onto the next flight leaving St Petersburg. So no calls and no slowing us down." His English was good, too good it seemed.

She sat back in the rear seat, the windows protected with metal, a barrier separating her from the two men up front. Very much the prisoner. She thought about Josée, who was also on her way to a prison somewhere, or a holding facility anyway, until they decided what they were going to do with her. How had it come to all that? How had things got so out of control?

Two hours later Anissa was sitting on the front row of the aircraft, a British Airways flight to Heathrow. The two officers stood at the doorway until the plane was fully boarded, only then handing back her mobile phone which had been switched off, exiting the aircraft at the moment it was ready for takeoff.

"You okay?" the female stewardess asked Anissa, a drink of something alcoholic passed to her in a plastic cup.

"I've had better days," Anissa said, as she downed it in one go before putting her head back onto her seat, the aircraft already beginning to taxi into position.

THAT AFTERNOON, the first Alex knew of anything having gone wrong in St Petersburg was Anissa calling him from Heathrow airport. As she spoke to him she sounded much calmer––clearly happy to have made it back to the UK––and asked if he could come and collect her.

He was there within the hour, Anissa having bought herself a drink and sitting in a coffee shop waiting for him when she saw Alex walk in through the doors.

"So the wanderer returns," he called to her across the coffee shop, going over and embracing his colleague. She looked terrible.

They stayed there for half an hour, Alex getting himself a drink, as Anissa poured out from her heart all that had happened, all that had gone on, besides last night's embarrassment with Sasha, which currently seemed the least of her problems. She realised she had been deported before she'd been able to see Sasha again. Now Anissa would have to wait for their next face-to-face––if ever that were possible––before she confronted that potentially awkward situation. She put that thought to one side.

She told Alex everything Sasha had discovered––Alex having

himself been kept in the loop somewhat as Sasha had been making regular contact through their shared draft email.

"So Kuznetsov made the call to take out Foma, a fellow T20 member? Who is Kuznetsov again?" Alex said, deferring to Anissa's better memory in that regard, having made it her job to study them all.

"Largely water treatment, I think."

"Sewage?"

"I think it includes that, but it's the full range, especially across Europe, not to mention western Russia."

"And Foma is a man of all trades?"

"Yes, like most in the T10, his wealth seemingly knows no bounds."

"But that wouldn't make them natural competitors in the real world? I mean, to want to kill a man, you'd have to be pretty cheesed off."

"Exactly. Which means it's Games originated. Something happened within that last event, that tipped Kuznetsov over the edge," Anissa said, before adding, "Anything back from Sasha yet regarding what else he might have found out?" She'd been on the plane for much of the day and hadn't been able to have any contact.

"Yes, there was a little, and he said he'd keep adding stuff as he gets it. Let's head into the office, and we can see if there's anything new. Plus it'll be good for you to show your face."

"If I'm still welcome, that is."

Alex gently punched her on the shoulder, Anissa breaking out into a smile, but only briefly. There was a concern there, worry too. Maybe he should have been more forceful with her about not going. He'd had his concerns, but had let them lie. He could see it was eating her up that Josée was still there, detained and awaiting her own trial date, something that made no sense. Anissa had scribbled a few notes down on the journey, thoughts to send to the lawyer––assuming she'd still be representing Josée anyway––things that just didn't add up. For starters, why would a perpetrator of a crime, someone whom the Russians knew nothing about, openly come forward, accusing another person in the process, thereby forcing a trial to take place in St Petersburg––whilst herself masquerading as the star witness? How did that make any sense? And for what? To somehow make a claim for the other person's money? Who would ever risk exposing themselves as the real killer just for some cash? She had been free, she was in Paris. Plus Anissa knew it was only the work of her and Alex with the team which had traced her back to France. She hadn't even put herself forward. Josée was broken, in fact, a mess.

It had been Anissa who'd coaxed her into making a statement, one thing leading to another––and then the trial.

Yet that had backfired. Somehow, and she wasn't sure she'd be able to get to the bottom of it, the defence had managed to turn the spotlight not only onto the witness but onto Anissa personally as well. That had been enough to cast doubt over Leona's involvement, enough, in fact, to acquit her entirely. Instead, it was Josée's turn to now face the same accusation.

Maybe she should have known? Perhaps Alex had been right––and she knew he had always been cautious about the whole thing, especially her personal involvement––but she'd silenced that warning, insisting it was their best chance of opening the entire thing up. Some good that had done. Now she was banished from Russia––that was no significant loss for her at that moment, though she would no doubt regret it if Alex got to make a future trip without her––and more crucially, she had almost certainly put herself on the FSB's radar. That was not something she'd planned to do.

WALKING INTO THE OFFICE, already past five o'clock, the main hustle of the place had started to dissipate. Both agents went straight into their shared room and shut the door. She locked it for good measure. Maybe what happened in St Petersburg really had affected her more than she was letting on. Alex let the thought go.

Opening up the email program, they could see there had been

some more information added. Alex clicked on the draft email, and both agents read it through.

"I knew it," Anissa said, having got a little further ahead than Alex, who reached the part where her finger was touching the screen. "An hour after the shooting, Matvey's personal jet left St Petersburg heading to Monaco. That had to have had Foma on board. He's alive."

"Why the mystery?"

"I don't know. Sasha has been remarkably thorough, though. Everything he's given us is good information. Do we also need to know what's in that safe?" Sasha had mentioned the garage he'd discovered, the key to which he had retained. No point leaving that in the BMW.

"I think we can discover that in time. Right now we have a more immediate puzzle to solve. Sasha has told us that Foma's jet is still sitting on the tarmac in St Petersburg. That is what caused some of the confusion. But he's been able to confirm from one of Foma's personal bodyguards that there was no hit. No one got shot. And Sasha already told us about what he found at the crime scene. There were no impact marks anywhere."

"So the shots fired weren't real?"

"No, I suspect they were blanks. Clearly whoever was really behind this––and it would appear to have Matvey Filipov's hands all over it, wouldn't you say?––wanted it to look like the original hit had been successful."

"Kuznetsov's contract killing, you mean?"

"Yes. Kuznetsov had hired the man, this guy was in place in the building opposite––the same one we used––and yet someone else got to him first. We have to assume they were Matvey's men. They killed the sniper before the oligarchs started leaving, switched out the bullets in the man's weapon with blanks, and then fired when Foma emerged from the building."

"So while most don't know what has happened, Kuznetsov obviously thinks that Foma is dead."

"Yes, that's my thought, too. The lack of public announcement could only add to that reasoning. Clearly, that's what Matvey wants them to believe."

"But why? What's in it for him?"

"I don't know. But secrets and mystery give men like Matvey a feeling of power––they control a situation others assume to have gone a different way. He'll have an angle on it for sure."

"He's making it look worse than it is..." Anissa said, her mind stirring with a new thought.

"Sorry?"

"My boys...they are mad about football. Neither Paul nor I are much into it, but because of our sons, we get to watch a fair amount. What annoys me most is when a player goes down clutching his face, yet the replay shows there had been no contact whatsoever. Yet the ref doesn't know that. Sometimes the apparent villain is sent off the pitch. Of course, sometimes the ref gives a card to the player acting on the ground. My point is––what if Matvey's using this situation to pull a similar trick? What if this is his way of making Foma writhe around on the ground––so to speak––play acting?"

"Playing dead, you mean?"

"Yes, exactly. One member of the T20 has dared to arrange the assassination of another––something Matvey obviously got wind off, something he stepped in and stopped––yet he allowed it all to be played out anyway, but on his terms and with blanks instead of live rounds, the apparent result the same. Foma dead."

"His next move will have to be to expose Kuznetsov as the culprit."

"Sasha has already managed to find that out for himself, so how hard would it be for others? Especially Svetlana Volkov, who treats that group like her own property."

"So Kuznetsov gets kicked out––sent off to continue your footballing analogy. Why bother to then make it look like Foma was killed? I don't get that bit?"

"I think it's just for added effect. Like those footballers. Stay down long enough––play dead for long enough––and it forces severe action to be taken. It could destroy the Games, as well as the culprit of course."

"Maybe that's the point. Maybe Matvey wants exactly that?"

"But he only joined the Games last year. Why try and destroy it?"

"We need to look into Kuznetsov. Why him personally? Maybe it was just the opportunity presenting itself; but seeing as the target was Foma, someone we know to be working with––maybe even working for––Matvey, we have to assume it was personal. Why is Kuznetsov now a target?"

Anissa had been typing away as they were speaking, scrolling through pages of results on Google, only now spotting something that made a little more sense.

"Here," she said, "it's a reference to Kuznetsov and Kaminski. Earlier this year there was some talk of the two working together. I bet it's financial backing from Kuznetsov to get Kaminski through his troubles, in exchange for something once Kaminski has run for President." The article didn't give much detail on anything––aside from the reference to some shared initiative––but it was a fair guess. On her growing wall of evidence, Anissa now connected these two men with their own piece of string. The ever-expanding web was growing––a network of interconnected behaviour, of shared business interests. A web of an increasing number of crimes, several murders now dotting her cork board, the pictures of each deceased person only adding their own personal reminder––when these men lashed out, they hit hard, fast and low, and didn't leave any prisoners. Alex and Anissa would have to continue to be extremely careful themselves.

19

It was already the closing weeks of August, the long summer days were starting to draw in, though in Moscow the days were never as long as they were further north in St Petersburg––neither were winters so dark.

Matvey travelled from the airport towards his meeting with Sergej Volkov. It was only his third time in Moscow in the last twelve months, and that already felt two visits too many. He wasn't a fan of his nation's capital––besides the Kremlin, with its history and symbolic importance––he much preferred where he most often resided and the relative quiet of Monaco.

He'd made the appointment the previous month to see Sergej––plus he hoped to catch a few words in private with Svetlana if that were possible––as he had continued his march toward building relationships with those not otherwise directly involved in the Games.

Sergej certainly fitted that bill––powerful and influential, if not quite as wealthy, even given the couple's combined assets––he was a man well placed, however. That made him extremely valuable. He was the Danny Ocean of the oligarch world, an incredibly resourceful go-to man.

The two men spent thirty minutes together in the garden––the property was significant, though nothing out of the ordinary and much smaller than their St Petersburg property—but the gardens were a real highlight. Matvey had to admire the couple for the landscaping they'd had done around the grounds. For a man who had seen so much, it still impressed him.

Svetlana watched from an upstairs window, keeping out of the way as much as possible. The fact that a member of her T10 was speaking with her husband was nothing new. Because of their shared business lives, the men often had reason to see one another. The fact it was Matvey speaking with her husband on their lawn, might well mean something, however. Ever since Egypt—when he'd first proposed to her the idea for the latest T10 event, picking the targets himself—she had become increasingly wary of him. Then, it had been the impossible challenge. Like a magician chained in a pool of angry sharks, no chance of escape. Yet he had managed just that—and in a matter of only months. The Banking Union he'd gone up against—a Goliath compared to his David—had crumbled. The impossible had been made possible.

And that kind of thing didn't happen by chance, nor was it possible in the timescale his team had managed. She might not know much about business—though because of her marriage, she was learning that aspect faster than most—but she didn't need to know much to understand Matvey had been planning that for a long time. He'd been planning that before he'd even taken up her invitation to join the Games.

Forbes was yet to update their rich list—that usually happened towards the end of each year, so there were a few months to go—but she was confident Matvey and his four other victorious oligarchs would climb the wealth ladder considerably. There would be some dramatic fallers, also. Kaminski had taken the biggest hit following that T10 event, and Kuznetsov had taken a similar hit during the summer Hunt. That one was still being worked through.

Most tragic of all, there'd been a shooting immediately following that last event. Foma Polzin was dead. She couldn't believe it had anything to do with the Games—how could it have—clearly something to do with the victim's own business dealings. These things were always possible, after all, and they didn't keep such levels of security around them continuously for no reason. They knew the risks. But even with that, she wondered how they could continue to keep going. With Foma out of the picture, and potentially Kaminski, and also maybe Kuznetsov, given their losses, the group would be down to seven. Yes, they could bring new Hosts on board––she'd certainly done that before––but who would she use, and could they be trusted?

She heard the doors to the garden open once again downstairs and went to the window to confirm––they had come inside. She went down the stairway, though she couldn't hear anything that was being said, so decided to join them.

"Why, it's none other than your beautiful and ever delightful wife," Matvey said as she entered the room. "Svetlana, a pleasure as always to see you," and he kissed her on both cheeks, as was usual.

"Mr Filipov," is all she said in reply.

"Svetlana, you show Matvey through to the sitting room, and I'll go and rustle us up some tea," Sergej said, leaving them both as he headed into the kitchen.

"What are you doing here?" Svetlana said immediately when it was just the two of them.

"Just talking a little business with your husband, so relax."

"I wasn't aware you had any business with my husband?" she said, the two now in the sitting room, taking chairs opposite one another, their voices not much more than an urgent whisper.

"Not yet, but that'll happen shortly. Look," Matvey said, handing her a sheet of paper, "we don't have long, and I wanted to bring you this."

"What is it?" she said, looking down at what appeared to be an email of sorts.

"It's the contract killing that Aleksey Kuznetsov arranged on Foma. This was taken from the dead sniper's property." Matvey's men had found the same thing that Sasha had discovered.

Taking in his words, she studied the information more carefully, catching the oligarch's name at the bottom, the reference to Foma clear and unmistakable.

"How did you get this?"

"Foma was a friend. He was like an uncle to my son. You must have known that I would go after the truth." She slipped the sheet of paper under the sofa as her husband came in with the drinks.

"There you are," he said, as Svetlana cleared some space on their coffee table for Sergej to put the tray on.

"What were you talking about when I was gone? Anything interesting?"

"Mr Filipov was just telling me a rather long joke, that's all."

"Oh, do tell me," Sergej said, as he placed the cups on to saucers, Matvey starting to stand up.

"Another time, I'm afraid. I am expected somewhere else five minutes ago already."

"And I've only just brought the tea in. Surely you can stay for one drink?" but Matvey was already on his way to the door, something that in some contexts would have been considered somewhat rude–– though, in their wealthy circles, such behaviour happened. Svetlana handed him his jacket, Matvey going in close to her ear.

"It wasn't a joke," he said.

"Am I laughing?"

He straightened and smiled. He took Sergej's hand when it was offered, both of their grips strong and confident, before he turned and walked out through the open door, his driver waiting for him on the circular driveway, opening the rear door to let him in as he got close. Seconds later they pulled away.

"A fascinating man," Sergej said, turning and walking back in.

"What makes you say that?" Svetlana said, keeping her tone inquisitive, even if inside she was still reeling from what he'd just told her.

"Just everything we talked about. Business stuff really, his plans for the future. Nothing you'd be interested in, but I'd like to see more of him. I think he's going places."

She'd heard that phrase from her husband before––going places––and knew it meant trouble.

It was the morning of the sixteenth United Russia party congress, President Putin's own party's annual gathering. Once more the party members were gathering in Moscow, as September nights were drawing in. Over the next four days, various issues would get discussed, the first two days acting as the primary days of that year's gathering, the first of which would be attended by Putin himself. He was widely expected to officially announce his intention to re-run for President at the elections the following March, something that he'd done at the 2011 congress, before his return to power. Not that he'd ever really laid down that power.

His announcement came just before the lunch interval. It was expected and planned––no one would be surprised to hear he was putting himself forward for a second six-year term––but the timing was such that as the delegates were just starting their lunch, the news was already beginning to spread.

Unlike previous years, Putin's chief media connection and financier Sokoloff was especially conspicuous by his absence. He would typically have been orchestrating the media angle––last time around it had been a foregone conclusion that Putin was coming back to power––but still Sokoloff had worked the media side of things hard. They were not going to miss a trick.

While there were many journalists present––there always were––crucially, now, Putin didn't have an inside track. The national broadcasters had been dramatically broken up following the Sokoloff collapse and subsequent suicide––which was still the only official story that had been released––and that continued to be an issue for the current President.

In his speech accepting the great honour and challenge of once again leading their great nation, Putin had talked about the growing tensions between Russia and the West––especially with America and the UK. He said that now was not the time to change leaders.

Now was not the time for Russia to go through the kind of meltdown Britain had had after its terrible handling of their own referendum on EU membership––something that would play into Russia's hands––nor the shambolic way America had conducted their own Presidential race. It was Russia's chance to show a different way––a United approach. The West was in tatters––those two votes had divided their own nations in half––and that wasn't to be the case in Russia. They needed to be a united people, people to rally behind their current President and allow him to carry through all the good he'd started.

His speech was met with a rapturous applause––what you'd have expected on home soil, anyway––and it was a full ten minutes before the crowd began to go silent, lunch already calling.

In St Petersburg, Sasha watched the speech from his office at the FSB. It was impressive, strong and bold––everything their President should be, everything the nation demanded and expected from its leader. Sasha had not been contacted about Putin's trip to England the following month, which wasn't a surprise. Nor was he bothered by that. Knowing that Alex and Anissa were tasked with that responsibility from the British side, he'd get to know what was going on, the two parties continually sharing information with one another.

It put Putin's words into stark relief––if these two Security Services would work together, instead of assuming the worst of each other––what more might be possible? Of course, he knew not everyone was like Alex and Anissa. He'd met Charlie in the past as well as Zoe. They seemed good agents. Open people. They were warm towards him, though he realised not everyone in his own agency would have been as welcoming. Anya had been––and that had got her killed. He was determined not to share her fate.

Dmitry Kaminski watched the speech from his London home. It was the only property he had left in England, the sale of his assets bringing in enough to keep the creditors away for the time being. Bitter lawsuits were being fought out in court, and Kaminski was struggling to keep hold of most of what else he had left. Kuznetsov's money wouldn't last long, and because of Kuznetsov's stupidity in the last Hunt, Kaminski wasn't sure if he now had much left anyway.

Kaminski knew nothing about who was behind the shooting, but believed the rumour that Foma was the victim. It might well work in his favour if Foma was out of the picture. Clearly, you couldn't pay out a bet to a dead man, and outside of those walls––the walls and floor of the Volkov Games Room––no legal documentation could bind Kuznetsov to pay out his debt to the Polzin estate. It had been a man-to-man agreement, and now one of those men was no more. Kaminski would back his friend to the hilt––his own campaign chances were reliant on the funds Kuznetsov couldn't afford to lose.

Matvey would catch up on the President's speech at a later point. He knew what was coming, Putin's announcement was nothing of a surprise to him––or anyone––but he would watch it anyway just to get an up-to-date picture of the man. What would his main points be, where was his strength and therefore where were his weaknesses? Matvey already had a clear idea where those weaknesses were. It was Putin's strongholds that he needed to undermine, and if not open them up, to at least expose them, to know what they were and where they existed. Then he might be able to do something about them.

He knew Putin was strong––that was why he'd been in power for so long, why the people loved him so much. You didn't get that type of following in the West, where they couldn't understand the Russian mindset, couldn't work out why they backed their President as they did. Yet what example had these Western nations shown to them? Public slanging matches by Presidential hopefuls in America? What had that done to galvanise the country, besides giving half of the nation a common enemy? They were now divided as a result. Britain very much too––their collapse had been catastrophic, the plummeting pound doing Matvey an excellent service, as it further reduced Kaminski's net worth, the man's fortunes so explicitly tied to the UK economy. Their leaders had led their nation to a vote–– only to all quit when the results were announced. A divided Europe––with the UK outside of the European Union could only be a good thing for the future of Russia. It made their nearest rival weaker.

The world had changed a lot in the last few years, and the next six would change it no doubt dramatically again. Russia held some keys to the future, a stable force in the face of challenging global conditions. Syria was an extensive dividing line between Russia and the West. It was the modern day Cuban missile crisis, waiting to explode, a potential flashpoint for direct conflict with America.

The next Presidential term would, therefore, include all these issues, and the next President needed to be prepared to be tough. Putin already held the office--and matched the criteria--but had he been in too long? Had the nations of the world started to work him out? There would be one or two other party candidates--those in opposition to Putin's United Russia who would also put forward a candidate. Did any of them really have someone who would be a challenge?

Then as well as himself there was Dmitry Kaminski. He was very different, but they were both from wealthy backgrounds, though the future for Kaminski, based in England, was now anything but secure. The next six months would see all these contenders come together. Only one could become the next President of the Russian Federation.

20

The month of September had raced by, and despite MI6 being busy ahead of Putin's Official visit to London just one week away, Dmitry Kaminski had demanded to see Thomas Price. They'd been meeting monthly, though this call had come only a fortnight after their last appointment. Kaminski had sounded rattled.

Once more Duke's club was the venue, there were few places in London like it, even fewer where the walls did not have ears. Such establishments were a dying breed––and that was a shame.

Thomas was once again the first to arrive, but Kaminski's arrival just minutes later confirmed somewhat the desperate nature of the Russian businessman. The DDG wondered for the first time if all their years of grooming, all their hours of working this man, were about to come to nothing. Price was seeing the man behind the curtain––and suddenly it wasn't looking like much at all.

They took their seats––same booth, same positions just as always––their drinks being prepared already at the bar, the barman having long since stopped actually asking them what they wanted, both men always ordering the same thing. It gave them more time to talk, without the added distraction of a waiter coming over.

"What is it?" Price said, a little shorter than he intended to be, his tone like that of an authoritarian teacher or parent speaking to a moaning child.

"I need to know I have your complete backing," Kaminski started, clearly not beginning with what was really on his mind, but Price would go with it, they would get there eventually.

"Do I have to repeat myself, Dmitry, you've had our backing for a long time."

"And Putin's visit next week?"

"He is still your current President, and it was announced to us rather than by invitation. Relax, it changes nothing."

"It does if he manages to convince your lot he's the right man to run the country."

"My lot? You mean our measly excuse for a government? One thing we do at least agree on is that we don't like, or trust, Putin. Haven't for the last decade. Ukraine, Syria, his own country's views on certain lifestyle choices..."

"You know I share much of those views, too," Kaminski said. He'd always found the West's openness to teach homosexuality to children as a way of life––imprinting the idea on such innocent minds––to be totally wrong.

"Relax, Kaminski, and drink your coffee," which had just arrived, the waiter now gone from their presence.

"How are things with Meridian?" Price asked, his own understanding entirely clear, the collapse and subsequent dismantling of the entire Banking Union having filled the business pages for months already.

"It will all be public knowledge before the end of the year, no doubt. It's all slipping through my fingers. Are you sure there isn't anything you can do?"

"About what exactly? The billions of dollars of debt you can't repay? I'm not sure you've exactly understood our relationship, Dmitry."

"Relationship?" he spat, "you make it look like this is two way, but

I'm just here to do your bidding, isn't that right, to be Britain's man in Russia? Is that all you see me as?"

"Are you thinking about your place in history, Dmitry, because, believe me..."

"Don't you dare patronise me!" and Kaminski got up, swearing at Price as he threw his teacup clean across the room and into the wall nearest them.

"Sit down, Dmitry!" Price warned, "you are making a bloody scene, and that's the last thing you need right now." Kaminski sat down, the barman calmly going over to pick up the broken pieces. It was far from the first time such a thing had happened––wouldn't be the last, either.

"I'm worried, that's all. There are rumours," Kaminski said, calmer again, as quiet as he could be with his pulse still racing, his blood pressure high.

"What rumours?"

"They're whispers really, but in my line of work, that's all we usually have to go on." Price had not come across anything that he could immediately fit these rumours Kaminski might be alluding to. "One is Matvey Filipov. He's a threat."

"In what way?"

"He's come at me––he's been victorious, too, it would seem. Why? Why take me out unless I am a threat to him? Unless he wants the same thing that I want."

"He wants to stand for President?" That was new information to Price. He knew of Matvey somewhat, due to his involvement with Kaminski––it paid to know who the other oligarchs were––but aside his vast wealth, which had always been considerably more than Kaminski's had been, he knew little else. Maybe that would now have to change regarding Matvey Filipov. If Matvey might also be a friend to the UK and could beat Putin, then he certainly warranted some of their attention.

"That's the rumour."

"Where did you hear it from?"

"From enough people who I trust to make it valid, okay," is all he said. He wasn't going to give MI6 that insight into his connections.

"A few months ago there was a trial in St Petersburg. A British national was charged with murdering a Russian janitor. She did it, I'm aware of that fact, anyway. A French woman was the prosecution's key witness. As was one of your own."

"Oh, yes, Anissa Edison," only now did Thomas make the connection.

"Yes, that one. The trial blew up in our faces."

"In whose face? Yours?"

"Possibly, yes."

"You said you had nothing to do with that? I asked you right here about that before I allowed my agent to take that bloody trip, and you sat where you are now sitting and categorically denied you had any involvement in that situation."

"There was nothing to connect me to it, plus it wasn't my girl on trial."

"Your girl?––you're connected to the witness?" Price couldn't believe what he was being told.

"Possibly, yes. I think Matvey has that evidence, somehow. I think he'll use it to implicate me in the crime. To at least muddy the waters."

"Then prepare for it; make a statement or something. Pre-empt the attack."

"That would be risky, and would certainly implicate me in the crime. I'd have to come clean about *certain involvements*, which wouldn't go down well with anyone."

"What option do you have? If Matvey does have this on you, he'll use it."

"It might just be rumours. I don't know for sure."

"You either are, or you aren't, I can't see what the problem is. Is this going to be a problem for you, Dmitry?"

"Is what going to be a problem?" he said, not liking the tone Price had just used as if looking down at a much weaker man in front of him.

"Being tough when you need to be. Striking out before you are struck."

"Of course it isn't! I just don't think wading into what is already a very delicate situation with too much truth is what anyone needs right now."

"You need closure on that one, Dmitry, before you announce you're running, I'm telling you. Something like that could come back to bite you when you can't afford it."

"Don't tell me what I need, Price, I'm more than capable of making such decisions myself." The Deputy Director General could see when arguing was becoming futile, instead placing his cup back on its saucer.

"Very good, I'll leave that in your capable hands." He'd called the Russian's bluff. It worked.

"I'm not saying I don't need your help and advice, my old friend." So they were old friends now were they?

"What are you asking for exactly, then?" Finally, they were getting to the crux of the problem.

"Is there nothing you can do about either man?"

"Putin and Filipov?" Kaminski nodded. "Do what, exactly?" Price didn't like insinuations––if the man were asking what he thought he was asking, he would have to say it directly.

"Stop them. Do whatever it is MI6 do when they need a threat––a problem––to go away. You've said all along that you want our two nations to work together, to heal our wounds and become stronger. You've said you will back me with everything you have at your disposal to help me win that race. And yet, I'm just about to be kicked out of my home, my entire UK operations are now in the hands of other people, and I have two very dangerous men standing in front of me, neither of whom I now have the financial clout to be able to remove."

"Assassinate them, you mean? You are asking me to order a British hit on these two men––one being your current President?" He sat back in his chair, arms raised to the ceiling, lost for words. He'd done some things in his time within MI6, but he'd never been asked to do something as potentially explosive as that before.

"Well?" Kaminski said, as if accepting it was asking a lot, but still he was there asking it.

"Well? Are you out of your mind? We can't be seen to do anything like that, you must know that by now?"

"Be seen? God, Price, I'm not asking you to share the details with the world. It'll only take one man––Putin has plenty of enemies in this country––to put a bullet through his skull as he tours your city next week."

"It can't be done here," Price said, conceding for the first time that he wasn't ruling out a hit.

"Where then? Moscow? You wouldn't have a chance. London is as close as you're ever going to get to him. You can take care of Matvey after."

"You would have us just kill your rivals?"

"You wanted me to be tough. Well, this is it."

Price sat there in silence for a moment, for the first time looking around the club, though it was as empty and private as always. He poured himself another cup of tea.

"We don't know where he'll be until he's already here. They aren't giving us that information."

"Still, you can have someone ready, no?"

"I don't know, Dmitry. It could force a war. If they ever found out..."

"Make sure they don't. Besides, if these men are out of the picture, I'd be able to step in. We can call an early election––there are enough people who know I've intended to run all along, even if it's not public knowledge. Once I'm President, you would have nothing to fear. As things stand, you might otherwise be heading towards conflict, regardless." It was true, the protests outside the Russian embassy in London had been growing more violent over the last year, ever since Boris Johnson encouraged crowds to gather and make their voices heard on Syria. That was something that made Putin's visit a surprise. Relations between the two nations were at an all-time low. Maybe that was why he needed to be seen here. Maybe he wanted to show his voters that the West didn't scare him, that he'd go anywhere he was still welcome.

"I'll have a look at the possibility," is all Price ended with. Kaminski smiling. He knew if something like that was going to be done, London offered them an ideal opportunity. No other location would give them as many options. Ironically, it was Matvey Filipov who appeared to be the harder of the two targets right at that moment. Putin putting himself into British hands––he would have his own unit, but MI6 was tasked with organising a lot of his protection––had made the President vulnerable.

"We'll meet here the morning of his visit, and we can toast each other to a bright future," Kaminski said, "drink some fine champagne next time, for a change."

Price smiled––he wasn't so confident that there would be anything to celebrate. Yes, he had some contacts, but such a move would be going way off the national agenda. For sure, they'd been courting Kaminski for years, and that alone was a highly risky action, if it was ever known. The circle which did know that––he represented MI6, there were two within MI5 as well as about eight cabinet ministers––was small, and even then, he knew he couldn't mention this latest request. He would be acting alone, applying what he understood as British foreign agenda, but writing his own contribution to that schedule.

The two men left––Price agreeing to meet Kaminski again on the morning of the Putin visit––though whether they would have anything to actually celebrate, depended entirely on what options he would be able to make work. Right now he didn't know what to think, who to speak to, who to trust.

21

That same week in China there was a World Economic Forum event, and for the first time in her life, Svetlana Volkov had joined her husband on a trip to the vast nation in the east, though it shared a northern border with her own land. Having an actress of her stature in the country was seen as a boost for the Chinese film industry, and she worked that angle a little while being there.

At the event itself––something she insisted on attending with Sergej, despite his suggestion that she would be bored there––were a number of the Russians from her T20 group. Not all could make it, nor was this a specific Games event, but the six who were there gathered in an upstairs room during the first break. The others would just have to be told the information later on.

She was not in a good mood.

"There will be no event this New Year," she said, the first time in the Hunt's nearly twelve year history that there hadn't been a gathering at that time of year, the cracks maybe beginning to show in what had otherwise been a solid partnership with them all. "It has come to my attention that the shooting of Foma Polzin wasn't in fact just a random killing, but something planned, paid for and executed by one of our very own. Aleksey Kuznetsov," who wasn't one of the six who had attended that conference, "is the man in question, the very man on the losing end of yet another cataclysmic day's betting. I fear therefore the novelty of what was always a little fun between us," yet that was an understatement, to say the least, "has now run its course. I can't be caught up in anything criminal. I will not accept or tolerate such behaviour. Gentlemen, for those who still deserve that title, anyway," and she looked at no one in particular, though the accusation was there for all of them, "I wish you every success in the future, but my part in this is now over. You shall as always never make reference to what we have been involved in, and should our paths ever cross in the future––as of course they will––I expect you each to walk the other way. Have I made myself clear?"

It was difficult to hear such a bitter tone, such heated words coming from someone so elegant, so graceful as Svetlana, though she was clearly fuming because of the whole situation.

The shooting had really got to her. When she'd been given that confirmation––she had her own suspicions following what had happened that day, but didn't want to believe the worst––that it was Kuznetsov, she'd gone into meltdown. Something she'd held so dearly––the Games––had been turned into something so ugly. Yes, Contestants had died before. The financial losses of one Host had even resulted in him taking his own life, though by that point she was long past mourning the death of Sokoloff, a man who'd slapped her across the face the last time they'd seen each other.

It had got wildly out of hand. The whole thing was ruined for Svetlana now and had to go. Even the T10––the last event multiple times bigger than anything ever attempted before, and won in a matter of months––was now ruined. She'd let the men get above themselves. Maybe that had been the issue, her mistake? To have allowed them to dictate what was going to happen, to come up with their own suggestions.

It didn't matter anymore. There was no going back now. Some of these men––the winning five in the T10 for sure––were becoming very powerful indeed. Matvey particularly concerned her. She'd seen his type many times, including her own husband before they'd married. She'd managed to tame him––he was now a reformed character. But she was sure the beast remained, however. Buried, yes, and under control, but tame? She wasn't sure. Gone forever? She was sure it wasn't. If Matvey got too involved with her Sergej, there was no knowing what it would do to her husband.

She left the meeting room fighting back tears of anguish and disappointment, taking the stairs and thankfully not seeing anyone else as she went up to her top floor suite. She would stay there for the rest of the day until her husband returned. They were due out that evening for dinner with some of the Chinese Communist Party leaders––it was a big deal––and she wanted time to recover, to prepare herself and be ready to impress everyone on behalf of her husband. Just like she always did.

IT WAS the final few hours of preparation before the Russian President was due to touchdown at a still unspecified UK airport the next morning. His precise plans were being kept secret.

Alex had been tasked with heading up the team and had gone at it somewhat head-on for the last few months, the previous week solid for sure. Senior technician Gordon Peacock was running the online surveillance side––so far there were no signs of trouble, nothing credible, anyway––but there had been plenty of chatter. The Russian President's visit was causing quite a stir, with various groups planning to stage any number of protests and demonstrations in the capital during the coming days, and especially on the day of the visit itself. Some had already been held. Gordon was keeping a close watch on where these were heading––both in their geographical meeting points, as well as their aspirations for the protest itself.

Anissa––coming back into things more strongly only in the last few days, everything a little in the air since her arrival back from Russia some weeks before––was working through the possible routes and stop-offs Putin might take. She ignored the irony that herself deported and banned from Russia for five years just a few short months ago, she was on the inside of the security operation looking to protect the President of the country that said she was no longer welcome.

One of the apparent locations she had detailed was the Russian Embassy in Kensington Palace Gardens, where for the last few weeks––and noticeably more so in the previous few days––crowds of protestors had regularly been gathering. They'd primarily been law-abiding––but there was always an element of social disorder that went along with such protests––and the embassy staff themselves had been complaining for days already about the situation. They wanted the British authorities to do something about it. Apparently they didn't like the idea of the British right to protest. It wouldn't have been allowed to go on for so long if it was Moscow they were standing in, not London.

The activity right along Kensington Palace Gardens made that area––and the embassy at large––a less likely possibility for a visit, bearing in mind the President's plan to hold several meetings across the city, with an as yet unknown number of dignitaries. Such an exposed and already volatile location as the Russian Embassy surely made it now off limits. She noted down her thoughts, regardless.

Alex had yet to hear anything from the Russians himself––he wasn't really expecting to, either, despite putting out multiple pleas for assistance from Moscow's end. Like the Americans had done before Obama touched down, everything was very much on a need to know basis, and Military Intelligence, it seemed, was not on that list. He would make do as best he could.

He had several military sniper units ready and on-call. They would cover most of the routes––once these were known––from rooftop locations. Teams of police with sniffer dogs would comb the streets before the Putin convoy was expected, to detect any explosive devices that might otherwise be in operation. The Kremlin convoy––as it had been with the White House vehicles––were bomb proof and largely bullet proof, but it paid to be diligent, regardless. Nothing could be allowed to happen on their watch. The Director of MI6 himself had made that very clear. Any type of incident while Vladimir Putin was on British soil could lead to a very major diplomatic incident.

Three divisions of army personnel were ready to be on the ground––a palpable presence. While the police would be involved, the whole operation was deemed to put too much of a strain on the Metropolitan Police force, so they instead would assist where they could, the strong army numbers taking most of the strain.

Alex had asked Gordon to check every soldier and policeman and armed response officer against the MI6 database. If anything was flagged up, that member of staff––from whatever division they served in––would not be allowed to be present on the day. He was taking no chances.

ALL WEEK ON THE BBC, special programmes were being shown in connection with the first Russian official visit for over five years, at a time when relations between the two nations could do with a vast improvement. The series of shows had been mainly looking at Russians who were connected to the UK––various famous names had been portrayed so far: football club owners, business leaders––men all based in London for many years already. Most were household names now, often appearing in references across many UK publications. Very much the public face of Russian wealth on UK streets.

Anissa had come across the series after its sixth part was released, which had focused on Dmitry Kaminski. It looked at his involvement in the Meridian Capital fiasco––a phrase coined some months ago, the full situation still not totally clear to the general public. The programme tried a little to explore what was happening to the previously large UK institution, now fallen on hard times, as well as a bit of the man himself. She was fascinated by it, and it portrayed Kaminski in quite a different light. She wondered how much the oligarch's own PR team had been behind that particular effort.

As that part of the series came to a close, they were already advertising the next episode. The words *Where is Foma Polzin?* flashing across the screen. Anissa focused on what it said--which was very little, as it was just a trailer--regarding the next show. She made a note of the time of the broadcast, which was to be shown the following lunchtime on the BBC News channel. She'd have to record it. Putin himself would have touched down by then, and she would be fully involved in that particular Russian visitor, though she would watch the recording with Alex as soon as she could, knowing the connections Foma had, knowing his involvement in the Games. She was fascinated to see what angle the BBC would be coming from.

IN JUNE 2003, when Putin had visited the UK with his wife, it had been a significant State visit. Met by Prince Charles at Heathrow, addressed by the Queen at Horse Guards Parade, troops of British Royal Guards saluting the Russian President before a band of guardsmen and women played both the Russian and British national anthems. That had been a four-day visit--by far his most extended visit to the UK in a decade--at a time when relations were better.

His last visit--over five years ago for a brief day--was at the beginning of the 2012 Olympic games. Much of the fanfare of those nine years before had gone. He'd met with the then British Prime Minister, David Cameron, and the two men had talked publicly afterwards about their strong connection, how trade between the two nations had increased dramatically, and how they looked forward to that continuing.

Putin then watched some of the judo competition--a personal favourite for him--before leaving. Half a decade later, it was clear how much distance their apparently growing relationship now had.

Touching down at London's Stansted airport--which was actually some distance north of London but one of the quieter airports, and the most suitable for the Russian President's large aircraft to land at--it was just gone nine in the morning when the convoy set out.

At Vauxhall House, Alex was notified by air traffic control--five minutes before the Russians themselves let him know––that the President's plane had landed. Stansted had been one of the most obvious choices, used by Barak Obama on his last visit, and therefore proven to be able to handle that kind of situation. Its location to London also meant several options could be taken. These routes were now coming through, Alex working with his team to monitor their progress. A no-fly zone was in place across that part of the city, besides the two police helicopters that patrolled the skies, following the convoy as it headed south.

It was understood by ten that Putin would be meeting with the Prime Minister herself at Downing Street for lunch. The location, already highly secure, made it one of their lesser concerns that day.

As suggested, there was no stop-off at the embassy scheduled––at least the Russians had taken MI6 advice on that––though Putin still wanted to meet the staff at some point. Details were sketchy as to when and where that would be. As far as the British knew, he was due to fly out that night.

With the roads kept mostly clear, the convoy reached the edge of the city by ten. Flying over that part of London was not so easy as it had been following the convoy down a motorway, so the two helicopters backed away as Putin made his first stops, at homes of two wealthy Russians.

Both of these addresses had been on Anissa's watch list––low priority, granted––but at least scanned. Because of the Russians involved, who had their own security teams in place, the locations were a safe bet for the Russian President. The convoy was reported leaving just before twelve––he'd been in the country for nearly three hours and had only spent time with fellow Russians––now clearly setting out for Downing Street, and the meeting with Theresa May at Number 10. He had ample time to make the relatively short journey, and Anissa and Alex were working on the possible route.

He'd taken none of them, however––in fact, they lost him entirely for twenty minutes––the team at MI6 getting a little frantic before communication was re-established, the convoy back on visual. They'd seemingly gone a slightly longer route––maybe being over cautious--and arrived at the gates of Downing Street five minutes before one, the front two cars of the convoy waved through, the other two vehicles speeding off to no doubt wait for Putin's re-emergence later.

Outside Number 10, Putin stepped from the car and walked quickly in through the doors. The waiting press watching from the gates--no one had been allowed into Downing Street to report his visit--could only strain to get a tiny glimpse of the President.

22

Thomas Price left the hustle of Vauxhall House––the Putin visit in full flow––as he headed out, going on foot to Duke's club, having agreed to meet again with Kaminski.

It was twenty past twelve, and he was five minutes ahead of schedule for the lunchtime meeting, only to be surprised by the man on the door.

"Your visitor is already inside, sir," he said. Kaminski was apparently losing his nerve, though in truth, so was he. It had been a wretched week since their last meeting, and he had little more to offer the Russian than the same rhetoric he'd given him the previous time they'd met, that there was little he could really do. He'd thought about taking up the challenge he'd been set, though there were too many people he would have to get past, mostly in his own agency, to successfully pull off a hit on British soil.

It couldn't be done, or more to the point, they couldn't get away with it.

He wasn't going to send someone on a suicide mission, that wasn't his style. The idea, though, as a whole held some merit. He'd drafted something briefly about the chance of a hit being carried out somewhere else––certainly not in Russia––but there would be other official visits to regions far more unstable than where he currently was.

Price came into the main room where the barman was already making a hot drink; the barman looked up, but as usual, he didn't otherwise acknowledge his presence. Price strolled over to their typical booth––Kaminski clearly already there, his back to him so that he couldn't see him coming––only for Price to get there, and realise it wasn't Dmitry at all. It was Putin.

"You seem surprised to see me, Mr Price." Thomas stood there in silence with his mouth open slightly. They were the only ones in Duke's at that moment. "Please, take a seat, I don't have long." Thomas sat down.

"Why in hell are you here?"

"Classic MI6, cutting right to the point." It was strange hearing that come from a man he'd only seen on a television screen, a man he knew so much about but only from a distance. A President and former KGB agent. If anyone knew anything about spying, it was the man sitting right in front of Price at that moment. "I've come to warn you, Mr Price," Putin said.

"Warn me? About what?" but his voice was quavering, far from steady.

"Someone in your position shouldn't be getting involved in Russian politics. It's not your domain."

"I don't quite understand what you are saying, sir?" he managed, this a little more controlled. Putin glanced at his watch. It was nearly time to go.

"Don't get involved in what you don't understand," and with that he stood, his team of minders coming in, one with a telephone to his ear, calling in the convoy to come to collect them. Just like that, he was gone. Price sank back in his chair, motionless. The barman, seeing the DDG in a state, came over moments later with a stiff whisky.

"Here, you look like you could do with this," he said, Price downing it in one go.

"I think I'll have another," he coughed, the alcohol burning down the back of his throat. The barman moved to prepare it. "How long had he been here?"

"Arrived a couple of minutes before you, sir. Cleared the place out as he waited for you, though there were only two others here. They didn't know who it was. Putin only entered when it was empty." He handed Price the glass, which he sipped instead now, taking smaller gulps over the next twenty minutes. He was on his third one--and given his empty stomach, starting to feel it too--when Kaminski arrived.

"Started without me, I see, but good to know you are in a celebratory mood, Thomas," he said as he took his usual seat--the one Putin himself had been in minutes before. When Kaminski looked into the eyes of the man sitting opposite him, he didn't see victory, only defeat. "What's happened?" he said, his heart already sinking.

Price told him what had just taken place, what Putin had said, how he'd been sitting there waiting for him.

"He was waiting for me!" he said not for the first time. "He knew exactly where I'd be, at exactly what time. I mean, how could he know that?"

"I don't know," Kaminski said again, getting a little paranoid himself. If Putin was to walk in right now--whilst there wasn't a problem with a London-based Russian businessman meeting with an MI6 operative--both knew their meeting was anything but routine. And if Putin somehow knew about Price, he surely had to know about Kaminski also. But how?

Price motioned to the barman for another drink.

"I think you've had enough, Thomas," Kaminski said.

"It's not for me, it's for you. I can see you need it." The Russian wasn't sure what he needed. A week ago he'd suggested that the man now in front of him should put together a plan that involved assassinating his own President, and also that of another rival. Kaminski had himself arrived in jovial spirits, keen to hear what Price had in place, seeing the man drinking as a sure sign his competition was about to be removed. And yet Putin had shown up in person, and at a time only the two of them had known--at least, he thought just the two of them had known––and then given an unambiguous warning to Kaminski's British connection. *Don't get involved in what you don't understand.* There was a lot the Russian didn't understand at that moment.

He took the drink, downing it in one go, the same fire burning his throat, though he held back from coughing.

"I have to go," Kaminski said, getting up right away and leaving Price on his own. Maybe the British end of things had run its course? Yet if his President knew about their meeting, knew the location––he, therefore, must have known about the content of their meetings. Kaminski no longer felt safe in London.

THE RUSSIAN DELEGATION left Downing Street just after three. Over the previous two hours, he'd enjoyed lunch with the Prime Minister––his first encounter with yet another new PM––and some of her key cabinet ministers. They discussed Syria a little, without going too deep. Some of the words spoken over recent months in public by lesser voices––each still senior enough in their nation––had been attacking the other side for too long. Both leaders agreed that peace should be the ideal they worked towards in the troubled region and left things at that.

From Downing Street he was due to meet with some business leaders––most of whom were connected in some way to Russia, if not, in fact, Russian themselves––and then was attending an evening reception at Roman Abramovich's London mansion. The embassy staff were being invited to that dinner, as well, to be given the honour of touching base with their President.

Routes were once again mapped out––this time the convoy seemingly sticking to the most obvious path through the maze of streets that made up central London––and the afternoon progressed well.

By mid-afternoon, with Putin confirmed as being inside a conference centre speaking to a business crowd, Anissa went and grabbed Alex.

"I want you to watch this," she said when Alex was sitting down in front of the computer. She pressed play on the BBC iPlayer page, that morning's case study into various Russian oligarchs playing straight away.

Ten minutes later, they were done. The programme had raised the question as to the health––and current location––of Foma Polzin, the billionaire who hadn't been seen for months, his companies running themselves in his absence.

The show led with the early rumours––really downplaying them, in fairness––that had surfaced initially about the reported shooting. It focused mainly on those working for Foma now. The share price had continued to grow––Forbes was about to declare Foma to be worth around $8 billion––though he'd not been at any of the significant recent business events, forums at which he had been ever-present for the last few years.

The programme ended with the shot of a private jet––last chartered by Foma and still sitting on the tarmac in St Petersburg. It questioned why it was still there before seemingly giving its own explanation. They confirmed the plane wasn't actually owned by the Russian and that it was in fact owned by a completely unrelated company which had since run into economic trouble, which explained why the jet had not been flown for some months.

To the average viewer, it all meant very little. A little smoke, a little suggestion but then the programme pretty much closed down most of the options, most of the conspiracy theories. The truth was, Foma just hadn't been seen for a while, which could have been for any number of reasons.

"Wow," Alex said as Anissa closed down the browser. "Do you think he's really dead?"

"I think we know he probably isn't. Maybe we should get them to investigate Monaco, see what they might dig up there?" she said with a smile. Alex knew she wasn't serious.

"It does go to show, we clearly aren't the only people watching these guys."

"Anyway, let's get back to the others. Until Putin has left British airspace, I don't want us to miss a thing."

Price finished his fourth and final drink five minutes after Kaminski had left. He didn't know where their special relationship had now landed them both. Was the game already up? He'd invested a vast number of hours into getting on the inside of a man who could one day become the President of Russia. It had been his own nudging that had pushed forward the plan to challenge Putin next time around, instead of waiting for the end of the second term. That would have been another six years, and relations between the two nations––between the West and Russia as a whole in fact––was getting more strained as the weeks went by.

At that moment, Putin seemed more dangerous than ever. Not only had he obviously known about what the Deputy Director General of MI6 was doing, but Putin had also made a personal visit to prove the point.

There were now a few others in the club as Price struggled to put on his jacket. He'd been there a total of only about thirty minutes, though with his head spinning from the whisky, and his world rocked by what had just taken place, it could have been much longer. It certainly felt it.

There was no sign of Kaminski when he got to street level––why would there have been, seeing as the Russian had left in a hurry some five or so minutes before––but his time and spacial awareness were entirely absent as he clumsily and slowly made his way down the street.

As he passed an alley, not twenty metres from the front door of Duke's, two men approached him from behind. He was manhandled into the alley, the British MI6 man unable to really do anything about the hands holding him firmly, especially given his reduced awareness and control because of his drunkenness.

One of the men slipped a needle into his neck, plunging in the liquid that would kill Thomas quickly, and peacefully, his body going limp almost immediately, the two men lowering him to the ground, before exiting out of the alley.

It was three hours later––the same two men about to board a flight leaving the UK from Heathrow––when they called the man they were working for.

"Is it done?" the voice at the other end of the line asked.

"It's done, sir." The phone went dead, the handset taken to pieces and left in a rubbish bin at the airport, as final boarding to Moscow was announced. They were up and away just twenty-five minutes later.

THE EVENING FUNCTION had been an expensive affair, all the stops pulled out for what was a once in a lifetime occasion. Abramovich had himself often visited Putin in Moscow––he'd given him a $35 million yacht a few years before––but this was his first time with him in the UK. Putin was looking for new financiers, something Roman had always been a little reticent to be. Gifts were one thing, actually being the one to finance an election campaign felt like something else. He declined to give Putin an answer straight away, much to the President's apparent annoyance. He was running out of options fast.

The convoy left the property at ten––a little later than planned. The convoy approached the airport, the Russians cleared through and were quickly on-board. Air traffic control confirmed they were free to go, the huge aircraft lifting to the skies just after eleven, heading straight for Moscow, where it would arrive in the early hours of the following day.

Getting the confirmation that the flight was in the air, a collective breath was let out in the MI6 offices. The day had ended without a glitch on their watch. Noticeable by his absence was Thomas Price, who hadn't been seen at Vauxhall House all afternoon.

23

It was the following morning before the call came through to MI6 about the body of Thomas Price being found. Alex and Anissa immediately went to the reported location––everything had been taken away by then, but they needed to see where it had all happened.

It had been around half past three the previous day when a couple walking past the alley had first seen what they thought was a homeless man just lying on the ground before they approached to take a closer look. The man on the floor was clearly well dressed, and he smelt of alcohol. They were going to just leave him to sleep off his drunken state, but there was something about how he was positioned that made the man take a closer look, much to his wife's initial caution.

He had found no pulse once the body was turned onto its side, and they had called an ambulance. That arrived, along with a police car, just ten minutes later. Because of the government offices in the area, two other police cars came to help in what might be more than only a fall.

He had been pronounced dead as soon as the medical team got a closer look, the police taking a statement from the couple as another officer taped off the entrance to the alleyway. Significantly, there were no identification papers on the body––Price had long made a point of leaving all that at the office when visiting Duke's, his bill paid through an eTab, his other identification papers not needed, as everything was done on facial recognition. Besides, he was a regular, those that needed to know who he was already did.

The body had been taken away to the nearest hospital at five––ninety minutes after it was discovered––where a full autopsy would be carried out to determine the cause of death. There appeared to be no impact to the head, which would have been the apparent result of a fall given his intoxicated nature, so that raised its own questions as to what had happened. They hoped to have the lab results back by the morning.

At six, coming to the end of their shift, two officers had returned to the street where the body was found, a photo of the victim in hand. They had wanted to try and see if any of the nearby offices and pubs knew anything. He'd been clearly drinking, so it made sense to speak to these first, plus most of the offices would be closing soon, if not already. There were a few pubs and restaurants in that square mile of London, plus some clubs.

They'd called at Duke's almost straight away, not getting anywhere further than the two men on the door, who barely looked at the photo before denying they recognised him. The police had moved on to the next option a little further down the street. Inside Duke's, a message was relayed upstairs about what they'd just been asked.

It was eight-thirty that evening––at the same time that Putin was arriving at Roman Abramovich's home––when the barman from Duke's had sneaked out of the back door and met the two officers by their car.

"I know who your man was," he had said, the bouncers on the door having reported that the man in question was a stiff. "His name is Thomas Price."

"How do you know who he was?"

"He was a regular."

"Where?"

"Can't say. Look, I've given you his name, you'll be able to find out who he is from that, I'm sure."

"Can we take your name?"

He looked at them as if they thought he was stupid. "I've said all I'm prepared to. I'm sorry to have heard he's dead," and he turned and ran the other way––away from Duke's––in case they would try and follow. When he was sure they hadn't, he doubled back twenty minutes later and sneaked in through the rear door, his break over, the evening crowd starting to arrive.

The officers had noted down the name. It was getting late, their shift was ending, so while they would make mention of the name they'd just been given, it would actually be the same two officers who would cross-check the name against the police database only the following morning after Putin had flown home.

That check happened just after eight. The body was identified as the high profile Deputy Director General of MI6–– there were no further details for security purposes––and the report got flagged and immediately sent upstairs. Within ten minutes the identity of the victim had been confirmed. A full investigation into a potential act of terrorism was set up. A call was made to MI6 to confirm what they'd just found out. They were waiting for the post-mortem results, which would be copied over to MI6 as soon as they had them.

Alex read the report from the police once more as they got out of the car, the blue and white crime scene tape flapping in the slight breeze across the alleyway.

"I guess that it's a local barman who knew the DDG. He called him a regular."

"That could mean anything. Massage, squash courts, doctors." Alex waved his hand theatrically around the area.

"Do you see many of those around, Anissa?" he said, a smile on his face. Besides some visible office buildings, there were only a few pubs and clubs visible.

"I guess not––though you never know."

"It says here there was a strong smell of alcohol."

"Well, the toxicology report will confirm all that."

"What I want to know is, why he was here? I mean, yesterday of all days, we were in the middle of one of the busiest operations we've had in a while, the visit in full flow, yet at some point in the afternoon, the DDG leaves to come here?"

They'd checked with the front desk. Though Price had never signed out with his card from Vauxhall House--a big no-no and something Price himself had screamed at juniors in the past for failing to do--he was spotted on the CCTV leaving just after midday. The body was found about a mile from the office--easily walkable--though it did beg the question as to whether he'd been attacked en route to somewhere, that he'd therefore just been passing through that area heading towards somewhere else?

And yet, an unknown local barman had named the victim.

Price was local, therefore, to that specific area. If they could locate the barman in question, maybe they could get some answers.

They were at the crime scene--beside the police tape, there was nothing else that suggested anything untoward had happened there--when the report came back from the autopsy. Blood alcohol level was high--that much they already knew--but not excessive. He had been restrained when his heart had stopped, and an impact wound in his neck suggested that a needle had been used to inject the fluid to kill him.

This was a professional job, he'd been murdered.

Time of death was a little harder to determine--clearly he'd died almost instantly, the type of drugs used lethal by design--and the temperature of the body when it had arrived for examination suggested a window of three to five hours before the autopsy when the death could have occurred. That gave a probable time of death of between twelve and half two the previous day.

CCTV footage from Vauxhall House showed him leaving at just before midday, his car was still in its parking space. No suitable public transport went where he was going so he must have had time to walk about a mile and down a few drinks. That pushed the time of death nearer two thirty. Clearly by half three, when the call for an ambulance was made by the concerned couple, he was already long dead.

There were no cameras in the alleyway or that part of the street––which was frustrating and annoying, given how much of the city was wired for video. Most of the establishments were yet to open––it was morning, and these places tended to start taking in crowds from lunchtime onwards, but mostly came alive in the evenings––so there seemed little the two agents could really find out.

The barman, whoever he was, had clearly been cautious about giving out the information on Price and didn't want to be put on record as having done so. That puzzled Anissa as they walked around, though there was nowhere they were really going. She pondered the situation a little, trying to work out why the barman had wanted––maybe needed––to stay so secretive? Who was he afraid of? What did he know?

They headed back to the office––the building on alert, but mainly in shock. No one at Vauxhall House really felt they were personally under threat, and a quiet group murmured amongst themselves that because of how their now former DDG treated people, it wasn't a surprise something like that had happened. There was a noticeable shock that it had––but they would have been mourning far more if it had happened to almost anyone else they worked with.

Now just the two of them again, coffee in hand and a pastry each before them, both purchased in the building's canteen, Alex and Anissa sat in their own office, talking it through. Because of what they knew about Thomas Price and his connection to Russia––something they had not told anyone else, besides Gordon who'd worked the technical angle a few times––it brought the whole Russian connection into suspicion.

Price had been meeting covertly with Kaminski, seemingly part of a small British-based plan to get the Russian elected President. Had Kaminski done this––not personally, probably, these men never did––but had their relationship broken down? Was he trying to make a statement, the killing happening on the same day Putin was in town?

Putin--and Anissa stopped dead in her seat at that thought.

"What is it?" Alex said. He knew that look.

"Jesus, where is it?" Anissa said, scrambling through the reports on her desk, finally finding whatever it was she was looking for. "We lost his convoy for twenty minutes yesterday."

"Whose? Putin's?" and Alex was laughing at the thought, though Anissa remained deadly serious.

"Here," she said, "between 12:05 and 12:25."

"He was on his way to Downing Street."

"A journey that takes thirty minutes max if you take any of the direct routes from where he'd just been, and he left there at midday."

"But he obviously got lost. Besides, Price was killed after that." But he was starting to buy into Anissa's idea. What they knew of the man--which wasn't much, but they knew plenty of men like him--anything was possible.

As far as they could tell, there was no connection between Putin and Price. Only the Director General himself had been introduced to the Russian President, which had been back in his 2003 visit. If there had been any informal meetings since then, they were unaware of them.

Anissa pulled open a map of London on her computer. She dropped a pin at where they first lost contact with the convoy--they hadn't had any visual contact for some time, just relying on trackers, which had stopped working for those twenty minutes--and then another pin at the point when a signal was received again. There were three miles between the two marks. Three miles in twenty minutes? It was possible, given traffic. With other routes closed off--routes they had assumed the convoy would pass through, and therefore kept clear--the areas around the side had taken the strain. If he'd been lost and caught in that traffic, it was possible that the two points on the map made sense.

But why go that way? There was really one main street between the two points on the map. Where Price's body was found, was something like another mile to the west of that road--some diversion.

"I don't know," Anissa said, throwing her hands into the air. "Is it possible? Maybe. Do I think Putin was involved in the murder? No frigging idea."

"I'll speak with Sasha. Putin's men must have had mobile phones on them during their trip. I'll see if he has an easy way of getting that cellphone data."

"He doesn't need to––plus if he tried, that would only put him in danger. He just needs to get us the phone numbers, and we can then check it out ourselves. They would have used British-based networks. We can see what signals were picked up during that time, once we have the numbers."

Alex was already typing a message to Sasha.

24

It was two days later before Sasha had been able to send through the details that Alex had requested, most of the numbers finally obtained for Putin's inner security detachment. He'd managed to get the information without exposing who he was or why he was collecting it. He sent it all across to Alex via their ongoing email draft thread.

"Gordon," Alex called, having gone to find the head of technical services, "I need you to map out the path of a series of mobiles. They should have all been on the same route, so once you have one back, it should tell us what we need to know. Is this something you can do?"

"How long ago are you talking?" If the information was too old, it might not still be readily available with the networks.

"It's recent. Last week or so." He didn't want to say anything about the source numbers--or the reason he was looking into where they had been--at that moment. There was still a thorough investigation going on, in collaboration with the police, into the death of Thomas Price. Because of his position, it was being treated as highly suspicious.

"Fine, leave it with me." The numbers were obviously Russian, that much was clear to him as he went off to get the process started.

Alex went back to join Anissa. She'd been trying to find out the latest from St Petersburg––she couldn't help but feel responsible for Josée still being locked up there, now awaiting trial herself––though getting news was proving harder to come by than she had thought. The French lawyer, maybe blaming Anissa in some way for the current situation, wasn't being as responsive as she'd been in the months before the original trial.

When Anissa finally did hear, things were reportedly still in limbo, and no date had yet been set, though the lawyer expected it to be in the next month or so. The lawyer then said she would let Anissa know as soon as she did—which Anissa doubted would be the case given her tone––and they ended the call.

Anissa updated Alex, who was by that point already standing next to her when she had finished speaking with the lawyer, before allowing Alex to fill her in on what Gordon had thought.

Now they just had to wait for information––doing nothing, not something that came naturally to either agent––so they instead started sifting through a pile of work that had been building up on their desks for the last few weeks.

IT WAS NEARLY lunchtime when Gordon knocked on the door. He wore a smile––which was instantly a good sign––together with his woollen jumper and his always a few seasons out-of-fashion glasses.

"I've been able to track all the numbers you gave me. They were in London last week." He didn't need to say any more; it was clear they all now knew these were the mobile devices in possession of the Putin party during his visit. "Aside from a period of silence, all the devices were operational from first being switched on," and Gordon pointed to a paper map he'd been opening on the table as he spoke, "here at Stansted Airport, until all the devices left from the same location in the evening."

"You said there was a period of silence?" Anissa said though she feared she already knew what this would show.

"Yes. All the devices at the same time––which is strange, though not impossible. But for such a long time, and considering there was obvious movement during that period, it is unusual that no other radio mast had picked them up before then. I mean, for there to be that much blackout and for so long within London, is a little surprising."

"So it's possible that the signal just dropped?"

"In London, it's possible in some patches that a signal might drop, yes. If a device is at an equal distance between two masts, then the signal can fluctuate between the two. When passing a tall building–– or going under a tunnel that hasn't yet been updated with the latest technology that allows radio waves and phone signals to continue–– then dropout does still occur." There was something in his tone that told them both he was keeping something back.

"But you don't think that happened in this case?" Alex said.

"No, almost certainly not. This route," and he made a line with his finger on the second map he'd opened––a more detailed map of Greater London––marking the space between the two points the mobile devices had radio silence, "has no tunnels, and the high tower-blocks are some way off. I also confirmed with British Telecom, only one radio mast services that area."

"So what caused the dropout?"

"It wasn't anything external, I'm almost certain. I suspect a cell phone jammer was deployed, taking out all their mobile devices at the same moment––more efficient than each being switched off simultaneously. We are talking eight separate devices here, after all."

"Is there any way that we can work out what route they took? Try to fill in the missing section?"

"I've had a thought about that," Gordon said, which didn't surprise them. Having worked out what they were looking for, his own natural interest then took over, and he dug as much as he could. "The challenge is there are multiple route options." It was like a coin drop game, no two paths were ever the same. "I did study their average speed both before losing the signal and then just after. Before the blackout, they'd been moving at around thirty-five miles an hour for the previous fifteen minutes, though some of that was on the motorway. After we pick up the signal again, they do an average of twenty-six miles an hour for the next ten. Even at this lower speed, they would have covered the section of radio blackout with about eight minutes to spare."

"So they didn't take a direct route?"

"That, or they stopped off somewhere."

"Would it have been possible that they went near the place Price was found?" Alex didn't need to say the specifics, nor really ask the question. He could tell that Gordon had not only asked himself that question, but had most probably already mapped out the diversion that would have taken the convoy to where the DDG's body had been found, and then on to where the signal was next seen.

"It's possible, yes. Even at thirty-eight miles an hour average--which is doable in these type of sides streets--there would have been time to get there and back." So he had indeed looked into it as Alex suspected, though his face suggested then he was about to throw a spanner in the works. "The only thing is, the timing doesn't work. Price would have still been alive when the signal came back on unless we got the time of death wrong?"

"No, that's as accurate as we can guess. We have Price on our own CCTV leaving on foot at around midday. Even if he ran--he was far from a runner, plus he was in business attire--he'd not have made it in time."

"And there are no CCTV images from the various streets the convoy might have used to give us a hint of where they went?" Alex said.

"No, and I've checked. Plenty of cameras, all temporarily offline at that point, most likely a wireless disruptor used that would block any camera footage." Both Alex and Anissa looked a little defeated by this until Gordon started drawing with red spots on the London map before them all. "But I correlated each of the unusual blackouts," he said, as he continued to make a path through the back streets--towards where Price's body was found--on the map below, "and this is what route they took."

"Gordon, you are a genius!" Anissa said, wanting to kiss him but she slapped him on the back instead.

They had the route. From the point the signals were lost for all the mobile phones in the convoy, to the point they were picked up again––and included with that was a significant diversion that had taken them down the exact road where Price would later be found dead.

"There's more," Gordon said, enjoying the obvious enthusiasm his work was being shown at that moment. "I timed the camera outages using a real-time process," he said, using the invisibility of the apparently blinded cameras to in fact show the passing of the convoy at that moment, give or take a few seconds. "These cameras here," and he pointed to the first dozen or so, the part of the route just after the mobile data went silent, "occur at the same average speed the convoy had been moving when we lost sight of them." They could see where he was going with this but waited in silence as he explained further. "But these ones," and he circled the gap between the two central cameras, which were two streets apart, "there was an eight-minute pause."

"They stopped."

"Exactly," Gordon said, triumph showing right across his face.

"This is bloody excellent work, Gordon," Alex said, breathing out in one long breath as if finally revealing some deeply buried secret. Anissa bent down and looked at the map, carefully inspecting where Gordon had drawn the circle.

"The alley where Price was found is just outside of this circle. What time did this camera go blind?" she said, tapping to the next one on the route, presumably once the convoy had started moving again.

"It was blind for around thirty seconds at twelve-twenty." Still, that was too early given Price's time of death.

"Might there have been an intercept before then?" Alex said, though tracing where Vauxhall House was––the route to the area that Price would have needed to take rather obvious now––the two paths didn't cross. They were each coming from the opposite direction.

"But the fact Putin and his convoy stopped at the exact same location where we know Price was--and where he later was found dead--surely isn't a coincidence? It's got to be connected."

"I've no doubt about that, but we still don't have enough."

"If you did, would you even be able to do anything with it?" Gordon said. "I mean, it's the President of Russia. What's he going to do, come across for questioning? It's a huge accusation even to suggest he had any involvement."

"But look, if this doesn't cast doubt on his innocence, I don't know what does?"

"Anissa, no one outside of these walls has any clue that he's even remotely involved. We need more before taking this upstairs." By upstairs, he meant to the Director General himself. A state-sponsored assassination--and by the Russian President himself, even if he hadn't actually been the one to do the act--would cause an international conflict.

"More? I mean, we have his route, we have him being there what, maybe twenty minutes before Price drops dead?"

"The non-appearance on a set of CCTV cameras wouldn't prove to any judge that he was guilty of involvement. It works for us to build an idea, but I don't think we can prove much beyond that. Plus it was Sasha who gave us the mobile numbers."

"I think I could have obtained them from the mobile networks here, anyway," Gordon chipped in, "I mean, a group of Russian origin SIM cards travelling together like that would have been easy to spot. So if it comes out, you can land that one on me. I'll say I sourced the numbers for you and used them to track the route."

"That's a good option, Gordon, well done," Alex said, "but I've got a better idea. We need to find out what actually took place if Putin actually met with Price. Such a meeting would never have taken place on the street, and we now know where the convoy seemingly paused for eight minutes. We need to find that barman."

"The barman who gave the police Price's name when the body was found?"

"Exactly. He knew who the victim was. We find out who this man is, I think we find out a lot more."

They could all see there was logic in his thinking. The information Gordon had put in front of them was good--it was an agent's dream to be able to see where others didn't want you to follow--but to take this on any further, to fully understand what was going on, they still needed more. Finding this barman, who presumably worked at the place where the meeting might have occurred, would give them a lot of answers. Alex grabbed his jacket.

"There's no point waiting here any more Anissa, so let's go, we have some canvassing to do," and he patted Gordon on the back, before putting on his jacket, Anissa following him out through the door and down the stairs to his car.

25

It was a beautiful autumnal day in Monaco, as Matvey Filipov finished writing out in precise English a paper he'd been working on, his French just not good enough yet, despite the years he'd been living there. He mostly operated in English or Russian. The fact he lived in Monaco was merely a side issue--he did very little actual business there or in France, though it was true some of his subsidiaries did do their own selling to the region.

He called in one of his men--he always had people available to run errands, people to do his dirty work--and instructed the man to take the sealed envelope and deliver it to a particular address. The address in question was a professional translator from English to French. The man left Matvey's office and took the document with him.

It was the following morning when the translated document was returned to Matvey. The translator--someone Matvey had used many times before when needing to word something correctly in the local language, had called him up the previous day after getting the document. It wasn't what he usually translated. Matvey--through a few minutes of listening to the man go on and on--became very blunt. He was being paid well to do a job--so he should just get on with it, therefore, and stop wasting his time was all the Russian asked.

Taking out the translation--he had no idea if it was any good, though he could make out some of the words--Matvey saw that his warning had worked. If the translation was anything other than what he'd demanded, there would be a high and swift price to pay.

He called in another man--a different one to the day before, as it was never good to allow one employee to know too much of his own personal business dealings. He gave this man the newly translated document, to which he'd added another sheet of paper covered in handwriting and a sealed envelope, provided yet another address, this time further north, a three-hour drive in fact from where they were.

"I need you to take this straight away to this man," Matvey indicated. The man in question was an expert forger, who specialised in handwriting and writing style. "Tell him he has three days to produce the goods, and the final product needs to be on this," and he handed his man a standard-issue legal notepad, as was common in France.

The man left his presence, Matvey going to a window and just standing there--something he liked to do and did very often--watching the water below. The sea had always fascinated him. Large and powerful, unforgiving too, the calm of the surface not giving any hint to the great depths or hidden dangers that might lurk just below. Just like himself at that moment.

IT'D BEEN a frustrating week of little progress for Alex and Anissa, as they had exhausted their search in that part of London based on the coordinates Gordon had given them. In the three-block area--nothing was that precise in this particular part of Old London town--they'd called in on all the possible places they were aware of.

There were only two they hadn't been allowed instant access: an Italian owned restaurant which was renowned for Mafia gatherings, and a private Gentleman's club, the two bouncers on the door just denying them access without a warrant. MI5 had confirmed they had been watching the Italian for some time.

When a warrant was finally issued for both, they returned. The Italian was empty of all but two couples, who continued to chat, oblivious of the two agents who were having a look around.

The bar staff were all female, and Italian––when Anissa asked about a man who might have worked there they said they didn't know him. The police report from the officer who'd spoken to the barman hadn't placed him as being unmistakably Italian, either.

When they went across the road to Duke's––this time with a warrant in hand which Alex held out before him––the same two bouncers who'd stopped them last time were at least a little more polite. They had seen the two agents arrive earlier to the Italian, taking in the fact that they now appeared to have a warrant which had allowed them access to that previously off-limits location, and they had then made their own guests aware.

The club was therefore empty as Alex and Anissa walked in from the stairway and through the double doors. The four patrons, who had been sitting there five minutes before, had been shown down the rear fire-escape stairway and were now nowhere near the building.

Alex looked around the room––small booths at the edges, a stage at one end, which was opposite the bar, and some sort of dance floor in the middle. The place was empty, besides one man standing behind the bar. Quite why two bouncers and a barman were needed for a place that was empty during the day beat them.

"Hello, can I help you officers?" the barman said, the word having been instantly communicated upstairs following their arrival, which explained the quietness. Neither agent bothered to produce their ID. The barman knew who they were––he at least thought they were police, which was as good as he'd get.

"Is it normally this quiet in here?" There were three dirty cups on the edge of the counter which the barman was removing, dropping them into trays, presumably for cleaning later.

"Comes alive mainly in the evening."

"This is a private members' club, correct?" Anissa said. "Men only, too?"

"We have some women," the barman smiled, before going serious. "Yes, it's a private Gentleman's club. One of the finest establishments in London."

She didn't doubt it, though the decor was plush, at best, and the ludicrous idea that a gentleman could possibly be someone who spent their nights watching naked women dance was always a bizarre notion to her. Her husband was a gentleman and had never seen the need to go to a strip club, which was all that place basically was, come the evenings. Cheap, slutty thrills.

"Have you ever seen this man," Alex said, holding out a photo of Thomas Price--not in uniform, so as not to give anything away--Alex himself glancing down at the image. Anissa didn't take her eyes off the barman.

"Can't say I have," he said, automatically, not having even glanced at the photo. That either meant he was not allowed to answer such questions about their clients, or he already knew why they were both there.

"Last week this man was found dead in an alley not far from here."

"Like I said, no clue about that, guv'nor." Suddenly he'd gone cockney on them, as he dropped the last of the dirty glasses into the tray and started hanging clean glasses upside down above the bar.

"And you didn't hear anything last week about the incident when it happened? Didn't see the police tape, the cars?"

"No, I probably was either working in here, or at home." There seemed an evasiveness about him, and he avoided eye contact with Anissa the whole time.

Alex left the man his card--they could both see they weren't getting anywhere--and went.

"He was hiding something," Anissa said when they were outside, walking back across the street and now out of earshot of the two bouncers

"Yes, possibly. Maybe he just can't answer questions about the place."

"We've covered every possible venue that Price might have been heading to. He'd been drinking heavily for a little while. His blood alcohol count was very high at the time of his death. He'd clearly been somewhere around here. Someone in his state couldn't have walked very far."

"That's assuming the murder happened where we found the body."

"But then again, who would risk carrying it very far before leaving it there? It was during the day."

"I've left my number," Alex said, which he had at several places, "so we'll just have to see if someone is willing to talk when we aren't face to face."

FIVE MINUTES after the two British agents left Duke's, the barman was on his telephone. The first two guests had started to return to the building, now that the coast was once again clear.

"I just had two officers in here asking about Price," the barman said. He retold the short account on what had happened.

"Thank you," the accented voice said in reply, "do nothing about it at the moment. I'll keep you posted," and the line went dead. The barman replaced the handset, as two more guests came back in through the doors. It was as if these politicians and businessmen could sense the danger that had just been there and stayed away. Indeed, the bouncers had warned two members from entering when Alex and Anissa were still upstairs. Now they were safe again. Now they could carry on their secret little conversations––conversations the barman, and therefore those who employed the staff there––were always aware of. It was priceless information.

26

As the nights started to draw in across St Petersburg––though it was hardly night, darkness falling around five already as autumn gave way to winter––the political system in Russia was starting to heat up, at a time when outdoor temperatures were plummeting.

By mid-December, three independent voices had named themselves as standing to challenge Putin at the following year's elections. It was big news around the world, let alone just Russia.

For British viewers, the announcement that London-based Kaminski was running for President, was met with a mixed reception. The stories from a few months before––in what had been a turbulent year for the Russian oligarch––started to resurface again after his self-nomination. Questions were raised by a few British newspapers as to whether a man who had seen his own bank collapse––leaving hundreds unemployed and tens of thousands with personal losses––could ethically be allowed to step forward at all. *Where was the money coming from to put together a campaign?* some said.

Matvey Filipov's name was less well known in the UK, though it came as a big surprise in Russia. Alex and Anissa devoured the reports, once again becoming fascinated in what was now finally a very public challenge––a very public race for the Presidency.

The final independent––someone who had a small but loyal following from Far Eastern Russia, enough to get a nomination––had run unsuccessfully before at two previous campaigns. He was not a vastly wealthy man, certainly not compared to his challengers in the race so far.

As independents––men who were not affiliated with a political party––they were required to step forward by that date in December. Putin was already on the ticket––as incumbent President, in the middle of a possible twelve-year term––it was no real surprise when he'd been the first to put himself forward in September. Within a month, by about the 18th January to be exact, the other parties in Russia would nominate their own challengers. Therefore another three––maybe four names––would be added to the four which were now already on the list. Campaigning started straight away.

The first round of public debates––the American style debates which were also increasingly popular in Russia, becoming explosive in 2012––were expected to be even more explosive this time around. As always, candidates were timed carefully. They would face off one against the other––there would be no mass debates between the challengers, but lots of individual head-to-heads. Putin himself wouldn't be involved in these until February. It was for the lesser men––it seemed––to prove themselves against the other challengers before they could be allowed to stand before their President, in front of millions via the live television coverage, and make their case.

It was always noticeable how the various candidates approached such debates. Some men were argumentative, really going at the character of the other person, accusing them of selling out their beloved Russia to the West. All would have to appear strong––men ready to fight one another at any moment, and indeed, fights often broke out, though never between the Presidential candidates themselves. But the threat needed to be there. Voters needed to see someone who could get tough when they needed to, who could stare down an enemy by the strength of their argument, while also being prepared to silence them at any moment with the power of their fists if needed.

Anissa watched from home as the announcements were made––to have her two boys running around the lounge, the Christmas tree on the floor ready to be put up that coming weekend and to see the names of Dmitry Kaminski and Matvey Filipov talked about in the open, as Presidential candidates, made it all very surreal. Something she'd been on the inside of for months––something she'd not been able to talk about with anyone at home––was now public knowledge, though how much the public would indeed be told was another matter entirely.

At least it was all out in the open. At least that much was known. In her pursuit of justice––if that was really what she and Alex were pursuing now––over the previous few years, so much of it had pointed towards this very event.

The race for the Kremlin.

Could either of these men––she hadn't heard of the third independent, though from what the reports were saying, it was clear he wasn't a genuine threat––really challenge Putin? A President who had served nearly fourteen years already over two periods as President, and someone whom most saw as a shoo-in for another six. Did either Kaminski or Filipov have the ground level support that would then be enough to challenge Putin? Would their joint involvement––therefore potentially splitting the votes of those who might want a change––still mean Putin would stay in power by default? Was not a united, unified opponent the best approach? These were the thoughts of those now discussing the news on a BBC show as Anissa sat there in silence and listened.

She certainly knew that for some in power––including her own former Deputy Director General––it was precisely what they had hoped. In Kaminski, they felt there was a man who could be the figure of opposition. His own downfall––as well as Matvey Filipov's nomination––had changed that picture dramatically.

Anissa thought of her former DDG. Had Putin somehow got to him? What did that say about the man who wanted another six years in office? What would that mean for the UK? She understood the desire to see a change in the political system––though knowing what she knew of Matvey, and the shadows he liked to dwell in, she was now concerned that he was potentially just as bad as Putin.

Should she take on board what Price had started? Was Kaminski the right man for the job? Should Britain even be having a say in another country's electoral process? She knew the answer to that one before she'd even formed the question.

The BBC finished their five-minute special report looking at the front-runners of the 2018 Russian Presidential elections––they seemingly already had their own logo for the event––with the news that the first of the debates was already about to be held in Russia the following week. It was the third of these debates––going out live on Christmas Eve––that most interested her. That would pit Matvey Filipov against Dmitry Kaminski. She would have to find a way of somehow watching that particular contest. Before that, both men would give the third independent candidate a run for his money. She was sure neither would be a fair fight––and so it would prove.

As the week progressed, the BBC continued their growing focus on the Russian political situation. The British Broadcasting Corporation was well known to have held a particular disdain for Russia and its practices and laws over the last decade, and that picture of a nation of thugs and lawbreakers was what led their lunchtime bulletin, as Anissa sat next to Alex at Vauxhall House.

"We're outside a Kaminski stop-off point on his tour around Moscow, and the scenes have been quite disturbing," the reporter in Russia said to the camera, the newsroom host then warning the audience that some viewers might find the following video offensive, as it cut to something that had been shown earlier.

"Men who have simply dubbed themselves the *Kaminski Enforcers* have been roaming the streets all night. At midnight they find their first gay couple," and the voiceover on the video being shown then went silent, as a mob of at least eight men are seen grabbing and punching two men, the first man knocked to the ground straight away, the other seen running off. The man on the ground was then kicked repeatedly until the footage was pixellated as just too graphic to show, the attackers heard shouting in clear Russian, their faces covered, as subtitles now came across the English screens: *When Kaminski is President, your lot will be burnt at the stake! Russia is no place for gays! Russia is our nation!* And the chanting repeated itself. It was one of the several videos that had been posted online over the last few days.

The camera went back live to the venue in Moscow, the reporter with his finger to his ear before speaking again into the camera.

"Those scenes were recorded last night, and they are not isolated events, either. The Kaminski camp––the man known to hold strict orthodox views in regards to homosexuality––has declined to comment though his office had released a statement which says they do not endorse violence of any kind, against anyone.

"And Philip, these are not limited to just groups associated to Dmitry Kaminski, are they? There have been pro-Putin, United Russia members seemingly doing similar things as well."

"That's right, Andrew," the Moscow-based reporter said, the camera back on him after the brief question from the newsroom in London. "Overnight a video was taken down from United Russia's official VKontakte social media page," and the video started to play on half the screen as the reporter continued to speak. "In this attack, a group of three people, two men and one woman, and dressed obviously as Muslims––later confirmed to be brothers and sister––were jumped on by a group of four men. All aggressors shouting pro-Putin propaganda," and a baseball bat appeared then on the video being played. The two Muslim men who were now on the floor were being repeatedly struck across their backs and legs as their sister pleaded with the attackers to stop. The men eventually did stop, punching the female in the face before moving off camera. "All extremely anti-Muslim. The three victims in this attack––and this is far from an isolated incident––were recent immigrants from the Caucuses––an area of the former Soviet Union which has for many years been very troubled and unsettled."

"And has United Russia made a comment on the action of these supporters?" the studio asked.

"Yes, as well as taking down the video––something they say was not posted officially by them but was the result of a hack––they have strongly condemned what happened in this video, as well as some other reported situations. They have stated that anyone carrying out such an attack was not a friend of Russia and that the Party would take seriously any allegations of violent behaviour towards any citizen. There have been no arrests made, however, following either attack."

"Philip, why all of a sudden are we seeing these types of events on our screens?"

"Andrew, what we've just witnessed isn't anything new. In fact, following the anti-homosexuality laws of two years ago, as well as the religious laws passed last year, these types of heavy-handed incidents have been on the rise. Clearly, the upcoming elections have focused such efforts––and while both candidates will be distancing themselves from such horrific events as we've just witnessed––you have to fear that such things will continue to happen, especially given their leaders outspoken views on these issues.

"It was Putin's own party––United Russia––which brought in these two new laws within the last couple of years, views that maybe Kaminski himself shares with his electoral rival?"

"Dmitry Kaminski––well known in the UK of course for his business side of things, and who famously lost control of his own bank earlier this year, at the cost of hundreds of jobs––whilst not outspoken on the matter, is privately known for his anti-homosexual policy. Four years ago, in a failed lawsuit, a former employee had claimed wrongful dismissal based on the fact he'd announced on social media the week before he was fired that he was gay."

"Indeed, interesting times," the studio said, coming back to London and moving on with the next story. Anissa switched off the computer at that moment.

"So, what do you think?" Anissa said, turning to Alex.

"It's ugly, that's for sure. And yet, there are still four months until the actual election. Get Gordon to have a look at these videos, though, see if he can make any sense of who these attackers were."

"Alex, these things took place in Russia. Besides, the attackers aren't easily identifiable. What do you expect to be able to do?"

"I don't know. Maybe work out who they are. Assuming there will be more incidents––I think that's an unfortunate certainty, given that the reporting of such events only gives rise to others doing likewise–– it'll be useful to know if it's the same group of aggressors each time, or multiple people."

"That's a good thought."

It was three days before Kaminski and Filipov were due to go head-to-head in their own debate. Dmitry had done well in the first one, which was before any of the videos had emerged online, and Matvey was due to face the other independent later that day.

27

"No, no, no, no, no!" Anissa screamed, dropping her phone onto the table, before falling in a heap on the floor. Tears were already pouring down her face as Alex ran in from the corridor to see what the problem was. He'd never seen Anissa in such a state.

A few minutes before, Anissa had taken a call from the French lawyer.

It's Josée, she had said, herself holding back tears, Anissa instantly on edge, the mere mention of the Frenchwoman's name enough to stop her in her tracks. *She's killed herself, Anissa, she's hung herself in the cell. I'm so sorry to have to tell you.*

"What is it, Anissa?" Alex said, coming alongside his colleague, as a few other heads poked around the door seemingly searching for the source of all the screaming. It was five minutes before Alex could calm her enough to understand what had happened.

Half an hour later they were sitting together in the canteen. They'd managed to call back the lawyer––she'd been happy to hear from Anissa again as there was something she needed to share with her––and the lawyer detailed a little more of what had happened.

Josée had been found the night before. It'd been four hours since her last meal had been brought to her––something she'd clearly not touched––when she was found hanging from a sheet tied to a metal girder in the ceiling. She had left a note––Anissa asked for a copy of it––which talked all about her reasons for ending her life, her misery, her sadness. She'd confessed to the crime, and more––she'd implicated a Russian in it all.

Anissa had quizzed her as to who had been implicated by Josée, and it took a while for the lawyer to mutter the name: Kaminski. Dmitry Kaminski, the man standing for President.

The fax came across while they were still in the canteen, Gordon himself bringing it to them. He had passable French, though they would pass it to an expert to get it fully translated.

"What does it say?" Anissa said, feeling as responsible for it all as much as anyone. If the note implied it was Anissa's fault––she already felt the blame for it all anyway––it would be too much. Her own guilt was more than enough to deal with, let alone if Josée, in her last moments, had blamed Anissa for her desperate situation before hanging herself. It would be more than she could cope with, Anissa knew that already.

"She says she can't go on anymore. She can't live with herself, not with what she has done, not with what she knows. She apologises for taking the coward's exit," Gordon said––pointing out it was a peculiar use of the phrase––before continuing to roughly translate, "but she couldn't live with the shame anymore. She says it was Dmitry Kaminski who got her into the event, that he hired her to represent him and that he knew her personally and had met with her before her arrival in Russia. She states he said he would protect her, but he hadn't. She was now in prison, with no obvious end to things, and Dmitry––a man she'd loved far more than she had told him––was now running for President as if she never existed. As if all they'd shared together now counted for nothing."

"That's it?" Anissa said, no mention of her own name in the note, no blame being obviously dished out her way unless Gordon had skipped that section or his translation skills had somehow missed it. Though how hard would it be to misunderstand: *I blame Anissa for this—she made me testify, she made me come to St Petersburg. And now look at everything. It's because of that stupid bitch that I've killed myself. She did this to me.*

"That's it."

"Are you sure?"

"Anissa, she doesn't blame you," Gordon said, understanding exactly why Anissa wanted to make sure. "I'll pass it to the experts, and you can read the transcript yourself."

She breathed out audibly. Inside something heavy had shifted—not a lot, but there was movement. Maybe Josée wasn't blaming her.

"You okay?" Alex asked, now just the two of them again, as Gordon left them, no doubt on his way to get the note expertly worked on.

"Yes, I will be. I still can't help but feel guilty."

"She doesn't blame you, so maybe you shouldn't either. Besides, she's directly implicated Kaminski for her being in St Petersburg in the first place. That's what you wanted, that's why you went to trial."

"This isn't how I wanted it to come about, though," she said, defensively, but softened as she looked Alex in the face. He wasn't the enemy, he was only trying to help. "It wasn't meant to end like this."

"I know, Anissa, I know. It's a crappy situation, but she's just handed us a lifeline."

"A lifeline?" Maybe it was the wrong choice of phrase, considering Josée was now dead. "Some lifeline for Josée."

GORDON HANDED them the English language version just before two––an hour after a British tabloid had published an article reporting the same on their website. The website promised to lead with the full exclusive story the following day, implicating British-based Kaminski in the murder of a man in Russia––the unnamed janitor in their online report––as well as some twisted love affair with a French personal trainer, before she recently committed suicide. It was precisely the type of sleazy story that that particular tabloid loved to print. How the hell they got the story, Anissa had yet to find out.

The note--part of the original, handwritten letter in French and pictured in colour in a prominent place on the website--was the same one the British had been faxed, though the English translation differed just a tiny bit in style. That ruled out the MI6 translation source as being the leak, at least.

28

It was the morning of the third round of debates--the one Anissa was most looking forward to watching--between Kaminski and Filipov.

All the previous day and that morning the papers across the UK were running with the story that had broken concerning Kaminski. With little else happening around the world, it seemed to spend longer on the front pages than might have otherwise been merited.

All sorts of conspiracy theories were being made up--the Kaminski camp had vehemently denied any connection--though no one had faced a camera and said that. That would inevitably happen that evening at the debate, which was already estimated to have the highest viewing figures yet, and that was before this story had even broken. The timing was terrible for the Kaminski camp, who had been running a robust underground campaign themselves for a few years, though they had seen things start to get out of hand for them increasingly over the last twelve months.

Overnight more videos had started to circulate--copy-cat actions of violence, it was assumed--across many cities, all in the name of either Putin or Kaminski, Muslims and homosexuals once more the targets. One Syrian man was in hospital--he was not expected to survive the week, his injuries had been that serious.

Putin had yet to feature in the debates by that stage--that was nothing new. Six years previously the same had been true. Then, the Sokoloff backed state television channels had carefully covered the debates, while all the time allowing seemingly unlimited airtime for Putin, who would be asked similar questions to those who had just been involved in the debate. Before a camera, and with no opposition, Putin had always come across much better than those argumentative types who had just taken part in a live show, Putin's official challengers--if they could even really be called that.

That time around--before Putin had even been involved in a debate--the polls had the would-be President with a thirty point lead. The debates had worked against his challengers.

This year that was all changed. With Putin remaining silent--a situation he'd allowed to happen, agreeing to take part in the debates only once things got a little more serious, when the elections were just a couple of months away--both oligarchs were coming across well on screen. They had effectively laid waste already to the other independent who was standing, his challenge all but over.

As the latest polls came out that morning--with the two oligarchs set to go head-to-head themselves that evening--crucially they were now level with Putin; something that would have been unheard of a few years back.

Without Sokoloff's relentless media push backing Putin every inch of the way, actual media exposure for any of the candidates had more of an impact in this upcoming election than it had ever done before. There was a genuine chance that by the conclusion of that evening's live debate--it was to be the last before the end of the year, sending Russians into their New Year festivities with a very positive image of at least one challenger--one, if not both of the oligarchs, could actually be ahead of Putin in the polls.

Of course, there was a long way to go. Once Putin got in front of the cameras himself--he was a pro at saying just the right thing at just the right time--then it could all change. The videos of obvious

Putin supporters—patriotic and applauding some of the hardline actions that were being shown online—could go either way.

Across Russia, Putin held the power of the general population. He was popular across the towns and villages. In fact, had the 2012 election been based on votes in the cities of Moscow and St Petersburg—hugely significant and influential centres in Russia—then Medvedev would have easily won. It was the broader vote that saw Putin return to power. The propaganda machine had done its work—despite the majority in the capital going with the current President at the time—it was the voice of the people far and wide, their sheer mass that won the day, and the election, therefore, for Putin. It was the voice of the media that had put Putin into every home and on every radio and in every newspaper right across the nation.

That was a voice that no longer had the chance to ring out. For the first time in modern Russia, that voice had been silenced. And now the polls were starting to record the outworking of that, putting the Putin camp into panic mode for sure.

Moscow's main arena had been made available for the third live debate. That allowed an audience of thousands in, though it was the estimated fifty-five million television audience that was the most significant draw. That represented nearly eighty per cent of people who might then turn up and vote.

Security was very tight. The audience—pre-selected people who were primarily residents of Moscow—were screened and checked before being allowed into the arena. A large number of journalists—not just Russian-based, but some of the world's biggest players—were also present. This was beginning to be global news, in much the same way that the US election had been. Might one of these two men be the one who played hard-ball with the new American incumbent? A billionaire President to go nose-to-nose against their billionaire President.

At eight Moscow time, the presenter entered the staging area, Anissa watching back in the UK where it was only five in the afternoon. The entire setup looked more like a game show than a political arena, though that was how things were going. She wasn't sure if she liked that. At least the British didn't go in for such theatrics.

Matvey Filipov was the first to take the stage, being generously received by the audience. Neither man was local––in fact, both were notorious now for not living in Russia, the only accusation that the other independent candidate had managed to make stick in the first two debates. Matvey spent most of the year in Monaco, Dmitry in London. Their opponent had argued: how could Russians vote for a man who didn't even consider his country worth living in?

When Dmitry walked out a minute later––after another lengthy, wordy introduction, more like two prize fighters entering the ring than would-be politicians––the crowd once again showing their enthusiasm. Clearly, both men had made sure they had some of their own supporters in that select and noisy mass.

Everything was done in Russian, of course. Anissa wouldn't be able to understand a word therefore as she watched it live, prepared to work through it all again at a later point to understand what was said. She wasn't watching it live for words, however, but all the other things the men were about to communicate. Would it get personal, or would they focus on their own policies? Would they unite in a common purpose against Putin? Or would there be direct conflict between the two men?

The show was an hour long. The format dictated that after each man had their forty-five seconds to outline their main stance. The opening forty-five seconds had been used by both oligarchs in the previous debates broadly to talk about their own policies, whereas their opponent each time had not held back from accusing both men of hypocrisy. They would then ask questions directly to the man standing opposite them, who would do his best to answer before asking his own question in reply. And so it would proceed, back and forth, no doubt getting more heated as the night went on.

Anissa had seen very little of either man––certainly far less of Matvey. She'd met Dmitry personally at a London conference the other year when she had headed up the security element with Alex. They had managed to mingle and get close to the man.

They had also once listened in on one of his meetings with Thomas Price, which had been when they'd first learnt he was going to run for President. She'd never really seen much of Matvey. How they would both handle themselves was going to be fascinating––she'd been tracking them for months, trying to pick apart their sinister little world, that it now felt surreal to actually be watching them on television, right there and in the flesh. Two men she knew to be a part of the Games. Two men who would be keeping that aspect of their life secret, for sure.

The host motioned for Dmitry to start speaking first––a large forty-five appeared in the centre of the debating floor. It started counting down as he spoke.

"Good citizens of Russia, it's time for a change. Gone are the days of one man dominating our nation, gone are the days of unequalled influence across our great land. We are a country that should be standing strong, we are a proud nation and one I will make proud again. No longer will other nations be able to take our honour away as freely as they take our gas, oil and minerals. I believe in a Russia that is united, not in the United Russia that Putin leads, a party of crooks and criminals, but a truly global family. The Russia I know we can be––the Russia our proud nation deep down has always been," and the counter hit zero, the crowd responding positively to what had been said.

Anissa had picked up the name Putin being mentioned––clearly making reference to a man not currently standing in front of him, who couldn't, therefore, defend himself. But that was expected.

The number forty-five once again appeared in the middle of the staging area, now that the crowd had quietened down, and the presenter turned to Matvey, the camera zooming in on his ageing, though still full of vitality, face. His greying hair gave him a commanding stage presence. He looked straight at the camera––which was behind Kaminski, to appear to be staring down his opponent as well, and started to speak.

"My great nation does indeed need a new vision, but this will not be brought about by someone like Kaminski, who has spent too long in London for his own good. No one who is that cosy with the West will ever be able to lead my country! Remember the way he treated this woman," and he picked up a piece of paper, Anissa not needing to understand what was being said to recognise it was a copy of Josée's suicide note. "That made him an accomplice in the murder of an innocent man. We know that from the woman's own lips--and it was your lies," and he was pointing directly at Dmitry now, the camera focusing on Kaminski suddenly at that point, building on the drama, "which caused her tragically to take her own life. And you stand there and talk about honour? Where's the honour in being declared bankrupt? In hundreds of jobs being lost and billions wasted? You think our country will be safe in your hands--never!" and the studio lights darkened as the time elapsed, the crowd erupting. Kaminski looked rattled. It had evidently become severely personal.

The presenter--a man unfazed by this sort of thing, a veteran of many debates--turned to Kaminski and told the oligarch; "You may now ask a question."

Kaminski paused for a second--clearly, the blow was still wearing off--before he seemed to form some element of order in his own mind again, his eyes darting around a little before he focused in on Matvey.

"You seem to be very easily led on, citizen Filipov," and by using the term '*citizen*, in that context, it was demeaning, as if saying he wasn't a contender, he was just one of the crowd, "if you believe what some tabloid newspaper might make up about me. Tell me, if you should win--which I doubt--are you going to remain so gullible then? Are you going to believe everything you get shown--despite it being a complete lie--and just run with it? Is that how you are going to lead, by accepting every lie? Because, believe me, you aren't fit to be our President. You need to seriously check out your facts before you jump to conclusions."

"Your question?" the presenter said, as he often needed to in such debates, as each man filled their seconds with multiple questions.

"Are you such a gullible man, citizen Filipov?"

The camera focused in on Matvey.

"I'm neither gullible nor a fool, something you appear to be. You think you can just brush this under the carpet? I for one will make sure that this woman sees justice, even if she is no longer alive to see you fall. It takes a brave man to make ten billion dollars––that doesn't happen to gullible people, nor to fools. To lose two billion, however––that only happens to foolish people." He didn't say any more.

"Your question, Mr Filipov," the presenter said now that it was Matvey's turn to ask.

"Having so gravely mishandled billions upon billions of dollars–– both your own money and vast amounts of other peoples––tell me, Kaminski, how in the world do you even think you are now qualified to run our country when you can't even run your own business empire?"

He wasn't holding back now. The camera focused in on Dmitry, who stayed silent, longer than was currently comfortable as if he didn't know how to begin his answer, as if he didn't know how to sound anything other than what Matvey Filipov was now portraying him as. He couldn't say how he'd been targeted––by Matvey himself––because that would expose the Games. Even if that wasn't bad enough, it would play right into Matvey's hands, proving to the Russian people that Matvey Filipov was a stronger opponent than he was. So he couldn't go there––he doubted that Matvey would go there either, though the way he'd started, he wouldn't rule it out completely.

"Russia has always operated from the top down. Men like Putin–– men like citizen Filipov standing across from me––who like to tell all of you what to do. I believe in strong leadership, and I'm prepared to be that, but not at the expense of my people. I believe that there is enough talent and there are enough entrepreneurs in our nation for the masses to be released and make our country proud. I believe that the days when men like Filipov––who openly boasts about the billions that he has accumulated just for himself––are over. These days are over. Russia needs to become more democratic. I want to give more power to the people!" That statement got some thunderous cheers from some aspects of the audience, but noticeable jeers from other sections, too.

The debate continued back and forth, each man asking the other increasingly scathing questions. *Did you recruit Josée in St Petersburg? Why did you so wholly mismanage your Banking Union? Are you a product of the West, someone willing to sell out our nation to minor powers?*

Kaminski did enough to fight back where he could--*had he personally gone out to destroy Dmitry Sokoloff*--being one of the most, to the uninformed observer, off-topic questions. He was apparently getting desperate.

As nine o'clock came round, the show came to an end. Anissa sat there speechless for a moment--she couldn't wait to see the transcript of this encounter when it was ready. Right now home was calling. It was Christmas Eve and already late. Time for a few days off.

AS THE CROWDS left the arena, polls were already being conducted around the country that night. They would report that Matvey now held a five-point lead over Putin, Kaminski himself dropping to one point behind the current President into third place. Round three of the debates had apparently gone in Matvey's favour.

Anissa picked up this information later that day, relaying it to Alex, who was home but doing very little. Without a family, Christmas Eve wasn't that much of an occasion for him. He would spend the following day with some friends.

Gordon Peacock had earlier sent through a list of faces from the various videos that kept appearing online--various anti-Islam or homophobic attacks. He soon noticed a match in some of the faces, particularly across the two groups. Groups that were meant to represent two different candidates, yet the men carrying out these attacks were often the same. He immediately compiled the faces onto one file--taking what he could find to be the best images from the various videos that they'd managed to pull from the internet before they were removed--and emailed them across to Alex.

Alex opened the message almost immediately, the notification coming through on his phone while the adverts were on during yet another Christmas film that was being shown. He decided it was too late to let Anissa know immediately; she would no doubt by that point be putting two very excited sons to bed and getting ready for Christmas Day herself. Instead, he dropped the file into the draft email message he had going with Sasha.

He wished the Russian a Merry Christmas––forgetting that for Russians it was all about New Year. For them, Christmas fell in January, solely a religious celebration. He missed Sasha at that moment, he realised––the thought making him stop short for just a few seconds. Were his closest relationships really only with fellow security service personnel?––be that within his own MI6, or further afield in the Russian's case? And what did that mean anyway even if that was true? Did that make him a bad person? Did that make him a loner in real life?

He realised that Sasha would be on his own, too, when he celebrated New Year. The last two years they had been able to join Sasha in Russia for that holiday––not officially, but there with him nonetheless. This year that wasn't possible––Anissa wasn't even allowed into the country anymore, not for five years anyhow. Might as well be forever, Alex thought, as far as his colleague was concerned.

Russia had affected her significantly, he knew it, they all did in the office.

Josée's death might just have been the last straw. And for what? What had they really achieved, what had they actually managed to bring to the table that they could use? What criminal activity––and they were clear, there had been loads of it––could they actually prosecute anyone over?

Alex watched the last half hour of the film he'd seen several times before and started to clear things away, dropping a now empty wine bottle into the recycling box. His wine glass was placed in the sink to be dealt with in the morning. Like all workaholics, however, he checked his computer before going up to bed. There was a short reply from Sasha. Clearly, the man was up very late.

"Thanks for this, I'll run the faces tomorrow through the mainframe and see what I can find out. Will be in touch. Merry Christmas to you too," he said, returning the greeting despite the next day being an average working day in Russia.

Alex smiled to himself, climbing the narrow flight of stairs up to his room and ten minutes later was in bed. It had gone midnight--Christmas Day had come.

29

Politically, not a lot would happen in Russia over the last week of December, when the life of the average Russian would build up in intensity, until the novogodnaya yolka—New Year tree—was purchased on the 31st and families started to finally celebrate.

Businesses began to wind down during this time—as did their leaders and owners—as Russia prepared for its ten day holiday at the beginning of January.

In the Presidential race, there would be no more polling until the fourth debate was finished, which would happen after the holidays when life was beginning to speed up again. A week after the holiday ended, all the candidates for the upcoming Presidential elections, less than two months away, would have been named. The date for the screening of the fourth live debate was timed to be able to include two of those yet to be announced contenders.

Kaminski would spend his first New Year in Moscow for a long time—the T20 events which usually took place in St Petersburg over that particular holiday were no longer happening. It would be the first time in the group's twelve year history that they hadn't gathered together at that time of year. It already seemed surreal. He felt a little disconnected.

He recognised that the group––the connections––had been good for him. Had it not been for his involvement in the Games over the last decade plus, he knew he wouldn't be in the position he was now in, running for the Presidency. He'd been a nobody before––yes, a billionaire, but there were plenty of them in Russia back then.

Not quite as many of that original group of oligarchs now remained, but plenty of New Russians with their expensive lifestyles were trying, anyway, to fill the gaps.

In reality, the gap between the super rich and just the rich had been snowballing. They would never catch up, and for every oligarch that fell––Sokoloff, Krupin, Kuznetsov even––it only made the others richer.

Kaminski pondered that some would most probably also add his own name to that list as someone who had fallen. And it was partly true. He'd lost a lot––more than he should ever have allowed to happen––and he'd seen it coming. There had been little he could do about it once he'd put himself in a vulnerable situation.

Of course, someone would find out about it.

Still, once he was President, he could change all that. He knew that he couldn't allow Matvey Filipov to win though he wondered how he would be viewed by the President if Putin remained in power, especially after some of the things he had said openly about Putin in the first debate.

Kaminski knew that the British had put a lot of faith––placed a lot of trust––in him, something that they were expecting a return on. He was sure they wouldn't stay around for long if everything they'd been working on with him now collapsed.

Yet Putin knew.

His meeting with Price––on the day he was killed, Kaminski knowing there was no coincidence there––had really shaken him. How much did the President know about him now? Had he known all along?

With Price out of the way––he'd been the spokesman from the

British side of things for many years as the UK courted Kaminski––it made that connection a little strained. Would there be someone else to liaise with? Price had always talked about there being support for him from within the government––had that just been spy talk, or was it true? Kaminski cursed himself for not having got a better understanding of where he stood. If he wasn't successful––his first debate with Matvey hadn't gone as well as he'd hoped, and the polls now suggested he'd dropped to third place––would he have a home in the UK anymore? With his business history there, would they not just think him no longer worthwhile?

Yet his downfall hadn't been just carelessness; he'd been targeted and by Matvey himself. His uncle had let him know about that; Lev's team had been unable to beat Matvey's in that contest and therefore unable to protect Kaminski from losing his Union. Like a chess move to take out his Queen, it was a strike he couldn't quickly recover from.

MATVEY WAS BACK IN MONACO. It was clear that he lived outside of Russia––something that he would be prepared to change only to take up residence in the Kremlin––so there was no apparent need for him to be seen around Moscow. Foma needed some company, after all, the man increasingly frustrated by his imposed isolation. Matvey's son Andre, who was still in Russia, would join them both in a few days and they would celebrate New Year together as a three.

SASHA HAD BEEN in early on the 25th and was finishing his third cup of strong coffee before nine o'clock. His computer was busy analysing the faces Alex had sent him for any possible matches. He was also running them through against the list of recent arrivals to the two cities––Moscow and St Petersburg––where most of the attacks had been reported.

As the week progressed, snow now falling quite heavily, especially further north, the reports continued to come in. These included a firebombing of a Christian Pentecostal gathering on Christmas Day––non-Orthodox Christmas Day that is. Again, Putin supporters claimed they were purging their country of false religions. Thankfully no one had been seriously hurt in that incident.

The Volkovs still travelled up to St Petersburg for their New Year celebrations––Sergej at various lecture circuit occasions as always, though mainly in a social context––Svetlana in their mansion. It had never felt so quiet to be there. She couldn't help but think about the previous years, her home a hive of activity, of action and excitement.

Had she made the right decision?

And yet to have had two Hosts turn on one another––leading to one man ordering the shooting of another and this carried out right outside her home––was an appalling feeling. What if she'd been walking out at the same time? What if she'd been down by the door and a stray bullet had found its way into her home? What then? It had all got too much, she'd been right to call things off.

Now two of these men were running for her country's Presidency.

She now fully understood all that Matvey had been attempting––she'd been the fool for having allowed him into the event after all his years of refusal. She should have known better, should have seen it coming. Matvey had used her group for his own gain. He'd set a trap for Kaminski by suggesting his Union be the target in his T10 Hunt––her event, she reminded herself, as she had always been the one to set the challenges. And yet she'd allowed him to get away with it, and to what purpose? So that he'd have one less challenger in his own personal race for the Presidency. And what would her country look like with Matvey in charge? Would it be a good change––or would it spell disaster for her? Would Matvey later look to expose her?

Could she really trust him?

Though as a couple they were not under Putin's thumb in any way––they didn't have much of a relationship with him, and she knew her husband had his own reservations––yet Putin hadn't done badly for their nation, always putting Russia first and foremost in his thinking and planning.

Should an oligarch even be allowed to run the country? Didn't their own wealth disqualify them from really knowing what real Russians needed? But wealth was such a powerful voice in their country––and she would know––how could it ever be anything different?

Svetlana realised immediately she couldn't just stay in the mansion, so she left, going to find her husband. He thought she was used to being alone and happy by herself as she had never wanted to join him for the past decade, so he was surprised when she showed up as were all the other guests. Having Svetlana alongside him was always very good for Sergej. It made the evening much more pleasant.

In Florida, Phelan was celebrating a wonderful Christmas with his family. Now it was just him, his wife and the boys. After months on the road––and seeing that all was not well between their children––the grandparents had left during the summer, both returning to where they had lived before, though because of a very generous gift, were able to buy much more beautiful homes in better areas. Time to start a new life––again.

Phelan had wanted to finish their time in America on the east coast. They'd travelled south over the last two months––their relationship improving the more time they spent together. They would see out the New Year period in sunny Florida before heading back to the UK. It was high time they started life again, and the boys needed proper schooling; his wife without the help of her parents was finding it all too much to do by herself.

Phelan hadn't really said much about what he'd been doing in England. When Matvey was announced as a runner in the Russian Presidential elections––his wife recognising the name––they had talked about it a little.

Nothing about Maggie––he would never mention her name again––but it did go some way to restoring what had been missing between them both. She understood that his work was aiding the man to become President. It added some justification to their months of separation.

In a small way––a stupid way––it was as if knowing that helped her to stop fearing the worst; she could cope if he had been away from them but doing something important. He'd assured them it was all over. The longer they were together, the more she could finally believe it.

Getting to Florida––the sun shining, though Christmas Day was upon them––those thoughts were largely forgotten. It had been a challenging year for them in America, especially with Phelan gone for so much of it.

The following year promised new opportunities, the chance to finally settle down, though they knew they would always be able to travel more in the future––shorter periods of time, for sure, and just holidays––but the world was very much their oyster.

As New Year approached, Phelan couldn't help but be reminded of the previous year––he'd been standing in Maggie's garden, during a party, calling his wife who knew nothing about what he was doing and wishing her a happy New Year.

He just needed to forget about all that, and he would be free.

The coming months would offer that––a change of scenery, a new life somewhere, anywhere was possible now––but more importantly the chance to just settle, to put some roots down. The boys had no friends, besides each other. Moving around wasn't right for them. They'd taken as much as they could. He was looking forward to seeing them growing up and making new friends wherever they ended up.

Wondering if Matvey Filipov might one day be President, was a perplexing thought. Just the mention of him brought back a whole mix of feelings and emotions. To think that this Russian might become the leader of one of the most influential nations on the planet––a nation that had troubles with the UK––was also worrying. Did Matvey mean it when he said he was done with Phelan? Was a man like that ever done? Could Phelan ever truly relax, ever truly be free with such an explosive secret kept locked away deep within––a lock that he didn't possess a key for, it being instead a President-elect who owned that key, and many others too, no doubt. Would he ever be free?

Aleksey Kuznetsov had gone into hiding. He feared those within the Games––especially Matvey himself––exposing him, coming for him. His sniper was dead; that made no sense. He had repeatedly tried to contact him, to pay the balance he owed him for having successfully completed the mission, only to get no reply. After finally learning the truth, it all remained a mystery.

Then Svetlana had closed them all down––he'd heard the rumour, so had stayed away. He wasn't going to be there when she stood before them all and no doubt cursed him before them all. He wasn't sure what more help he could be to Kaminski, though his own wealth was relatively untouched.

He'd got away with a considerable loss.

With Foma removed from the picture––with the Games dead as well––he had got away with it. They were leaving him to it. Once Kaminski was President, Aleksey would rise again, his standing in the new order of things promised to be even better than it was before. He would no longer have to hide. Others would need to hide from him, but he would be free.

IT WAS GETTING LATE on the 30th December, as Sasha cut his way through the razor wire that was meant to keep people out of the private airfield in St Petersburg. In front of him––in relative darkness despite the airport's lighting––a group of men were waiting to board a plane.

Sasha had been on their trail for a couple of days. His search on the FSB database had managed to put a few names to the faces, and through known associates, a more comprehensive group could be named. It wasn't clear if all these names––there were men and women listed––were all involved in the incidents which were growing more violent by the day, but apparently some were.

Standing in the shadows, he was keeping as far away as he could.

Too far to be able to clearly make out who was who. He didn't want to be following the wrong group––mind you, there were not many private jets at the airport at that moment.

He took a few quick photos just as a cry went up––he'd been spotted by someone, and a dog started barking soon after. It was apparently the security patrol. Maybe they'd found the gap in the fence?

Sasha started running. The group that was boarding the plane had stopped. They saw the commotion, saw a dark figure running along the tree line. A few of the men turned and gave pursuit themselves.

Sasha worked his phone steadily in his hands, nearly tripping as he typed, adding a photo for good measure. The dogs were getting closer.

Look who I spotted, he said in the message, about to board a private jet with the faces—your man Andre Filipov.

He fumbled for the save function––he hadn't found it––when a loud order of *Freeze!* was shouted from behind not more than metres away. A dog was growling very aggressively. As Sasha slowly turned, the dog being restrained just inches from him now, his own hands were behind his back––phone still in hand, trying to save the draft and close the phone––though it was all backwards and he had no idea if he was doing anything. He was in danger of deleting it entirely if he wasn't careful.

Another security officer arrived, his dog too leading the way. Both had their guns trained on Sasha.

"On the ground, now!" the first man demanded. Just then, the four who were about to board the jet arrived at the scene, weapons visible, though they put them behind their backs as they approached the scene before them.

"Stand back, we have this under control," commanded the second security guard, who covered their approach with his own weapon, not yet entirely sure what was going on. Both dogs continued to growl angrily just inches from Sasha's face, as he lay on the cold, snow-covered ground.

"I'm unarmed." Sasha said, showing his hands which had now dropped the phone. He was carrying a weapon, but he wasn't holding it, which is what they needed to know.

The four from the jet were starting to move closer.

"Stand back!" the second security guard demanded, dragging his dog back and turning to face the four men, who were just ten feet from them all. They held one arm behind their backs.

"Who is he?" the leader of the four shouted, Sasha having recognised him from the video of the Muslims being beating up. When the two men had been attacked, he was the one who had punched the sister right in the face.

"We have this under control!" the security guard shouted back, the air filled with the sound of the aircraft starting up its engines. "Move away!"

"Who is he?" the lead man demanded again, all four men bringing their weapons out.

Then the shooting began.

AUTHOR NOTES

Setting out in this series was something new for me. I'd written mainly stand-alone books before this (which people loved) but writing these first three books, so close together, was something else entirely! I hope you have felt that too.

I was always very excited about this idea and knew early on there was more to dig the further I got into the story. This part concludes the initial opening trilogy, but there is more to come (as you'll see in the following pages). *The Machine* will take the current story on (so don't worry, things will get resolved) but will also reveal something far more profound, delving into some of the histories of the main characters, giving you a greater understanding about who they are, and why they do what they do. It also uncovers who runs the nation.

These first three books were written and timed to be a build up to and ready for the Russian Presidential elections. *The Prey* was therefore 2015; *The Pride* covered 2016 and this book which you've just finished covers 2017. If you've read the book in its launch month (December 2017), then you are bang up to date on the timeline!

The Machine takes us to the election next March/April.

There are many ways to stay in touch to be told when my latest books have hit the shelves. You can follow me on the website you usually purchase books from. Here are two other ways:

BookBub
Goodreads

If you follow me on any of the above, each time a new book of mine is ready, they'll email you and let you know. Try it; it works well.

THE IMPORTANCE OF A REVIEW

NOW YOU KNOW!

Reviews should be automatic. Think of it as a tip left for the waiting staff after a meal out. Except, the book you've just devoured wasn't prepared in just the last twenty minutes—the author has possibly spent months agonising over it.

Sadly, very few people leave a review.

Reviews greatly help an author. They do not need to be wordy (but they can be), you do not need to talk about all aspects of the book (but you can if you wish), they just need to be there. Visual. They help other readers to choose a book, thereby increasing the author's readership. They also affirm, encourage and help the author to keep going. Believe me, there are days when you just want to quit.

So now you know. I make it a matter of principle to always review a book I've read—how about you?

CHARACTER GLOSSARY

WHO'S WHO IN THE HUNT SERIES—AS OF THE START OF THIS BOOK

MI6 - Alex Tolbert, Anissa Edison, Gordon Peacock (head technician), Thomas Price (*DDG*)

FSB - Sasha Barkov

T10 - Mark Orlov (*Grey Eagle*), Roman Ivanov, Lev Kaminski (*Lion Man*), Vladimir Popov (*the Priest*), Matvey Filipov, Viktor Gavrilyuk, Dima Petrov, Yefrem Fyodorov, Valery Holub, Timur Budny (*Iron Man*)

T20 - Foma Polzin, Arseni Markovic, Rurik Sewick (*Mr Grey*), Akim Kozlov, Aleksey Kuznetsov, Dmitry Kaminski, Motya Utkin, Andre Filipov, Dmitry Pavlov, Osip Yakovlev

Matvey Filipov—father of Andre Filipov, oligarch and Presidential hopeful.

Andre Filipov––son of Matvey, in contact with Alex at MI6 under the name Andre Philip.

Sergej Volkov (*the Wolf*)––Billionaire and husband of Svetlana, with huge influence within Russia, though otherwise unconnected to the Games.

Svetlana Volkov (*the Lamb*)––Wife of Sergej, world famous actress and founder of the Games.

FREE BOOK

Not yet on my mailing list? It's the best way of keeping updated—–and never spammed!

Be the first to know when the next **Hunt** book is released!

For your free copy of my second novel (retail price £3.99/$4.99) just click through on this link, complete the steps and you will be emailed a copy of:

The Last Prophet
www.timheathbooks.com/books/the-last-prophet/freebook/)

ACKNOWLEDGMENTS

I want to thank God for the gifts He's given--all I can do is use them to the best of my ability. He requires nothing more.

I want to thank the fantastic team of people around me who help me at each of the levels of edit and scrutiny through which this novel has gone. All remaining errors are purely my fault (you are welcome to email me and let me know--I'll make corrections so that future readers don't find what you found).

Thank you to my wife Rachel, for always believing in me. It's been a horrible year on some levels. I'm glad you've found some joy in my books. You seem to rave about this one particularly.

Thanks once more to my editorial team; the brilliant Elizabeth Knight, Steve Dunn and Chelsea Bielskus.

Thank you to Taaniel Malleus, who has once again come up with a cover design that fits the story perfectly (and to the dozens of you who chipped in with comments as I put the covers on Facebook and asked for feedback).

Thanks to my ART members who have once more spotted some things that slipped through--Maxine Heath and Zan-Mari get a mention here. Thank you (and congratulations!) to the baby girl of

Zan-Mari who waited until mummy had finished reading ***The Poison*** before making her arrival.

This novel has once again also passed the eyes of my BETA team––thank you in advance for your reviews and encouragement.

Finally, thank you, the reader, for buying a copy, for reading it, and hopefully anticipating what is to come next.

THE MACHINE (THE HUNT SERIES BOOK 4)

A brand new three part series concludes *The Hunt series*, and the first of these books is coming out (at the time of the Russian elections, no less!) in April 2018.

The three titles are:

The Machine (April 2018)

The Menace (TBC)

The Meltdown (TBC)

ALSO BY TIM HEATH

Novels:

Cherry Picking

The Last Prophet

The Tablet

The Shadow Man

The Prey (The Hunt #1)

The Pride (The Hunt #2)

Short Story Collection:

Those Geese, They Lied; He's Dead

ABOUT THE AUTHOR

Tim has been married to his wife Rachel since 2001 and they have two daughters. He lives in Tallinn, Estonia, having moved there with his family in 2012 from St Petersburg, Russia, which they moved to in 2008. He is originally from Kent in England and lived for eight years in Cheshire, before moving abroad. As well as writing the novels that are already published (plus the one or two that are always in the process of being finished) Tim enjoys being outdoors, exploring Estonia, cooking and spending time with his family.

For more information:

www.timheathbooks.com
tim@timheathbooks.com

26172189R00151

Printed in Great Britain
by Amazon